MANKIND MUST WIN . . . OR PERISH

I would be the first human to touch the moon since the days when major league baseball used wooden bats.

As I waited I thought of something. "Metzger? How do we pee?"

"Use the little condom thingy in the leg. You hooked it up, didn't you?"

Air bled from the lock.

"What thingy?"

"Sorry. Should've told you. Just hold it."

He opened the hatch. Before me another world, as dead and white as bones, stretched to a black horizon. I turned around, felt for the descent ladder's first rung, then stepped into airless nothing cold enough to freeze helium. I hopped off the bottom rung into the Sea of Fertility's dust, then focused my vision on the object a half mile away.

Peeing my pants was the least of my worries.

"ORPHANAGE is a witty, fast-paced, and solid military story that sharply illustrates each character as well as the action they are engaged in. The vibrant voice of Jason Wander engaged me from the get-go."
— **Karin Lowachee,**
     author of *Warchild* and *Burndive*

ORPHANAGE

ROBERT BUETTNER

ASPECT®

NEW YORK   BOSTON

Aspect® is a registered trademark of Warner Books, Inc.

Cover design by Don Puckey and Shasti O'Leary Soudant
Cover illustration by Fred Gambino
Book design by Giorgetta Bell McRee

Warner Books

Time Warner Book Group
1271 Avenue of the Americas
New York, NY 10020

ISBN 0-7894-5031-X

Printed in the United States of America

For Senior Drill Sergeant DeArthur Burgess,
wherever the winds of war carried him,
and for all the other special ones

Acknowledgments

For opportunity, wisdom and enthusiasm, thanks to my Editor, Devi Pillai and Editorial Director Jaime Levine. Kudos: for perfection, to Anna Maria Piluso; for stellar Art Direction, to Don Puckey; for telling the world, to Joy Saveriano; for copyediting, to Sara Schwager, and to all the others at Warner who contributed so much.

Thanks to the best agent between the orbits of Mercury and Jupiter, Winifred Golden, for all that and more, and to the most brilliant, visionary cover artist inhabiting this planet, Fred Gambino.

To the shy military and aerospace folks who kept me on the technologic straight-and-narrow, cheers. You know who you are.

To the Capitol Hill Gang and the Boulder Bunch, past and present, whose flinty critiques made this book, thanks. Your turns are coming.

To Robert A. Heinlein for inspiration and to Joe Haldeman for that and for his generous humanity, my gratitude forever.

Most important, to Mary Beth, more than thanks for all of the above and for everything that matters.

We crabbed shoulder to shoulder down cargo nets to our landing craft bucking in the Channel, each GI's bilge-and-sea-soaked boots drenching his buddy below. In that moment I realized that we fight not for flags or against tyrants but for each other. For whatever remains of my life, those barely met strangers who dangled around me will be my only family. Strip away politics, and, wherever or whenever, war is an orphanage.

> — Anonymous letter fragment,
> Recovered on Omaha Beach,
> Normandy, June 1944

ORPHANAGE

ONE

"THE SUN WILL COME OUT . . . TOMORROW . . ." Our pilot hums through her open mike into zero-Fahrenheit cabin air fogged with four hundred GIs' breath. And fat with smells of gun oil, vomit, and fear. The sun never comes out here. In Jupiter's orbit, Sol is a pale dot. It's joke enough that I smile even as my hands shake the rifle propped between my knees. I'm Specialist Fourth Class Jason Wander, one of the lucky orphans who in one hour will save the human race or die trying.

We sit helmeted in paired, facing rows, so red cabin light paints us like eggs cartoned in the devil's incubator. Eternad-battery-heated fatigues warm us against a cabin cooled to the surface temperature our enemy manufactures a hundred miles below.

Our backs mold against the ship's "pressure hull" that seals out space's vacuum. "Ship" my ass. It's a 767 fuselage looted from some airplane graveyard in the Arizona desert, tacked to a streamlined parachute and reinforced to drop us from the mother ship to the surface. Like most of the 1900s antiques we have to fight this 2040 war with, it was built when *Annie* was a live-acted musical, back before the Millennium turned.

That red cabin light preserves night vision. A hundred miles below our parking orbit, it's always night on Ganymede. Or so the astronomers say.

We'll be the first humans to see it. If our groaning hull doesn't pop when we fall through vacuum or melt as we thunder through the artificial atmosphere the Slugs have slathered around the rock below. If we don't slam into Ganymede like crash-test dummies. If our demothballed weapons can kill the Slugs waiting down there.

And who knows, since I'm the only human who's ever seen Slugs alive?

My gunner shivers warm against my shoulder clicking her Muslim beads, praying like her hair was on fire. Yeah. My boss is a four-foot-eleven Egyptian girl. But Munchkin can shoot.

My teeth grind, I close my hand over her beads, and she stops clicking. Divine help's improbable for agnostic me. As improbable, I suppose, as Pseudocephalopod Slugs from beyond the Solar System camping on Jupiter's largest moon and killing millions by bombing Earth from out here.

They say that an infantryman's life is boredom punctuated by intervals of sheer terror. After six hundred days traveling in the mother ship's mile-long steel tube, finally being in the dropship liquefies my guts even though I asked to be here.

We all asked. So many volunteered for the Ganymede Expeditionary Force that they only accepted ten thousand soldiers who'd lost entire families. Munchkin lost parents and six sisters to the Cairo Projectile. I'm an only child, and the Indianapolis Projectile took my living parent. Such things now pass for luck.

So the media calls us the Orphans' Crusade.

Munchkin hates "Crusade" because she's Muslim. So she calls us Humanity's Last Hope.

Our platoon sergeant's seen combat. So he calls us meat. He says "Orphanage" is true because in combat your only family is these government-issued strangers.

Intercoms crackle. "Begin drop sequence on my mark . . . now!"

Somebody sobs.

The mother ship releases all twenty dropships like dandelion seed. Red light flicks black for a skipped heart-beat as electricity switches to internal. Our cut umbilical scrapes our hull like a handcuff unlocked.

Which is how this started for me three years ago, a week after my eighteenth birthday.

TWO

"JUDGE DON' LIKE 'CUFFS IN HIS CHAMBERS." The bailiff of
the juvenile court in and for the City and County of Denver bent and snapped metal bracelets off my wrists. He
stared me down, dried blood still measling his lip where
I'd coldcocked him.

"I'm okay now." I wasn't in the mood to hit anybody
anymore, but "okay" was a lie.

They'd backed me off sedatives this morning, except
for Prozac II, of course, to polish me up for my hearing.
It was two weeks since my mom, on a visit to Indianapolis, died when the city blew up. Also two weeks since I'd
pounded the crap out of my homeroom teacher. Social
Services, sharp as tacks, thought my loss and the pounding might be related.

The bailiff knocked, then opened the door, waved me
through, and I made the acquaintance of the Honorable
Dickie Rosewood March. It was just me and the judge in
his office. He wore a gray suit that matched his hair,

stretched across wrestler's shoulders. No robes. His furniture was antique, even down to a computer with one of those television-screen boxes and a keyboard. That must've been the zoo for him because his right sleeve was pinned up at the elbow. In his remaining hand he balanced a paper file. Mine?

His chair creaked when he looked up. "Mr. Wander."

"Sir?"

"Are you mocking me?"

"Sir?"

"Your generation doesn't call veterans 'sir.'"

"I called my dad 'sir,' sir." If the drugs had *really* worn off, I probably would have cried at that. Even though Dad was ten years dead.

He looked at my file again. "I'm sorry. Your courtesy is appropriate, generous under your circumstances."

"How long have they had me sedated?"

"Two weeks. Two weeks since that first Projectile hit Indianapolis. Why the hell did you go to school the next morning, son? You must have been in a state."

I shrugged. "Mom said not to cut while she was out of town. What do you mean 'first Projectile'?"

"Jason, since your episode with your teacher, we're at war. New Orleans, Phoenix, Cairo, and Djakarta were also destroyed. Smashed by Projectiles as big as the Chrysler Building. Not nuclear bombs. Everyone thought Indianapolis was a bomb, at first. Terrorism against America."

"That's what my teacher said. That Americans in Indianapolis deserved to die for the way we treat the third world. That's when I pounded her."

The judge snorted. "I'd have pounded her myself.

These Projectiles came from space. Jupiter. More are coming." The old man choked and shook his head. "Twenty million dead." He removed his glasses and wiped away tears.

Twenty *million*? I only knew one of them, but I teared up, too.

His eyes softened. "Son, your problems are a drop in the bucket. But it's your job and mine to deal with them." He clung to my file like a life preserver and sighed. "You're old enough to charge as an adult with assault. But your circumstances mitigate your conduct. Your home was in eviction proceedings before I ever heard of you. Now complete. Rent deficiency."

I felt dizzy. "Our house is gone?"

"Personal goods are in storage for you. Do you have relatives you could live with?"

Mom's great-aunt sent an annual Christmas letter, the old, copied-paper kind that always ended "Yours 'til Niagara Falls," followed by "Ha-ha" in parentheses. Last year's came from a nursing home. I shook my head.

He reached across his body with his huge, good hand, hugged his pinned-up sleeve like a bear, and glared. "Do you know how I lost this arm?"

I froze. Beating a juvenile defendant snotless? I realized he didn't expect me to know the answer. I relaxed. "No, sir."

"Second Afghan Conflict. The military could channel your anger, and the discipline wouldn't hurt you, either. The court has broad sentencing discretion. And this is a just war. Have you considered enlisting?"

He sat back and fingered a paperweight. It was some kind of bullet. It might as well have been a dinosaur tooth. For years now the military, especially the ground forces, had become like plumbing. Necessary, unpleasant, and out of sight. Not that you could blame people. The terrorism years had given way to *Pax Americanum*. Everybody wanted to buy new holosets and to travel on cheap airfares and to be left alone. In the contest between guns and butter, butter finally won. The army? Not me.

"What do you think, Jason?"

My eyes narrowed. Since organic prosthetics, nobody had to display a stump. Was Judge March's a recruiting poster or a warning?

"I think I don't want to go to jail."

"I'll take that as a 'no' to enlistment. Jason, do you think your violent episodes are over?"

"I dunno. I don't feel like hitting anybody now." I had a nice float on from the Prozac II and whatever else they'd been pumping into me. Or else I was just numb from what he'd told me.

He nodded. "Your file says you've never been in trouble before. That's true?"

I supposed he meant like armed robbery, not the cafeteria pudding fiasco with Metzger. I nodded.

"Jason, I'm going to dismiss this matter. You're too old for foster care, but I'll backdate papers and sneak you in with a family. It's a roof over your head."

I shrugged while he wrote with a pen in my file.

He buzzed, and the bailiff returned and led me out. I reached the door as Judge March called, "Good luck and God bless you, Jason. Don't let me see you again."

Three weeks later Judge March saw me again but not because I let him. No office visit this time. The bailiff called "All rise!" when Judge March swept black-robed into his courtroom. He sat between two American flags and scowled at me over his glasses.

I looked out the window at leafless trees. Weeks ago the difference between the day sky and the night was blue compared to black. Now the Projectiles had vomited impact dust up into the stratosphere and day and night were just different shades of gray. They said rain and crops might disappear for years. People were hoarding broccoli.

We were at war with somebody we didn't know, who wanted us dead for reasons we couldn't understand, and all we could do about it was slow down the End of the World. And cling to stupid rituals of civility.

"You broke the windows out of your foster family home with a bat? And slugged the arresting officer?"

"The world sucks."

Judge March rolled his eyes to the ceiling. "So does a cell down at Canon City, Mr. Wander."

Mr. Wander. What happened to the judge's pal, Jason? I swallowed.

The courtroom door tapped shut behind me, and I turned to see who'd come in. A guy in a board-stiff green uniform whose chin and skull were shaved so shiny they looked blue stood at attention in the aisle with a recruiting brochure under one arm.

Judge March peered down from the bench. "Your choice, son."

THREE

IT TOOK FIVE MINUTES FOR JUDGE MARCH to assure me that if I chose to enlist, then quit the army, he would have my ass.

Then the recruiting sergeant and I sat on a bench, in a courthouse hallway awash in disinfectant smell. He spoke up to be heard while the whines of handcuffed crack heads echoed off puke pink marble walls. "You sign here, here, and here, Jason. Then we'll talk about branch preference."

Branch, schmanch. My preference was that Judge March didn't jail me with mother-rapers and father-stabbers and throw away the key. I took the pen, signed, and eyed the sergeant's chest. Ribbons, silver jump wings. He actually looked pretty wick.

I pointed the pen at his badge, long and skinny and powder blue, with an old-fashioned musket stamped in the middle. "What's that one?"

"Only one that matters. CIB. Combat Infantryman's Badge. Means you've seen combat."

"You have to be Infantry to get it?"

He shook his head. "You have to see combat. But the way to do that's Infantry."

"Isn't that like marching and stuff?"

"Everybody marches. Infantry marches for a reason. It's my branch. The Queen of Battle."

He really did look wick with his beret tucked under his shoulder loop. Unless the army had a sex-and–rock 'n' roll branch, it was all olive drab to me. And I liked hiking as much as the next Coloradan. I checked the "Infantry" box and the sarge and the Queen and I shared a special moment. The moment lasted as long as it took for him to tear off and fold my yellow copies.

I had a month to jerk off before my orders said report for Basic. The only foster family that would take me were the Ryans. Mr. Ryan spent hours in the yard watching his trees. He'd planted them around the turn of the century, and they'd grown old and brittle like him. Their leaves fell after the dust darkened the sky.

Every Sunday morning Mrs. Ryan clicked down their walk in high heels and off to church while Mr. Ryan hunkered in their living room glued to the pregame. They seemed very normal.

Mrs. Ryan held a turn-of-the-century-style bowl, probably virgin plastic, across the kitchen table. "More peas, Jason? They're the last of the fresh. From tomorrow it's all frozen." She wrinkled her brow. "After that I don't know."

I shook my head. She poked the peas at Mr. Ryan.

He grunted and kept watching TV. Yeah, TV. The dust in the atmosphere was screwing up holo signals, but the land lines from Cablevision days were still buried in place. So if you had an old cathode-ray-tube television box—and what the Ryans didn't have only the Smithsonian did—you could still watch news.

TV's like a holo, only flat. You get used to it.

The anchorman asked a professor, "Ganymede?"

The professor wagged a pointer at a studio holo, hanging over the desk between them, of a slow-rotating rock. "Jupiter's largest moon. Bigger than our moon yet with less gravity than Earth. The only other place in the solar system with liquid water. Of course, Ganymede's is in a layer far below its surface. This image was taken by the Galileo Probe thirty-seven years ago, in two thousand. Ganymede looks hard edged. It had no surrounding halo back then. No atmosphere but wisps of released ozone and oxygen." He spun his chair and pointed at the twin to the image alongside the first. The twin had blurred edges. "This telescopic image is a week old. *Voilà*! Atmosphere!"

"And that means, Doctor?"

"These aliens have set up a forward base on Ganymede. They've generated an atmosphere for an entire world."

"And what does that tell us?" The anchorman knit his brow.

"They covet a world with water and an atmosphere. Which is why these Projectiles are being fired at us instead of nuclear warheads. Precisely large enough to slowly strangle us but clean and small enough to allow Earth to escape true 'Nuclear Winter.' "

"They don't want permanently damaged goods?"

The TV professor nodded.

Mr. Ryan waved his fork. "So fly the Marines up there! *They'll* permanently damage some goods!"

Mr. Ryan was very upset about his trees. But the human race couldn't fly a gerbil to Jupiter. We hadn't had the hardware or the will to send a person as far as our own moon since the 1970s, much less attack some super-race that could air-condition a whole planet.

"Walter, two wrongs don't make a right." Mrs. Ryan tweezed individual peas into Tupperware like pearls.

Mr. Ryan clamped his jaw as he'd done it for a life-time.

The anchorman faced the screen. "When we return. Military unpreparedness. Worse than Pearl Harbor?"

Mr. Ryan clicked off the TV box. "I'll just read the paper."

They were actually publishing daily news on paper again. The Greens didn't bitch since the trees were already dying.

Mr. Ryan turned to me. "What branch did you pick?"

"The Queen of Battle." It sounded so cool.

"Christ on a crutch! Not *In*-fantry?"

Uh-oh. "The sergeant recommended it."

"I was in sales. You always push the shit first. Besides, if we ever win this war, it'll be the rocket jocks that do it."

Actually, I'd thought of that. The United Nations Space Force was already up and running. But you had to be a math brain like Metzger to get in. My verbal test scores were so high that I had to sit through weekly counseling about the tragedy of underachievement. However, I C-minus'd precalc and took the Computer-Repair-Shop low road junior year. Even though it split up Metzger and me for the first time since third grade.

Mr. Ryan shook his head. "Infantry. You better spend next month getting in shape."

I spent next month dropping Prozac to forget Mom, drinking up my signing bonus on a fake ID, sleeping and downloading porn. The rest of the time I wasted.

The day before I shipped out I went down to the recruiting office to pick up my travel allowance. A guy in Space Force cadet uniform was coming out. Khaki jumpsuit, high boots, royal blue neck scarf. Even through the gloom, *that* looked wick.

"Wander!"

It was Metzger. His face reddened. "I heard you, uh, signed up after . . ."

Metzger was sort of my best friend, but we hadn't spoken since I got suspended after my monstrous homeroom assault.

"It's okay." I shrugged. What could he say? It wasn't his fault that he still had parents and a life. I don't know if I'd have called him up if the situation had been reversed. Mom would have said adolescent males form dysfunctional friendships and told me to forget about it.

I said, "So check you out! I thought only delinquents with a court order could enlist without graduating."

"If you score high enough and your parents consent, you take ROTC while you finish high school. After graduation . . ." He put his hands together and swooped them toward the sky.

Already the military was shooting missiles up from Earth, swatting away some Projectiles. But within months Interceptors, really updated space shuttles, would patrol space between here and the moon. It was going to be a holofantasy come true. Metzger succeeded at everything.

But on hologames he was the best anybody had ever
seen. They said game reflexes were success predictors for
an Interceptor pilot.

"So whadya get, Wander? Rotary-Wing Flight School?"
Metzger acted like an adult, sometimes. Tactful. We both
knew I couldn't do rocket-science math. Helicopter gun
ships were the next-sexiest thing.

I flipped his blue braided shoulder cord with a finger.
"Flight school's for pussies."

"So? What, then?"

Two girls walked by. The blonde looked Metzger up
and down and whispered behind her hand to her friend.

He grinned.

Girls always looked at Metzger like that. Now he was
Luke Skywalker, too. I rolled my eyes, then squinted at
the gray sun. "Infantry."

"Infantry." He blinked. "That's good. Really." He looked
off at bare trees. "So. When do you go?"

"Tomorrow morning."

"I guess you've been getting in shape."

"Naturally."

"We gotta get drunk tonight."

In next morning's darkness I slouched, hungover, in
the airport lounge and watched the transport parked outside the window. It squatted on its landing gear, its floodlit paint as gray as every dawn had been since the war
began.

I'd never seen a propeller plane except in a museum.
But jet engines sucked in so much Projectile-impact dust
they chewed up their own insides. Two jumbo jets had
crashed, so the commercial fleet got grounded and be-

came parked aluminum scrap. Airports these days were all military.

The dust ate propellers, too, but they'd rigged filters for prop planes so the old, mothballed crates could operate. Filter bags hung under the four engine nacelles like udders.

I rubbed my throbbing temples. Metzger and I had bought beer, driven out to the country, kidnapped a goat, and let it loose in the school cafeteria. Metzger's idea, as always. Roguish daring was another trait prized in fighter pilots.

I turned to the guy beside me, who looked as hungover as I felt. "You think that old cow's safe to fly?"

Big and black, he sprawled, like the other fifty of us enlistees, across a departure-lounge chair.

He scowled. "Cow? A Hercules? The C-130 was an outstanding ship in her day!"

Another gung ho letter-and-number spouter. These recruits actually wanted to enlist. I was the only sane one.

"Saddle up, ladies!" The corporal from the plane was more fanatic than the recruits. We fifty stood, stretched, groaned, and drooled. If milling around could win a war, we were going to kick ass.

We boarded and took off. The Hercules' saving grace, besides not crashing, was that it was as loud as riding in a trash barrel rolling across cobblestones. None of the gung ho crowd disturbed my misery. We landed twice to change filter bags, then hit the runway—not a figure of speech—for the last time around noon, local time, wherever local was.

"Saddle up, ladies! Welcome to Indiantown Gap, Pennsylvania!"

That sounded civilized. Not Greenland or the jungle or someplace.

The plane's back ramp dropped, and Antarctica whistled in. By the time they ran us down the ramp and lined us up in four rows on the runway's cracked, weedy asphalt my teeth chattered so hard my eyeballs rattled. Pennsylvania wasn't so civilized.

"Platoon! Atten-*shun*!"

I'd watched enough holoremastered war movies to know that meant stand straight and still. Like your mommy stood you up against the doorjamb to mark your height with a pencil. What crapola.

Wind scraped curled leaves across snow as it carried away the last Hercules exhaust fumes. Somebody coughed.

I stared straight ahead. Indiantown Gap was snow-dusted hills carpeted with the gray, leafless hardwood forest a pine-sniffing Coloradan seldom saw.

I said to the big black guy from the airport, "We should've joined the Hawaiian army."

He laughed.

It wasn't my best laugh line. Once, while he lunched with a cheerleader, I made Metzger snort milk out his nose.

"What's your name, trainee?" The voice boomed behind me and hair stood on my neck.

"Me, sir?"

"Sir? Commissioned officers are addressed as 'sir!' " He stepped around in front of me and stared into my eyes, so close that I thought he'd poke my forehead with his brown, Smokey Bear hat brim. He was leather-faced and so old that the hair fuzz above his ears was gray. Like his eyes. They were colder than Indiantown Gap.

"I am Senior Drill Sergeant Ord and am so addressed! Name?" A spit bead arced from his mouth. It froze before it hit my chin and ricocheted away like a foul tip.

"W-Wander, Drill Sergeant!"

"Trainee Wander." He paused. He was talking loud, so everybody could hear, even over the wind.

I bet he pulled this routine with every incoming group. And some poor dweeb—me—was made an example. Maybe I rolled my eyes at the thought.

"At the position of attention, you may blink, swallow, and breathe! Not joke, roll your eyes, and dance the macarena!"

The what? I shook in the wind like an out-of-tune Pontiac.

He turned away, hands clasped behind his back. "The platoon will move out of this mild breeze and indoors as soon as you assume the position of attention, Wander."

I could feel the hatred of every frozen-ass person on that asphalt. It was so unfair. I couldn't stand still. Shivering was an involuntary reflex. I hadn't done a thing. Well, maybe I shouldn't have talked.

I was freezing inside my ski fleece. Drill Sergeant Ord wore just an olive drab, starched-cotton uniform shirt and pants bloused over laced boots that shone like glass. And that fool hat. But he strolled back and forth like he was poolside.

It was probably three minutes but felt like thirty until my body went numb and motionless.

Ord faced us, hands behind his back, and rocked on his boots. "Very well. When I dismiss this platoon, you will shoulder your gear, face right, and move out smartly to the quartermaster building." He pointed at a whitewashed shed on the horizon. It was probably four hundred yards away but looked like it was in the next county.

Somebody whimpered.

"There you will receive a hot meal and be issued uniforms, including field jackets with liners. These you will find to be the finest cold-weather protection ever devised."

Somebody whispered, "Dear God, let's go!"

Ord seemed not to hear. "They are provided to you at no small expense by this country's taxpayers, whom you are privileged to defend."

The wind howled.

Somebody whined through clenched teeth. "My dick's frozen, or I'd pee my pants." If he did, we'd all be trying to warm our hands off the steam.

Ord ignored all these other whisperers. I'd bet the taxpayers would be pissed if they knew they were paying Ord to pick on an orphan who got railroaded into the army.

"Dis-*missed*!"

Evidently, "move out smartly" was army talk for "stampede." If I'd known what came next, I'd have run the opposite way.

FOUR

WE THUNDERED IN FROM THE COLD to the quartermaster shed like we were taking Omaha Beach. It was a barn of a room split lengthwise by a waist-high counter. Behind it loitered vacant-eyed men in olive fatigues and behind them shelves sagged beneath clothing and equipment just as drab.

We lined up and one by one got piled chin-high with clothes that smelled like Grandma's closet.

I said to the gung ho black guy from the airport, "This stuff's used!"

"Not since the war."

"Second Afghan?"

"Second World."

I laughed.

"Seriously." He plopped his gear on a wooden table and jerked a thumb at rough, whitewashed board walls. "The army's overcrowded. Last time they opened Indiantown Gap was Vietnam."

A bored clerk behind the counter tore plastic from another packet of field jackets. Mothballs trickled onto the counter.

I stuck out my hand to the black guy. "Jason Wander."

"Druwan Parker." His hand swallowed mine.

"How come you know so much, Parker?"

"I always figured to enlist. My uncle's a general. Adjutant General's Corps."

This smart guy picked Infantry! So I *had* made a good choice.

"He says I gotta do time in hell before he'll swing me a branch transfer to AG Corps. So I'm starting in Infantry."

My heart sank, then rose. "Branch transfer?"

He shook his head. "Unless you got connections, it don't happen in wartime. Most everybody here's Infantry 'til they die."

"Maybe the Space Force is at war. The war's out by the moon."

"That's not the point. The economy's tanked. Unemployment's the highest in a century. The army is America's soup kitchen. They're demothballing posts like this and dragging out old equipment to train us all."

"Train us for what?"

He shrugged. "Clean up craters that used to be cities. Evacuate new targets. Shoot rioters when food runs out. Don't you watch the news?"

Why, when I could get the Cliff Notes version from Parker? He was a nice guy and smart to boot.

A garage-size door at the building's end rumbled, rolled aside, and let winter in. Snow shot at us, horizontal on the wind. A canvas-topped truck backed up and plugged the opening. Framed in the truck's cargo bay stood a guy in white fatigues, hands on hips. Fumes belched into the building. The military was still allowed to use diesels.

I never believed that back before the turn of the century internal-combustion-engine cars rumbled over the roads like stampeding buffalo and turned the air brown. Until now.

I coughed. "That's bad!"

"No, that's good!" Parker stood and tugged me toward the truck. "That's the mess truck."

Parker's quick action put us fourth of fifty in the chow line. This was a relationship to cultivate.

The white-suited cook tossed us each a cardboard box maybe eight-by-five inches and we walked back to our table.

Parker muttered, "Botulism in a box!"

"Huh?"

He tore open his box and undersized green cans and brown foil packets spilled onto the table. "C-rations. One can's a main course, then there's dessert and stuff. These have been in some warehouse since Vietnam! The army never throws nothin' away."

He shrugged and read one of his cans. "Some of the main courses are edible. Like this one. BEEF WITH GRAVY."

I tilted my box toward me, peeked in, and read a can top, stenciled HAM AND LIMA BEANS.

"But," he said, "there's one, 'HAM AND LIMA BEANS.' Recycled barf."

"Trade boxes, Druwan?"

Fifteen minutes later I stood in line burping up lima beans, realizing that Parker was even smarter than I thought, and pushing my civilian bag forward with my foot. At the head of the line Drill Sergeant Ord sat at a table while each of us emptied out all our crap for his inspection.

Ord didn't look up as I scooped my stuff onto the table.

"Warm now, Wander?"

"Yes, Drill Sergeant."

He tossed my Chipman into a big, green poly envelope labeled with my name. "You'll get it back after Basic."

"How'm I supposed to mail people?"

He snapped his head up.

I added, "Drill Sergeant."

He nodded.

I figured it out. You just had to use their little suck-up words.

"You know the satellites aren't receiving, trainee. And there are no land repeaters in these hills. Your little personal assistant is good for nothing here but stored porno and hologames. You'll be too busy for either."

He reached into a box and pulled out a dull green Chipboard. "This is yours to keep."

"Some trade! Army-surplus junk that nobody's mailed with since before the Broncos won the Worldbowl."

"The army encourages you to write home, trainee."

A lump swelled in my throat. The bastard probably knew I had no home to write to.

He dug through my shaving kit, tugged out the shaving-cream squirt can, and chucked it into the envelope. "You will shave daily but with this cream." He tucked an old-fashioned, capped squeeze tube in my kit.

I was an orphan. War had taken my mother. War had

taken my home. This war-loving bully had nothing better to do than take my shaving cream?

Annoyance rose in me and spilled. I raised my voice to be heard over all the sniffling and milling and whispering behind me. "Begging the drill sergeant's pardon, why is he harassing us about this crap instead of teaching us things that might save our lives?"

The place went morgue-still. Somebody whispered, "Oh, fuck."

Ord stared at me, then his eyebrows twitched one millimeter. "A fair question. And you asked with appropriate military courtesy, Trainee Wander."

He stood, hands on hips, and addressed the assembled multitude. "Many of the weapons-control, vehicle, and other systems on which you will train were designed before the advent of reliable voice-recognition technology. Chipboard practice will allow you to refine or develop keyboard and handwriting skills today's generation lacks. That may save your lives and those of your fellow soldiers."

He held up my shaving-cream can. "Your unit may on a moment's notice be transported anywhere in the world aboard aircraft which are, or may unexpectedly become, depressurized. Pressurized aerosols become bombs that at a minimum can ruin your gear and at a maximum could bring down an aircraft. You will be clean-shaven at all times because your gas mask will not seal against a beard. Additional questions?"

I smiled to myself. "Military courtesy" meant you could be a smart-ass and not get in trouble.

"Trainee Wander, your question indicates you believe

you know better than the command structure what is best for your unit?"

Uh-oh. "No, Drill Sergeant."

"Are you cold?"

Was there a right answer?

"It's a bit chilly, Drill Sergeant."

Ord nearly smiled as he nodded. "Then let's all warm up. Platoon! Drop and give me fifty push-ups."

Anonymous groans as fifty bellies hit the deck. I supposed that if I'd said I wasn't cold Ord would have said how nice, the temperature was perfect for exercise. We'd be doing push-ups either way. Could Ord be a bigger dick?

"No, Wander, not you. You have earned your opportunity to lead the group. You will stand and count cadence."

Yes, he could. I stood. "One!"

Someone hissed, "Asshole." He wasn't talking about Ord.

When they finished all I wanted was to crawl in some hole as far away from Drill Sergeant Ord as possible. No such luck. He held up my pill bottle and raised his eyebrows.

"Just Prozac II, Drill Sergeant."

It went in the green envelope. What the hell? I mean, I'm no 'Zac hack. I'd drop a couple if the Broncos lost or something, but who didn't? It had been over-the-counter for years. They did say Prozac II was hugely stronger than the old stuff. Maybe since Mom died I did too much of it. Who wouldn't?

Ord stood again. The platoon would lynch me for this.

"Gentlemen, there is one thing that will get you out of this army or into the stockade in a New York minute! That thing is drug abuse. Impaired performance may kill your buddies. If you are wounded in combat, the medic lacks the time, training, and material to match lifesaving drugs to those already in your system. In that case drug abuse may kill *you*. Nonprescription mood lighteners are regarded as severely as cocaine and the like. If you have any now, it will be packed away, no questions asked. If you have any later, *you* will be packed away. Are we clear?"

"Yes, Drill Sergeant!" Fifty voices together.

After an hourlong orientation lecture we stumbled into Third Platoon's barracks, just a long, whitewashed room lit by double-hung windows. A regular combat-infantry company was four platoons, fifty soldiers each. A training company was the same, except each platoon had no regular officers, just a drill sergeant who lived in an office at the end of the platoon's barracks and rode everybody's ass. Third Platoon's drill was supposed to be a guy named Brock. Parker said he heard Brock was soft for a drill, a good deal for us. Parker probably thought a cold was a good deal because it created jobs for germs.

Upper-lower metal bunks piled with rolled-up mattresses lined the room in two rows flanking a center aisle. Each bunk pair shared a metal wall locker backed against frame walls that were just whitewashed siding, an inch of wood between us and the Pennsylvania winter.

Druwan Parker tossed his stuff on an upper bunk.

I chucked mine below. "Unless you want the lower?"

He shook his head. "Never had an upper." He grinned. "It's not a job. It's an adventure." His breath swirled as white as cotton against his cheeks.

I shucked my field jacket, then shivered. They couldn't turn up the heat in here soon enough. The jacket was lead-heavy but as warm and windproof as Ord had said. The bad thing about Drill Sergeant Ord was he was always right. The good thing was that he was senior drill sergeant for a company of four platoons, so we wouldn't see much of him anymore.

"Gentlemen!"

Ord's voice froze all sound and movement.

His boots tapped down the center aisle. "Carry on. You have not been called to attention."

Unpacking resumed.

Ord said, "I am saddened to announce that Drill Sergeant Brock has been transferred. He is as fine a noncommissioned officer as you will find in this army. It would have been your great privilege to be trained by him. However, I am pleased to announce that I will assume his responsibilities for this training cycle in addition to mine as senior drill sergeant. Therefore, I will bunk in the NCO's office at the end of this barracks. I will have the pleasure of getting to know each of you in Third Platoon, twenty-four hours each day."

Lucky us.

"Your questions?"

Someone, not me thank God, spoke. "Where's the thermostat, Drill Sergeant?"

Ord stood at the end of the aisle and clasped hands behind his back. "Heat for these barracks is generated by coal-fired boilers. As you know, coal-fuel burning and mining was discontinued in this country before some of you were born. Supplies are being imported from Russia. We expect them momentarily."

Momentarily turned out to mean sometime after 10:00 P.M. lights-out.

Before bed, Parker had shown me how to shine my
boots and arrange my locker and stretch the sheets over
my mattress. The one thing I'd done right all day was
choosing a bunkie who knew the ropes. Meanwhile,
some people even found time to write letters home on
their Chipboards, like Ord suggested. There was an old
machine at the end of the barracks where you plugged
in your Chipboard and actually printed a paper letter
and put it in an envelope to be carried by mail. Ord
thought up some bullshit about how we should soften up
our new boots, as if he hadn't invented enough chores
already. Walking around tomorrow would be soon enough
to break them in.

We all bunked under coarse blankets, in field jackets,
long johns, and three pairs of wool socks, towels around
our necks like scarves.

In my pocket burned two forgotten Prozac II tabs. I
was terrified either to take them or to get caught flushing
them. I hadn't had a 'Zac in a day.

I stared at the mattress above me, sagging under
Parker's weight while fifty strangers snored, scratched,
and farted.

It was the first time since Mom died that I'd really
thought about her without the warm fuzz of drugs. She
was gone. Not for the weekend or to the movies. Forever.
In a roomful of people I was completely alone for the first
time in my life. I sobbed until the bunk frame shook.

Finally, I closed my eyes.

"Zero four hundred hours! Fall out, gentlemen!"

It couldn't be 4:00 A.M. I'd just closed my eyes. Overhead lights seared my eye sockets. Metallic thunder rattled the barracks. Ord stood in the center aisle, stirring a

stick around the walls of a galvanized trash can. His uniform was perfect, his face glowing. Feet and bodies thumped floor tile. I sat up.

"Hunnh!" Above me, Parker woke in his new upper bunk. The mattress bulged as he rolled off the bunk edge, didn't find the floor, and crashed. He screamed and clutched his leg. I looked, then looked away and gagged. Under his long johns, Druwan's lower leg bent at the knee where no knee was supposed to be.

Parker was our first training casualty. If he had been our last, human history would have been different.

FIVE

ORD SHOWED TWO GUYS HOW TO LACE their arms to make a basket Parker could sit on, an arm around each of their necks. They shuffled him off to the infirmary while his complexion turned from ebony to putty. He clenched his teeth but never said a word while the platoon stood at attention on the company street's frozen, floodlit dirt.

Ord faced us. "Good morning, Third Platoon!"

"Good morning, Drill Sergeant!" Forty-nine voices feigned enthusiasm.

"Would you enjoy a tour of the post?"

Like a needle in the eye. "Yes, Drill Sergeant!"

"Physical training is normally conducted in sweat suits and running shoes. Those are expected to arrive momentarily."

No doubt being imported from Russia on the coal boat.

"We will therefore conduct PT in fatigue uniform. I am certain you all heeded the advice to soften and break in your combat boots last night."

Oboy. Ord faced us right, converting our four squads from four rows to four columns, marched us forward, then brought us to a double-time jog. He jogged alongside calling cadence without breathing hard. You'd have thought the bastard would have said something nice about Parker. He would either be offered a discharge or be recycled and start training over again when his leg healed. I had no bunkmate.

After four hundred yards I broke a sweat and friction from the stiff boots warmed my heels. We'd have to stop soon.

By the time we reached the edge of the board-building cluster that was the post, sweat stung my eyes, and I panted. My heels burned. I glanced at Ord. His boots skimmed the ground as he sang cadence. We would be turning back any second.

"Anyone who doesn't care to extend our tour to the pistol range?"

Maybe they were all out of breath like me. Maybe they were chicken. Nobody spoke.

"Out-*stand*-ing! Marvelous day for a run!"

We labored on.

By the time we turned around at the pistol range, which was somewhere near Los Angeles, I hobbled fifty yards behind the pack. The problem had to be the high-topped boots and the jacket. I was a gazelle during soccer season. Okay, maybe I should have spent some time getting in shape like everybody had warned me.

Deathlike wheezing sounded at my left shoulder. I glanced back. The guy flailed along, head peeking out of his field jacket's neck like a spectacled turtle's from its shell. At least I wasn't last. His glasses bounced on his nose, and he sobbed and stared ahead of us. "Oh dear God."

I saved my breath. I figured he wept from blisters or exhaustion until I looked where he was looking. Ord drifted back from the pack toward us like a vulture. I almost sobbed myself.

"Difficulty, trainees?"

The Turtle shook his head on a scrawny neck.

Ord smiled. "That's the spirit, Lorenzen. Trainee Wander is seeking a new bunkmate. I believe you two are a perfect match."

Ord was saddling me with this geek! I wasn't some nerd. I was just a tiny bit out of top condition. Not only had I lost Parker, who knew his way around, now I had to babysit this dork instead.

Ord sped up and circled the platoon's main body like a great white as they tromped along.

The geek panted. "Sounds. Like the sergeant. Wants us to get. To know each other. Walter Lorenzen." He tried to hold out his hand as we stumbled along side by side but it flopped like windblown Kleenex.

"Jason Wander, Walter." I clenched my teeth as much at the prospective relationship as at my blisters.

When we struggled back to the company street, Ord made us police the barracks to cool down before breakfast. If the blister-footed march to the mess hall cooled us down any more, we'd be ice sculptures. A white plume curled from the stovepipe that poked through the hall's green-shingled roof. My heart leapt. Where there's smoke . . .

Side-by-side horizontal ladders stood basketball-rim tall between us, heat, and food. The first two guys in line peeled off gloves, climbed onto wooden steps at one end, and swung monkey bar–style across the ladders to cheers, then dashed up the mess hall steps to warmth and sustenance. The pair behind them followed.

Lorenzen and I stepped up. Icy steel stung my palms as I rocked across the ladder. I've always had good upper-body strength. Halfway across I glanced back. Lorenzen dangled one-handed like an olive drab booger stuck on his ladder's second rung.

"Pair drop and go back to the end of the line!" We dropped as Ord motioned the pair behind us up onto the steps.

Lorenzen whispered as we hopped up and down at the line's ass end. "I'm sorry, Jason."

"No big deal." I blew into my fists.

At the building's rear, next to us because of our preferred position at the line's end, some idiot had planted a six-foot-tall twig of a sapling. A squared-off rock border made it into a scruffy garden centerpiece, awaiting spring.

Someone needed to clue the army that there wouldn't be spring as long as the sky only rained dust.

After three tries and three drops we were the last pair into the mess hall. Walter had never made it past rung two. He rubbed blistered palms. A few seated guys glanced up and snickered. We two huddled like lepers.

I stared across the tables while circulation revisited my extremities. Steam rose from pancakes, fried eggs, and bacon heaped on compartmented plastic trays. Bacon aroma made my saliva gush.

Lorenzen said, "Good. No SOS."

"Huh?"

"No shit-on-a-shingle for breakfast. Creamed, chipped

beef on toast. It's supposed to be awful. My grandfather was a soldier, and he always complained about it. He won the Medal of Honor."

"For eating it?"

Lorenzen grinned. "Good one, Jason."

Yeah, it was. I smiled back and straightened up.

The next few training days blurred into a muck of cold, sweat, and exhaustion. Instruction consisted of crap like drill and ceremony and how to boil water so you didn't get sick. The only thing halfway interesting was a demonstration of plastic explosive that scared me nuts. Explosives terrified me since I was ten, when Arnold Rudawitz blew off his fingernail with a Fourth of July cherry bomb. They said we'd have to throw a live grenade before we graduated. I'd have to get sick that day.

Rifles I liked, though. We got M-16s a couple weeks later. Ancient but deadly.

In the classroom building they lay on tables atop cloths stenciled with outlines of their various components. First the army teaches you how to take your weapon apart and put it together and clean it and care for it like it was your puppy. Then they teach you how to kill with it.

We stood at attention, each man behind his chair and his weapon, the whole four-platoon company.

Excitement was palpable. It's not that males want to kill living things with guns. It's that hosing down targets with a '16 on full auto is the ultimate extension of writing your name in the snow with urine.

Captain Jacowicz, the company commander, mounted the room's foot-high stage. There was the usual preclass bullshit as each platoon demonstrated bloodthirsty esprit de corps by chanting some doggerel about how much more excellent they were than every other platoon in the entire army. Third Platoon growled "WETSU! WETSU!" Short for "We Eat This Shit Up." Then silence.

"Take *seats*!"

A brief symphony of metal chair legs scraping floor-boards as we sat was followed by more silence. Hands folded, we looked up. Not a few fingertips brushed the rifle in front of them.

"Gentlemen," Jacowicz began by addressing our cluster of teenage nose-pickers with that obvious lie. "The war is going well." Jacowicz's tight lips said it was going poorly, indeed. Not that any of us had time or spirit to care. Life's victories were squeezing out an extra sleep hour or a hot shower.

Without personal communicators, not even TVs, we knew about the outside world only what the guys who got mail passed along. The word was the converted-shuttle Interceptors were flying and knocking aside Projectiles, but still imperfectly. Imperfectly meant people were dying by the millions. I wondered if Metzger was among the pilots. And if Projectiles shot back.

Captain Jacowicz cleared his throat. We rarely saw him, except watching training from a distance, arms folded. He was hardly older than we were. A West Pointer, they said. His fatigues were even more razor-creased than Ord's, if that was possible, his chin shaved even shinier. He wore no Combat Infantryman's Badge. Even among the drills, only Ord had seen combat.

He had spoken to us in this classroom once before, lec-turing that the Geneva Convention banned mistreating prisoners. Considering any potential enemy prisoner was half a billion miles away, I slept through most of it.

"Today your training enters a dangerous and challenging phase. This company has never experienced a range casualty. With care and attention, that is a record we will all preserve. Lights!" He stood aside as the lights dimmed and a flatscreen hushed down out of the ceiling. The title of today's after-lunch epic faded in on-screen, "Introduction to Firearm Safety."

Nobody could train on six hours of sleep that were really four. So everybody napped every time the lights dropped for a holo or a video. The drills had to know it. And since the Russian coal had arrived, the classroom buildings were sweatboxes. Lunch stew rolled in my stomach like a bowling ball. My eyelids drooped.

Our uniforms were so old-fashioned that they had pin-on collar brass. The stay-awake trick was as soon as you felt drowsy you undid the pin, reversed it, and held it under your chin with a thumb. When you drifted off, your head nodded and you got a wake-up call and lost only a little blood. It was a stupid ritual, but you had to do it because there was hell to pay if a drill caught you asleep.

I was fumbling to get my collar pin pointed against my chin. I swear I was.

Crash.

My head rested on the jigsaw-puzzle rifle cloth in a drool puddle. My M-16 spun on the floor.

"Soldier!" The lights flashed on, and the captain stood over me.

I popped to attention. "Sir!"

"Firearm safety bores you?"

"Sir, no sir!"

"You disrespect your weapon?"

"Sir, no sir!"

"Then pick it up!"

I did. Godammit. Everybody slept during the flicks.

"Sergeant Ord!" Jacowicz snapped.

The Great One appeared alongside, a statue at attention.

"Trainee," the captain peered at my name patch, "Wander is Third Platoon?"

"Yes, sir."

I supposed there was nothing a drill sergeant liked better than having one of his own fuck up in front of the commanding officer.

"See that Third Platoon learns to appreciate its weapons." Captain Jacowicz spun an about-face that did West Point proud, remounted the stage, and the flick resumed. I stayed awake.

That night after chow we broke down, cleaned, and reassembled our M-16s six times before we returned them to the company armorer. In addition to policing barracks, shining boots, and the usual bullshit. Drill Sergeant Ord left us four glorious sleep hours by generously extending lights until midnight.

Lights went out, Ord closed his office door, and disappeared. My forty-nine roommates lay silent until somebody hissed, "Wander, you fuckhead! You should be shot!"

I waited in vain for the expression of an opposing view.

Four hours from now we would wake and march out to the range, where every one of these guys would be armed with an assault rifle loaded with live ammunition.

SIX

THE NEXT DAY BEGAN ORDINARILY ENOUGH.

"The girl I marry she must be . . ." Trainee Sparrow stood six-six and weighed 160 pounds without his pack. But Ord had designated him to count cadence because he sang like the black choirboy he had been.

"Airborne, Ranger, Infantry!" Third Platoon sang back as we marched rangeward, rifles slung, in the gray morning. In the name of equal misery, women had served in the combat branches—Infantry, Armor, Field Artillery—for decades, even though they trained separately. But still the lyric seemed mythic. Actually, women seemed mythic.

I envisioned Metzger lounging poolside in trunks and a star pilot's scarf while twin blondes—no, one blonde, one brunette—ministered to his blistered trigger finger, suffered while he zoomed through outer space, saving millions of lives weekly. Here at Indiantown Gap, my idea of living large was seconds on something the army called apple cobbler.

It was what you'd call a nice day since the war started. The haze was almost bright, and it was a windless thirty degrees or so. Then something in the air went funny.

Of course, it was overpressure. As everybody knows now, a Projectile is so big that it piles air in front of it when it plows into the atmosphere at thirty thousand miles per hour.

Walter spun his head toward me, brow knit beneath his Kevlar pot. "Do you feel—"

We saw it before we heard it. I never want to again.

Sun-bright light boiled in a streak that seemed as wide as the sky and a hundred feet above us. It was actually twenty miles up. The noise and shock wave as it roared by knocked us all flat. Then the impact-flash bloom blinded me like an old film-camera flashbulb, even half a state away.

The ground rolled underneath us, like a bedsheet snapped over a mattress, then we all tumbled and fell back onto the road. It knocked the wind out of me, and I saw stars.

Somebody said, "Holy shit!"

Then the blast wind swept across us, whipping house-tall, bare trees like goldenrod straw in a breeze.

For too long nobody moved, just lay and breathed.

Ord was first up. It was the first time I'd seen him even faintly impressed. His eyes seemed wide, and he stood close enough that I heard him whisper, "Holy Mother of God!"

He dusted his uniform off, straightened his hat, and called out, "On your feet! Third Platoon, sound off!"

Everybody was up, rattling off names by squad. Nobody admitted being hurt. He had us marching before we could think.

We all stared west, toward the impact flash.

Somebody whispered, "What's over there?"

"Pittsburgh. Was."

I teared up, and my throat swelled.

I'd have thought Ord would call off training. We had just witnessed people die. Stunningly. Horribly. Massively. But he kept marching like something else mattered. Nobody sang the rest of the way to the range.

The M-16 is no marksman's weapon. It's short-barreled. The bullet wobbles, the better to tear through flesh once it strikes. The bullet is small, so a GI can carry more ammunition. But those characteristics reduce accuracy. At ranges beyond 300 meters without telescopic sights you might as well throw rocks at the target. Which didn't stop the army in its wisdom from setting the farthest rank of range targets at Indiantown Gap out at 460 meters.

Lorenzen stood chest deep in one of a firing-line row of foxholes, popping away with his '16. I sat cross-legged on the ground beside him, serving as his "coach" and marking his scorecard. The shooter-coach pairing was repeated up and down the line. I scored using an antique lead pencil and sniffed drifting cordite.

"Did I hit that last one, Jason?"

How the hell did I know? The close-in targets were easy to shoot, but I couldn't even see the far row through the dust-dimmed twilight. I checked off Walter's card. "You nailed that mother!"

"Wow! A perfect score!"

Nobody talked about it, but if an infantryman scored less than expert, his coach's pencil failed, not his marksmanship.

Everybody switched places, me and the other coaches now hunkered in the foxholes, plinking away. I whacked the close-in targets, then sighted on the far row.

Walter squinted downrange. "I think you missed that one Jason."

"Nah."

Walter shook his head. "Maybe you need to bear down more. Like I did."

I exhaled. "Christ, Walter! Just mark them hits!"

He shook his head again. His helmet misfit him so his head moved while his pot sat still. "That would be cheating."

Ord strolled by behind us. I shut up and shot.

Later the drills sat around a wood outdoor table adding scorecards while the rest of us eyed three deuce-and-a-halfs parked behind them. The old, internal-combustion-engine kind that ran on diesel fuel. As heavy as they were, battery power wasn't an option. One truck had litters and a medic aboard. A makeshift ambulance. Anytime we practiced live fire the army made sure we had plenty of Band-Aids close by.

The sight moved me near tears. Not with emotion at the army's concern for our well-being, but at the realization that there were three trucks. Four platoons. Lowest-scoring platoon was going to walk six miles home with full pack.

Ord stood and read from a Chipboard. "In first place, Second Platoon."

Those dicks whooped and piled into a truck.

Ord watched them go, then said, "First Platoon *also* achieved perfect scores across the board. Most impressive!"

Everybody perfect? I got a sick feeling. Maybe the other drills had tipped their platoons off about the creative scoring system. Ord had left us to figure it out for ourselves, and at least Walter hadn't. We were screwed.

Fifteen minutes later Third Platoon trudged toward the post, six miles away. Ahead of us the last truck disappeared, leaving us to eat Fourth Platoon's dust. At least we didn't have to listen to them hoot and make sucking sounds at us over the tailgate anymore.

"Nice work, Wander! The only guy in the company who scored less than perfect!"

If I said a word about how it happened, Third Platoon would kill Walter. Even the stress of field-stripping his rifle made his hands shake. If the other guys crapped on him for this, he'd crumble. They already hated my guts. I could take it.

But still, as I marched alongside Walter, the injustice of it all made my hand quiver as it clutched my rifle sling.

"Jeez, Jason. If you'd asked me I would have helped you practice. I bet you could learn to shoot just as good as me."

I don't know what happened. Maybe it was Pittsburgh. Maybe it was that Ord and this idiotic, insensitive army kept us playing target practice when all those people had died. I just grabbed Walter by his scrawny fucking neck and choked him. His helmet popped off and rocked on the ground.

"You ignorant, four-eyed toad! Get a clue!" We fell and rolled in the road while the rest of the platoon gaped.

"*At* ease!"

My fist froze midway to Walter's nose. Ord's voice could stop a falling piano thirty stories up. He dragged us to our feet by our field-jacket collars.

A blood string trailed from Walter's left nostril. He peered at me through cracked glasses, with hurt-puppy eyes.

Ord frowned at me. "Wander, when will you learn that you will all get through this together or you will all fail separately?"

Me? I was Mr. Teamwork here. These other assholes were the problem.

Ord moved the platoon out, and as we marched, he walked alongside me, and said, "Wander, *after* you have cleaned your weapon and returned it to the armorer and attended to tomorrow's uniform requirements and your policing duties you will report to my office."

"Yes, Drill Sergeant." My heart sank. But at least the rest of the platoon wasn't getting screwed for my fuck-up.

"Oh. That's right. I should be sure you get back early enough to get all that done, Wander."

Forty-nine pairs of boots crunched Pennsylvania's frozen earth. What could be worse than six more miles of this drudgery with full pack?

"Platoon! Port *arms*."

My heart shot into my throat. When you walk with a rifle, you carry it over your shoulder. You carry it across your body, at port arms, when you *double-time*.

Ord was going to run us all six miles back to camp. As a favor to me.

I should change my name from Mr. Teamwork to Mr. Popularity. Nobody had breath to curse me, so it was a quiet six miles.

Lights were out when I stepped up to the wedge of light that spilled from Ord's open office door. He sat behind a gray metal desk, hat alongside him. How his uniform looked morning-fresh off the hanger at 2200 hours I couldn't fathom. I rapped on the doorjamb.

He didn't look up. "Come! And close the door behind you."

Oboy. I stepped in front of the desk and froze at attention. "Trainee Wander reports, Drill Sergeant."

He was reading an old, paper greeting card. He slipped it and its envelope under his hat brim while I swallowed, blinked, and breathed.

I survived many a pop quiz by reading somebody else's paper upside down. Ord's card read "Happy Birthday, Son."

The envelope's return address was Pittsburgh.

My God. Ord had just lost his mother. When I lost Mom I beat the crap out of everyone who crossed my path. And here I stood in front of Ord. I clenched my jaw and braced for the worst.

Finally, Ord swallowed, then looked up. "Why are you here, Wander?"

Was this a trick question? "Because the drill sergeant told me to be."

"I mean in the army."

Because if I wasn't here, Judge March would lock me up with the scum of the Earth until I was so old I creaked. "I want to be Infantry because Infantry leads the way, Drill Sergeant!"

"I don't mean the bullshit answer. I know how you came to enlist. I know about your mother. And I am genuinely sorry." His eyes were soft, almost liquid.

I wanted to tell him I knew. Knew what he had lost. Knew how he had suffered. But soldiers don't do that. I thought.

"I don't know, then."

"Son."

Now there was a word I thought was outside Ord's vocabulary, until now.

He rocked back in his chair. "I'm not sure you belong here. This really is about working together, eye-rolling cynicism to the contrary."

"Together? Those other assholes cheated at the range!"

He nodded. "Lorenzen scored you honestly at seventy-eight of eighty. I doubt anyone else in the company really broke sixty. I've seen lots of perfect scores, but only two trainees have actually hit seventy-eight targets in the last ten years."

My jaw dropped. I should have realized that Ord knew about the scoring. Ord knew everything. And my chest swelled a little about the seventy-eight.

"Wander, your Mil-SAT math score was average, but your verbal pulled it up so your overall score is higher than Captain Jacowicz's was. And he's a West Pointer! Infantry seems like a lowest-common-denominator exercise to a bright guy like you, doesn't it?"

Another underachiever lecture. I sighed loud enough that Ord heard.

"Mock foot-soldiering if you choose. But it's really about the toughest thing men or women can discipline themselves to do."

I swallowed. I wasn't mocking. I understood the discipline that let Ord carry out ordered training even though he had just watched his mother die.

It wasn't disrespect, but wonder, that made me roll my eyes.

But Ord didn't know I knew, didn't know I understood. Whatever softness had been in his eyes disappeared. "The world's dying, Wander. I don't know whether the Infantry is destined to reverse that. But I do know that it is my job to assure that every infantryman I train is ready if destiny calls. An infantryman who's not part of the team isn't just a pain in the ass. He's dangerous to himself and to other soldiers. Would you like to quit?"

Like to? I'd love to. But I couldn't, or I'd go to prison. I shook my head.

He sighed. "I can't order you to quit. But I can make sure you consider carefully how badly you wish to stay."

I swallowed. I didn't wish to stay.

He bent, reached into a desk drawer, and came up with a plastic bag. From it he drew a purple, pencil-size object and displayed it between thumb and forefinger. A manual toothbrush strung on a cord loop. "Wander, do you know upon what you gaze?"

I squinted. "Toothbrush?" It was stained in that way that Mom would say you didn't know where it had been.

"Toothbrush?" He exploded.

I stiffened. "Toothbrush, *Drill Sergeant!*"

He smiled and sauntered around his desk to stand in front of me. "No. No, no, no. Trainee Wander, you gaze upon the Third Platoon Memorial Nocturnal Hygiene Implement."

"Silly me." Had I lost my mind?

Ord just kept smiling. He held his hands apart so the brush dangled between them on the spread string loop. "Once every few training cycles, a very special trainee earns this." He lifted his hands above my head and lowered the little necklace onto my shoulders. The brush passed my nose. Now I knew exactly where it had been.

It was midnight when I crabbed sideways across the latrine floor to the third of six toilets and continued to scrub and swear. Ord said it was going to be a nightly exercise.

He said I had to wear the brush at all times. He said the reason was to give me time to think about my future.

Right. Usually, if you weren't on KP or CQ or taking your hour wandering the barracks as fire guard, you got to sleep. Ord was royally fucking me over to make me quit.

Well, fuck him instead. I scrubbed harder.

If fifty guys in an open platoon bay was a bit unprivate, the latrine was a living, breathing rape of the Fourth Amendment. The toilets sat in an open line facing the sink row six feet away. You crapped counting the hairs on somebody else's bare butt while he shaved. The showers were at the end of the room, just as open.

If they ran a prison like that, we'd all get released on grounds it was cruel and unusual punishment.

The first few weeks people were so intimidated that they got up in the middle of the night to crap in relative privacy. Gradually most of us got desensitized. Not everybody, though.

"I'm sorry you have to do that, Jason."

I looked up. Walter shivered in his field jacket, bare, pale legs spindling below the hem. They ended in sock-blobbed feet, so he seemed to wobble on a pair of Q-tips.

"You here to crap or talk?"

"Do I really look like a toad, Jason?"

"No." Of course he did. I stared at the floor so he couldn't see me smile.

He smiled, then frowned. "It should be me down there scrubbing. I'm the platoon's biggest fuck-up."

"No." Of course he was. "The army's just not for you."

"It has to be."

I scuttled sideways and massaged the next ivory throne. "Why?"

"You remember I said my grandpa won the Medal of Honor? He saved a man's life. Everybody in my family served. My mother won't be proud of me unless I win a medal."

"That's crap, Walter. People get medals when things go bad. Medals are just ways that armies hide mistakes. Nobody in my family ever served. Now they can't." Tears blurred my vision, and I scrubbed harder. Somebody's army killed Mom, for the crime of taking a trip to Indianapolis. It killed everyone in Pittsburgh. It even killed Ord's mother. "It never ends. It's wrong. What's the point, anyway?"

"My grandpa was a hundred when he died. He served in World War II. He said the point was to make it stop."

He rocked from sock to sock, and his intestines gurgled. Walter needed his privacy. Soon. But he was still too shy to ask even me for it. I stood and arched my back. "I need a break. I'm going outside a minute."

I stepped out into the cold dark and looked up. Beyond the dust, constellations still shone. Somewhere up there star pilots like Metzger waged the battle to save the human race. I'd watched a million people in Pittsburgh die today. Did I really want to be just a smart-ass scrubbing toilets with a toothbrush?

I didn't know who or what took Mom and my life away. I didn't really want revenge because that wouldn't bring my old life back. But if I could help to make it stop, that would be worth everything.

Walter stuck his relieved head out the door into the cold and smiled. "Thanks, Jason. You're okay."

My breath curled out into the dark. No, I wasn't. But I could be.

SEVEN

THE NEXT MORNING WE DREW OUR M-16s from the armorer and went straight to hell.

Not just Third Platoon, but the whole eight-hundred-man training battalion mounted an olive drab convoy of antique deuce-and-a-halfs, belching diesel soot in volumes unseen since cars went electric years ago. We rolled west toward Pittsburgh's ruins beneath a drifting grit plume that a day before had been strip malls and skyscrapers and children. Exhaust soot seemed irrelevant.

We rocked and shivered on facing benches under our truck's canvas top.

Somebody asked, "Why'd we draw weapons? Did the fuckin' aliens land this time?"

"Looters."

"Fuck! I ain't shootin' no brothers."

"Brothers all gone, hombre! So's the loot."

"We're gonna feed fuckin' civilians."

Troop-truck discourse isn't Question Time at the House of Lords.

Rural Pennsylvania unreeled beyond the open tailgate. At first, we saw the occasional cow trying to graze a frozen field. Closer to Pittsburgh the cows stumbled, deaf and disoriented even a day later from blast-wave overpressure.

The trucks slowed to a crawl in the gloom as we closed on the city. Civilians lined the roads, headed away from the grit plume. Cars were outbound, but also well-dressed people pushed shopping carts piled with plastic trash bags. Parents walked, pulling kids in coaster wagons and yard carts.

Some kids waved. Their parents shielded their eyes against our convoy's headlights and stared at us like we were insane. Or they were.

It was dark by the time we got close enough to smell it.

Burned buildings and flesh. "Dark" is inaccurate. Pittsburgh still burned, and red glow reflected from low clouds lit our faces. We dismounted the trucks, grateful for the leg stretch, and formed up.

The residential streets around us were a flat, tract-house neighborhood of undamaged two-story homes. They were old enough that the now-dead trees in the yards had grown to be as big around as my leg. Soot piled inches deep on everything and kept falling.

Captain Jacowicz addressed the company. Drifted soot grayed his hair and made him cough behind his government-issue paper mask.

He put hands on hips. "You know what happened here. They pulled us out of training to assist. We'll search for survivors, secure property against looters, aid displaced civilians, and assist MI teams."

Our back-of-the-truck brain trust had guessed right about most of our mission. But MI teams? MI was Military Intelligence Branch. What was that about?

We played hurry-up-and-wait for an hour in the cold while ash snowed down, and Jacowicz talked on the radio. Candles or lanterns lit the house windows around us. They silhouetted curious heads, grown-ups and kids peeking around curtains. These were the lucky survivors. But they had no power, no water, no heat, no groceries.

A smaller truck pulled up, dropped its tailgate, and we unloaded boxes. C-rations. The civilian population was about to learn why war was hell. At least if our mission was to distribute food back here, that was safer than going closer to the burning city core.

When the truck emptied, a drill motioned to me to climb in back.

"What's up, Drill Sergeant?"

He shrugged. "The spooks need a warm body. You just volunteered, Wander."

Spooks. Why would Military Intelligence need one half-baked trainee? I bounced against the truck's canvas sides as it lurched away from Walter and the rest of Third Platoon. As they faded away in the ashfall my throat swelled. It wasn't fair. They weren't much family, but they were all I had, and now I was losing them.

I bounced along for minutes feeling sorry for myself before I realized that the light was redder, and I wasn't shivering. The smell got worse and the fire's roar louder.

I snatched up the canvas side flap. Toppled wooden power poles wrapped in black cable made the streets an obstacle course. Cars lay on their sides. House windows gaped black and shattered.

The truck stopped, and, again, I dismounted. Closer to the blast zone!

The fire's heat baked my exposed cheeks. It sucked air to itself, making wind that snapped at my uniform sleeves. I guessed I was a couple miles from downtown, if the Projectile had hit dead center. This neighborhood remained recognizable, brick warehouses or old offices, half-flattened. Even after a day, the flames at city center volcanoed a half mile high. Their roar shook the street so the broken glass that paved it shimmered as it reflected the orange firestorm. The truck turned back before I could blink.

Fifty feet away, a middle-aged captain was silhouetted against the firestorm. He stood alongside a folding table, and above him rose an ash-coated canvas canopy. The canopy centered three sides of a square formed by olive drab trailers. Floodlights on poles glared down on the canopy while a portable generator buzzed somewhere.

He shouted through cupped hands. "You're not in hell, but you can see it from here."

I saluted. Instead of returning it, the captain waved me closer, with a tired hand untrained by Field Manual FM 22-5, Drill and Ceremony.

He looked me up and down, his hands on his hips. "Ever had experience with extraterrestrials?"

I smirked. "My drill sergeant's pretty strange."

He sighed. "Well, I told them I just needed a strong back. Coffee?" He waved at an aluminum pot and stacked cups on the table.

"I'm Howard Hibble."

I shook his hand. It was so thin he'd never make one dead-hang pull-up. His uniform was contemporary camouflage pattern, not like our last-century training togs. Captain's bars hung crooked from one side of his collar and the Military Intelligence Compass-Rose-Dagger from the other.

Captain Hibble ran a lean hand through flattop gray hair and dragged on a tobacco cigarette. "Don't expect drill-sergeant crap from me. You've probably been in the army longer than I have. Until last month I was Walker Professor of Extraterrestrial Intelligence Studies at the University of Nevada. Believe it or not."

I believed. He'd never spent time with the likes of Drill Sergeant Ord. His uniform sagged over his scarecrow frame, as wrinkled as the skin of his face. His boots looked like he shined them with a Hershey bar.

"All my life I hoped we weren't alone in the universe." He hacked and looked around at the flames. "Now I wish we were."

"What am I doing, here, sir?"

"For now, bunk in that truck over there. I'm the only one in this menagerie still awake. We go when its cooler and lighter."

I'd been bouncing in a deuce-and-a-half since before the previous dawn. The "extraterrestrials" remark sounded ominous, but "bunk" was music to my ears.

By morning, the firestorm had burned itself out. The wind had died, and only scattered fires flickered.

I stumbled, scratching, into the dawn and toward the latrine.

Other soldiers wandered the quadrangle formed by the truck trailers. I use the term "soldier" loosely. Unlaced boots and stubble sprouted everywhere. Ord would explode if he saw this bunch. This whole unit had to be

Intel weenies. I'd heard outfits like this existed. "Unconventional" assemblages of brainy weirdos. I eavesdropped on yawned conversations. This platoon included aerospace engineers, biologists, even psychics and aboriginal water-sniffers. As a race we were grasping every straw in the search for answers.

Under the center canopy, Hibble scavenged through a cardboard doughnut box. He stepped away, chewing, while powdered sugar flurried onto his chest. "Help yourself. Then you and I are going into the city core to hunt Projectile fragments."

I spit crumbs. "In there?" The city center was still a molten, orange pit.

"In protective suits."

"Protective? But the fragments—"

"Aren't radioactive." He nodded. "Not even explosive. These devices are just large masses moving at high speeds. Enough kinetic energy to incinerate a city. Last century, humans bombed Dresden and Tokyo into firestorms with incendiaries. But big rocks from space work, too. Ask the dinosaurs."

"Why hunt fragments?"

He rolled his eyes at the smoke. "What *else* have we got to study? But we pegged the enemy as extra–solar system that way. The metals were too exotic for our neighborhood."

I had a feeling Howard's neighborhood and mine differed by light-years. He fitted me out with a goggled, rubber respirator mask. One of those firefighter-technology deals with the little sidepack that manufactures oxygen. Over our uniforms we each wore fire-resistant coveralls and boot covers. I also got to wear an empty backpack.

We drove toward the city center until the rubble deepened, then left his ancient car, he called it a Jeep, and hiked.

Smoke, flickering firelight, and my goggles blurred tipped, brick walls that towered above us, poised to crush us at every turn.

My heart pounded. I glanced around at the debris, expecting to find a bloody, severed limb or a charred body under every drywall slab.

"Jason, don't expect this to be a graves-registration detail."

"A what?"

"We won't see many recognizable remains. When a skyscraper collapses on a body, a person disappears."

I squeezed my eyes shut at the image. Respirator or not, I breathed through my mouth and still smelled burned flesh.

Howard held his aluminum walking stick out for balance and high-wired across a blackened girder that bridged a brick pile. I followed, knees shaking. I joined him on the other side as the girder groaned, snapped, and a ton of bricks cascaded next to Howard.

"Watch out!"

He waved his stick. "You'll get used to it."

Insulated suit notwithstanding, sweat trickled down my cheeks inside the mask. My lenses fogged. As we closed on ground zero, buildings no longer existed separately. I recognized only occasional doorframes or papered walls. A corkscrewed electrovan bumper wore a charred sticker, MT. LEBANON HONOR STUDENT. I swallowed.

"How do you find things in this mess, Howard?"

He shrugged. "Practice. And instinct. My grandfather

was a prospector." He paused. "Did you lose family in this, Jason?" His voice buzzed through his respirator.

"All of it. My mom. Indianapolis."

He stopped. "I'm sorry."

I shrugged. "You?"

"My only living relative was an uncle who lived in Phoenix."

"So we're both orphans."

"Lot of that going around, these days." He duck-walked under a blackened wood beam angled between two rubble piles.

"Howard! That looks shaky!"

"I have a nose for these things." He waved his hand without turning around, then poked ashes aside with his walking stick. "Holy Moly!"

Definitely an Intel weenie. Any self-respecting GI would have said "fuck!"

He bent and tugged at something. "Jason, come over—"

The debris mound that supported one end of the beam rattled. Above Howard's head, pulverized brick pebbles trickled.

The beam above him teetered.

I lunged. "Howard!"

Whump.

Dust swirled. Where there had been Howard there was now a wall-board-and-charred-lumber mound.

"Howard!"

No answer but the fire's roar.

I had liked Howard. He was as goofy as Walter Lorenzen but as genuine.

I dug, flinging board and plaster and found a boot, a pant leg, then all of Howard. The beam pinned his chest.

I brushed dust from his mask lenses.

"Howard?"

He opened his eyes and gasped. "Holy Moly!"

The beam's charcoal surface crumbled warm in my hands but on the second try I budged it, and he wriggled out.

I dropped the beam and made an ash cloud, then faced him.

He stood staring down at an object he turned in his gloved hands.

"Howard, you okay?"

"Perfect. Thank you, Jason. You saved my life. More important, you saved this."

"What is it?"

"Not sure. But it's alien."

He held up a prune-size twisted metal bit, so hot his insulated glove smoked. "This iridescent blue's characteristic of a Projectile hull. Like titanium, but with trace elements rare in the solar system."

"It's worth getting killed for?"

He frowned inside his mask. "Nah. This shrapnel is all we ever find." He waved a hand at the ruins. "We have no idea where to look for anything larger. We've tried every sorting and detection device and methodology."

We walked as he talked.

I pointed at rubble. It looked . . . different. "What about there?"

Howard turned. "Why?"

I shrugged. "I dunno. Something."

Howard shrugged, and we dug.

Two minutes later, I touched it. Inside my suit, hair stood on my neck.

"Howard . . ." I wrapped my gloved fingers around something curved, then yanked.

It popped loose, and I stumbled back.

The thing I held was iridescent, blue metal, dinner-plate size, and so hot it warmed my skin through my gloves.

Howard pounced from where he had been digging and snatched it away, muttering, "Holy Moly, Holy Moly."

He rotated the fragment. The convex side was scorched black. "This was the exterior surface. It was coated with ceramic that friction burned away as the Projectile entered our atmosphere."

"It's important?"

"Biggest frag we've ever found. Most of the Projectile vaporizes." He drew his finger along one side of the fragment. It was a round edge, like somebody had taken a bite, and silver. "But this part here is the prize."

"What?"

"My educated hunch—the army puts up with me because I have good educated hunches—is this is a rocket-nozzle edge."

"So?"

He punched a button on a handheld global-positioning unit, and it beeped. I supposed he was marking the location where we found this little treasure. He motioned for me to turn around, unzipped my backpack, slipped the frag into an insulated bag, and dropped it in. My light pack got heavier. Now I understood why Howard requested an infantryman. He needed a pack mule.

"The radius of this nozzle is too small to be a main propulsion system for a vehicle that was as big as a building. It's a maneuvering nozzle. We've been of two schools on how these vehicles are so accurate. One school of thought is they're ballistic. Fire-and-forget, like a bullet. But from a range of three hundred million miles that seemed unlikely to some of us. This confirms that they make midcourse corrections."

"Like remote control?"

He shook his head. "That's what the others will say, now. But neither radio astronomy nor any other monitoring has picked up any signals to these Projectiles. And we've certainly been listening."

"What do you think, Howard?"

He snugged my pack, spun me, and we again picked our way through debris. "You tell me, Jason."

Professors. The Socratic method. I was coming to appreciate the army. They just told you how it was.

I pushed my helmet back and scratched my head through the protective suit. "I dunno. I have a hard time hitting a rifle target with a bullet past three hundred meters, much less three hundred million miles. I think the Projectiles must be guided. But I wouldn't do it by remote control. I had a radio-controlled model car once, with one of those antenna boxes? Every time our neighbor hit his automatic garage-door opener my car turned left."

Howard stepped over a fallen lamppost. "Great minds think alike. Why would these aliens risk signals that we could jam?"

Well, then, how did Howard think they steered these things? I shuddered. "Pilots?"

He nodded. "Kamikazes."

I shuddered. "We're looking for alien bodies?"

"The chances of finding one after impact are infinitesimal. But an alien corpse could teach us enough to turn this war."

"Like why they hate us enough to exterminate us."

He stirred bricks with his walking stick. "Hate us? We didn't hate the AIDS virus. We eradicated it because it was killing us. Maybe *I Love Lucy* reruns we broadcast into space last century cause birth defects in their young."

For the next six hours I jumped every time Howard poked rubble with his stick, expecting to see ET's charred carcass. We had no more narrow escapes. We made no more Holy Moly–provoking discoveries. But we collected enough scrap to restore an antique Buick. My pack clanked with every step.

Dusk fell as we returned to spook camp. Howard actually whistled behind his mask, pleased with the day's loot. Of course, he wasn't carrying the Buick.

In a trailer, Howard helped me out of the pack. "Jason, why did you dig there? Where we found the big hull fragment?"

I shrugged. "Seemed right."

"Very right."

We shed our protective suits, now soot-blackened. He caught one foot in a leg. As he pogoed for balance, he asked. "You're in Basic, now?"

I nodded.

He stared at my pack on the trailer floor. "You have a permanent assignment when you finish?"

"If I finish. I'm kind of a fuck-up."

Evening chow was over by the time the spooks released me back to Third Platoon. Civilians trickled away with the last of the distributed C-rations. Walter asked, "Whadja do, Jason?"

"Same ole', same ole'." I shrugged. The last thing that happened before Howard released me was a Judge Advocate General's Corps major made me sign in triplicate a paper that said I'd never tell that Howard's outfit existed. Hell, after I read it I wasn't sure I could admit that Pittsburgh existed or I existed.

Walter had scrounged me a bacon-and-scrambled-eggs C-ration meal and even a plasti of Coke. My mouth watered, even at the prospect of C-rations.

My back ached from humping Hibble's war souvenirs, my face blistered from blast-furnace heat where the mask hadn't reached. I ate seated with my back against a deuce-and-a-half tire. The day with Howard Hibble taught me that, quietly, humanity hadn't quit. If I hung in, maybe the army and I could make a difference.

EIGHT

AFTER WE CONVOYED BACK FROM PITTSBURGH, the battalion commander gave us a day off. Most people slept. I went to the day room and discovered books. Not Chipbooks. Paper books.

Every company area has a day room. It's a lounge for soldiers to spend their free time. Of which there normally is none in Basic. I think the army named it because an hour there feels like a day.

Ours had a manual Foosball table with one of the little men broken off, a tray of yesterday's mess-hall cookies, coffee, and ancient orange furniture covered in the skin of animals so extinct I'd never heard of them. Really. I read the labels. "Naugahyde."

Shelved books lined the walls, the way libraries used to be. Not exactly the *New York Times* most-downloaded list, of course. There were yellowed field manuals on everything from first aid to the ever-popular FM-22-5 Drill and Ceremony. Better were *The Art of War* by Sun

Tzu and General Eisenhower's *Crusade in Europe*. Whole shelves held histories of the campaigns of Napoleon, Robert E. Lee, and Alexander the Great, complete with color maps that folded out just like a wide-screen you could actually touch.

Books aren't like chips. You feel them and smell their age.

Some have a life of their own. Inside one's cover was handwritten, "DaNang, Vietnam, May 2, 1966—To a short-timer who won't have to study war no more." Another read, "For Captain A. R. Johns, KIA Normandy, France, July 9, 1944." It didn't say if he had a family. He could have been orphaned, like me. But he had an outfit forever. The First Infantry Division.

I devoured the books shelf by shelf and just made it back to barracks by lights-out. I persuaded myself my obsession was just because I was starved for intellectual stimulation after Basic's moribund mud. The alternative was that Ord and Judge March foresaw that the army and I were a pre-destined match, a notion too bent and knobby to contemplate. I snuck Benton's *The Sino-Indian Conflict: Winter Campaign 2022* back with me and skimmed it while my free hand scrubbed commodes with Ord's brush.

The nights that followed, for me, were stolen moments to read the day-room library. The days we spent in the woods learning small-unit tactics.

The Reformed Me enjoyed small-unit tactics. You see, one soldier with a rifle is just a serial killer with a hunting license.

But even a squad of twelve can multiply its combat power if it's properly coordinated and armed. The mission succeeds, and fewer GIs come home in bags.

Our instructors said stuff like "Today you will become familiar with the force-multiplying capacity of crew-served weapons integral to the Infantry platoon." In other words, why a machine gun was good even though it took two soldiers to carry it.

Our training now involved more field maneuver and specialized-weapons familiarization. Firing the M-60 Model 2017 was even grander than humping all forty-five pounds of the machine gun cross-country. The loader has it even worse because the ammo's even heavier. For the rest of tactical training, I carried the machine gun. My offers to let others share the fun fell on deaf ears. Esprit de corps went just so far. I shut up and got used to it.

After a few weeks Walter whispered during noon chow, "One of the guys said you were okay, Jason."

We were eating in the field, seated backs against trees amid dead piled leaves in the perpetual twilight draped over Pennsylvania—and Earth—by stratospheric dust. By the calendar, it was summer, now, but felt like dry winter. I missed green leaves.

I squeezed brown glop from a foil pouch into my mouth and swallowed. The slightly less antique successors to C-rations were MREs, Meals-Ready-to-Eat. Three lies for the price of one. "I already know I'm okay, Walter."

"But it's the first time I've heard anybody else say it. I think that's good."

So did I. Good or not, the world worsened.

The pancake-flat stock market stayed that way, so retirees like my short-term foster parents, the Ryans, couldn't live off their investments. The Armed Services maxed out in taking new recruits like us. There were only so many holes soldiers could dig just to fill them up again.

For all our bitching, GIs were eating okay, and the enemy had left humanity with fewer mouths to feed. Civilian fresh food was rationed, supermarket prices were sky-high and going higher, and there was an active black market in things like apples and coffee. Even in places that hadn't suffered like Pittsburgh.

It looked like my machine gun's principal utility after training ended would be dispersing food rioters. An M-60 Model 2017 was a Vietnam-era blunderbuss sleeked up in post-Afghan neoplast. But it could turn a rioting crowd into a Dumpsterful of guts. Pulling that trigger didn't bear thinking about.

Still, I figured to graduate in two weeks. They'd given us each a pack of old-fashioned postcards engraved with the Infantry crest. Graduation ceremony announcements to mail out to our loved ones. Refreshments immediately following in the mess hall. Maybe goodies would be ham and limas and everybody's mom would have to hand-walk the horizontal ladder to get in.

At first I cried, being short of loved ones. Then I sucked it up and sent a card to Druwan Parker. I'd only known him a day before he broke his leg, but he was the next best thing to family. I mailed one to Metzger for grins. He had made captain, deflected two Projectiles while flying in space between Earth and the moon. His smiling face and chestful of medals made the *People* homepage. I sent a third announcement to Judge March. I figured it might make the old boy smile before he clapped some other delinquent in irons.

An M-60 gunner—I had become quite the dead-eye— was a specialist fourth class. After Basic, I'd be assigned to a line unit.

I might even live dormitory-style with a roommate and regular heat and a john with a door. After Basic Training, that sounded like promotion to chairman of the Joint Chiefs of Staff.

A few months ago I was a homeless orphan looking at jail time. Today, I was collecting a paycheck I didn't even have time to spend, learning about things I hadn't even known existed. I had three hots and a cot and belonged to an extended family the size of the US army.

Life was sweet.

I thought.

NINE

WE SHOULD NEVER HAVE EVEN *BEEN* at the hand-grenade range on the training cycle's last day. But there we sat in bleachers, while Ord lectured up front. Behind him a trench maze zigzagged down to a line of four sandbagged pits.

We would soon waddle through those trenches to the pits, from which we would hurl live grenades. Ten yards downrange beyond the pits, splintered, dead tree trunks stood. A grenade exploded into four hundred shards of metal shrapnel. If the trees weren't reminder enough that this was live fire, at our backs idled an ambulance, medics dangling their feet over the tailgate.

Would the medics give me oxygen if I told them I couldn't breathe? Every one of us trainees was tight about this. But for me it was worse. All I could see was Arnold Rudawitz's fingernail, cherry-bombed and dangling bloody from his index finger as he ran screaming to his mom while she barbecued Fourth of July chicken.

Normally, Basic Training climaxed by playing war out in the boonies for a couple days, sleeping in tents and foxholes, and eating only rations we carried. Kind of a doctoral thesis of dirt grubbing.

But one Basic Training rite of passage is to throw a live hand grenade. We hadn't. The army was supposed to have sent Indiantown Gap live grenades long ago. For twelve weeks the grenades were expected momentarily, like the Russian coal that arrived late and the physical-training gym shoes that arrived never.

So we had already completed our final field exercise, and we had the last day to kill. I can't believe I just wrote that.

Everybody wore helmets. Except the drills, of course. They swaggered around in their Smokey Bears, as if a felt hat would intimidate a short-fused grenade. They dragged rope-handled wooden boxes of grenades forward into the pits, then returned.

Walter whispered, "A guy last cycle got one with an instantaneous fuse. He was lucky. It only blew his arm off."

A guy behind us said, "I heard the primers are so old there are lots of short fuses."

My heart battered my ribs as I saw again Rudawitz's bloody finger.

I felt Walter's shoulder warm against mine. Goofy as he was, I had come to depend on Walter. He was always there, and I always knew what he was thinking, like Metzger and me. I suppose to people who grew up with siblings that's normal. To me it was amazing.

A drill demonstrated grenade-throwing. The grenade top has a spring-loaded hammer in it that's held back by a lever that curves along the grenade's body. A pin holds the lever down. You pull the pin while you hold the lever with your thumb. When you throw, the lever flies off, the hammer snaps like a mousetrap and sets off the primer. Four seconds or so later, the primer detonates the main explosive. Wire wrapped inside and the ball-shaped metal casing blow to pieces. They gut everything for a five-meter radius.

My vision blurred. All I could see was blood and severed fingernails.

I had done many new, scary things in Basic. But I couldn't throw that live grenade. Yet I had to or fail to graduate.

"Jason? You're shaking. Are you alright?"

"Yeah." Until about a minute from now, when I'd puke.

Against my shoulder, Walter shook. "I know how you feel. About now it would be nice to have Prozac."

Yeah. I slipped my hand into my trouser pocket and touched two pellets. I had worn these fatigues the first training day. My two leftover Prozac IIs still lay in there. I fingered them. Flattened by countless launderings but still potent inside their indestructible plastic wrap, they defied the zero-drug-tolerance regs.

My hands trembled. I'd drop the fucking grenade right at my own feet. If my hands would just stop shaking for twenty minutes, though, I'd be okay. I'd waltz through the trench lineup, into the throw pit, march back out and back to barracks to brush down my Class-A uniform for graduation.

The drill showed how the exercise would work while the breeze twitched his hat brim. He held the grenade in one hand with his thumb pinning that lever down like his life depended on it. Because it did.

He stuck the finger of his nonthrowing hand through the ring that was attached to the pin that held down the lever.

The drill said, "Short fuses are extremely rare. A bigger problem is trainees dropping the weapon. Don't!"

Easy for him to say. I truly could not breathe. The drill stood in a throw pit and jerked his grenade's pin.

While everybody concentrated on him, I skinned the plastic off the 'Zacs and smeared a hand across my face. I gagged them down, dry.

The drill threw. We all ducked and covered while he dropped behind the sandbag wall.

Nothing happened.

Well, nothing happened for the longest four seconds you ever heard.

Boom!

Dirt and spent shrapnel rained on those of us forward in the trench.

Up ahead, the drill stood and dusted himself off.

I smiled as the Prozacs' tingling glow spread through me.

Ahead, the first trainee in line stepped forward into the sandbagged pit with a drill smack on his elbow. The drill unwrapped a grenade from a cardboard sleeve, talked the guy through everything while he looked him in the eye, then handed him the grenade.

Somebody behind us shouted, "Fire in the hole! Fire in the hole! Fire in the hole!" We all ducked and covered in the trench.

I felt myself breathe, nice and easy. Beside me, Walter still seemed tight. I whispered, "Cakewalk."

"Sure."

Boom! It rained dirt clods. We all looked up as the trainee and the drill stood and dusted themselves off.

The procedure was the drill tackled the thrower instantly after the grenade left the trainee's hand and knocked him behind the sandbags. Evidently people had a tendency to watch the grenade fly downrange. Nobody understood why people did that, since there were no points for distance or accuracy.

So, unless the thrower got a short fuse, then so long as the grenade even dropped a couple feet beyond the sandbags nobody got hurt. Your aunt Minnie could throw it far enough.

We moved to the on-deck circle.

I wasn't exactly smiling, but with the Prozac II kicked in, I could do this, now. The drill and trainee ahead of me moved up into the sandbag revetment. I looked over my shoulder at Walter, crouching twenty feet back. His eyes were wide. I gave him a thumbs-up, and he stretched a smile.

Prozac or not, my heart pounded. Second Platoon's drill hoisted me by the elbow. "Our turn, Wander."

The last thrower passed me on the way back, grinning and working his jaw to get the ringing out of his ears.

In a few seconds that would be me.

We moved into the sandbag revetment. I could feel Walter's presence twenty feet behind me in the on-deck circle I had just vacated.

My blood chilled. What if he fucked up? Walter always fucked up. What if I got through it and Walter blew himself up?

I started to look back.

The drill grabbed my shoulders and held my eyes with his. "Wander? Listen up!"

"Yes, Drill Sergeant."

He was just running through the procedure, saying something. If anything happened to Walter, it would be like losing Mom again. Walter was my little brother.

"Got it?"

I felt myself nodding, then something heavy pressed into my right hand. Prozac or not, I shook.

It was going to be fine. What was going to be fine? I didn't know, and I didn't care. I just wanted things to be over with.

"Throw it! Wander!"

I looked down at my hand. The grenade trembled there, but it looked different. I could see the little hammer quite clearly. There was no lever. It spun through the air and tinged against a sandbag. I'd pulled the pin and released the lever and the grenade was still here. How interesting.

"Fuck!" The drill grabbed my wrist, and the grenade dropped from my flexing fingers.

Not flew.

Dropped. At my feet. It rocked there in the dirt, trailing a white-smoke thread from its top. The primer had detonated.

I had dropped my grenade with us inside the sandbag wall. In four seconds I would die.

The drill rammed into my chest and wrapped his arms, like a linebacker. Sandbags thudded against the backs of my thighs and we toppled backward, across the sandbag wall and out of the pit.

Two thoughts floated across my mind. So this was what happened when a trainee dropped a grenade. The drill just knocked himself and the trainee over the sandbag wall. As long as grenade and people ended up on opposite sides of the sandbags, nobody got hurt. I was going to live.

The second thought was that Walter was running toward me, his mouth open, screaming. "Jason!"

Behind him, a guy in the on-deck circle grabbed out at the place where Walter had lain.

Walter dove headfirst, arms out like Superman.

I saw his eyes, scared and proud at the same time as his torso fell across the grenade.

Then the drill's momentum carried both of us backward over the wall, and I saw only my boots silhouetted against the sky's gray shroud.

My back hit the ground, the drill's shoulder drove down on my chest, knocked wind from me, and I saw stars.

TEN

BREATH EXPLODED FROM MY BODY like a detonating
grenade. I lay paralyzed and tried to suck air. The grenade
must have been a dud, thank God.

Plock. Plock, plock. Dirt clods rained down. One
struck my cheek. Not a dud. The grenade had exploded.
The drill lay across my body, so heavy his heart thudded
against my ribs.

The dirt on my cheek was warm. I wiped it away and
held it in front of my eyes. It dripped red. Flesh.

I tried to scream, but I still had no breath. I couldn't
hear anything anyway. Ruptured eardrums?

A silhouette jerked across the sky. A Smokey Bear hat.
Fourth Platoon's drill vaulted the sandbag wall alongside
us. "Jesus. Fuck." It sounded like he spoke through a pillow.

He yelled, "Medic! Get the fuckin' medic!"

Walter! I shoved the drill off me, sat up, and rolled to
my knees. Other heads bobbed on the opposite side of the

sandbag wall. I scrambled up, pulled myself across, and looked down into the revetment.

Smoke swirled around people kneeling beside Walter. He lay facedown where he landed, his arms still stretched out. His cheek rested against the earth and his eyes were open. He looked fine, though his glasses were crooked, the way they got, even with that elastic band he wore around the back of his head.

Except that below his belt he was gone.

Just gone. He was just a head and torso, like a GI Joe doll thrown in the trash.

Somebody was screaming, over and over. It was me.

ELEVEN

THE MEDIC KNELT BESIDE ME and pressed me back against the sandbags. "Easy, man! You're okay."

He inspected me. Somebody else looked over the drill who had knocked me out of the sandbag pit and maybe saved my life. To the extent Walter hadn't.

"Not okay! Walter's dead!" I wept.

A voice drifted from beyond the medic's shoulder. "This one's uninjured?" Ord bent forward, hands on knees.

"Yeah, Sarge. Shock, bleeding from the nose and ears. Maybe lost an eardrum. The other kid you saw . . ." The medic leaned toward Ord. "Sarge? This one's on something."

Ord stiffened. "What?"

"Look at his pupils."

"He's just agitated."

"No, Sarge. Maybe just Prozac II. But he's on something."

"I was scared. I didn't think I could do it. It was just two pills I had left."

Ord grabbed my shoulder and squeezed, hard. I couldn't tell whether he was mad at me, or he was trying to get me to shut up. I shut up.

The medic said, "You know regs, Sarge. I gotta write this up."

Ord crossed his arms over his chest. Behind him they were loading a bag onto a litter. Walter.

I couldn't breathe. The medic held my cheeks in his hands and made me look at him. "You just took Prozac? Like within an hour? Nothing else?"

I nodded.

He slid my sleeve up, I smelled alcohol, and felt a needle prick my forearm. "This will calm you down, man."

"Thanks."

"You may not thank me later."

Things got fuzzy.

The next thing I remember was the infirmary ceiling. White-painted boards strung with naked lightbulbs. A plastic IV sack full of clear liquid hung beside me and connected to my forearm with a tube. I lay in a room as white as the ceiling, rowed with a half dozen empty beds.

Double swinging doors at the ward's end were half-paned in frosted glass. Two silhouettes moved gray beyond the glass.

"You should have washed him out weeks ago, Art!" The speaker had Captain Jacowicz's square-jawed profile.

"He's bright, sir. He was coming around." Ord.

"He was an accident waiting to happen!"

"Sir, they're all accidents waiting to happen. It's our job to make them soldiers, not wash them out."

"And Lorenzen? What kind of soldier will he make, now?"

The silhouettes didn't move.

"You're right, sir. It's my responsibility, not the trainee's."

"Bullshit, Art! You're too good a soldier to bust your career because a druggie disobeyed standing orders. With your age and record you should have been a division sergeant major driving a desk years ago."

"I prefer field assignments, sir."

"Well, I prefer to lay blame where it's deserved. And that's not on you. Even if you did fuck up. You know the procedure. He gets admin or a court. You know I'll keep an open mind. But if he chooses administrative punishment in front of me, I'm presently inclined to take it to the maximum. That's still a lot better deal than he'd get in a court-martial, if I'm giving odds."

"Sir, a court would require presentation of evidence—"

"Evidence? He told the medic he was on drugs!"

More silence.

"I never expected you of all people to have trouble understanding an order, Sergeant. Explain his options to him as soon as he's coherent."

I watched my IV drip.

"Yes, sir," Ord said.

Boot clicks faded away down the hall, and one silhouette remained on the frosted glass. Ord bent his head forward, removed his Smokey Bear hat, seemed to look down into it, and sighed.

I felt myself drift away again. I smiled. I had to be dreaming. I might have believed it was real, but Jacowicz said Ord had fucked up, which was impossible.

They released me from the infirmary two days later.

When I got back to barracks, it was tomb-quiet. Mattresses lay rolled up across wire bed springs. Packed duffels piled on the buffed floor waited to be carried off. Third Platoon graduated today. My boots echoed in the empty bay as I walked to Ord's office.

I saw him through his open doorway, seated at his desk, writing on paper with a pen.

I swallowed, then knocked.

"Come!"

"Trainee Wander reports, Drill Sergeant."

He looked up and put down the pen. "You're well?"

"The doctor says well enough, Drill Sergeant."

He nodded. "Wander, was the standing order regarding drugs unclear?"

I read upside down. It was becoming a habit when I visited Ord. Ord's letter was addressed in cursive handwriting to Mrs. Lillian Lorenzen. It began, "Your son was a fine young man and a fine soldier." That was as far as Ord had gotten. Three balled-paper sheets nested in his wastebasket.

Tears burned my eyes. I swallowed.

"It was clear, Drill Sergeant. I made a horrible choice. But it was my choice, nobody else's."

He nodded, again. "Whether I agree or not, you have two options, now. You can elect a trial by court-martial on charges or you can elect administrative punishment. The first means you will be defended by a member of the Judge Advocate General's Corps in a trial before a jury. You choose whether the jury's noncommissioned or commissioned officers. Most enlisted men choose commissioned officers. The conventional wisdom is noncoms are hard asses."

"Surely not, Drill Sergeant."

He nearly smiled. "The second option is administrative punishment by your commanding officer. No appeal if you don't like what he dishes out. A crapshoot. But the conventional wisdom is that admin is the way to go because you just have to persuade one guy who knows you, not a bunch of strangers."

"That commanding officer would be Captain Jacowicz?" Jacowicz hadn't sounded sympathetic outside the infirmary door.

"It's true Captain Jacowicz goes by the book—"

My future was on the line. No time for tact. "Goes by it? The guys say he rams a fresh copy up his butt every morning to make himself stand stiffer!"

Ord looked down, covered his mouth with his hand, coughed, then said, "Be that as it may, Captain Jacowicz is a fair man. He comes from a distinguished line of soldiers. I served under General Jacowicz in the Second Afghan War."

Captain Jacowicz was the same guy who had lectured that we would be shot for abusing enemy prisoners, when the human race had about as much chance of taking prisoners as I had of flying to the moon. Throw myself on Jacowicz's tender mercies or get court-martialed. Fat chance or no chance. "What's the worst I could get?"

"Worst? Stockade time, likely less than a year, and a dishonorable discharge."

"I can do time. Just so I can stay in."

He frowned. "The likely result is the other way around, Wander."

My heart sank. Ord was right. I'd heard Jacowicz say outside the infirmary that he would kick me out.

"I want to stay in. I *have* to stay in."

He covered his letter with his hand. "Son, that result may not be in the cards."

"Walter was all I had in the world, Drill Sergeant. Now the army is all I have." Until the words rattled out I hadn't realized what Walter and the army had come to mean to me. But I had just told the truth. If Jacowicz wouldn't save me, I'd take a chance. "I want a court-martial."

Ord drummed his fingers. He looked down at the letter under his palm. He shook his head and looked me in the eye. "Son, you pick a court, you're out. I've seen enough of them to know."

My throat swelled shut, and I tried to blink back tears. One squeezed out anyway and ran hot down my cheek. Ord put a hand on my shoulder. "You'll get through this, son. We all will."

I looked down at Ord's letter. Walter wouldn't get through it. I might as well put the army behind me. Get out of Ord's hair, out of this mess.

"If I just want out on a DD, would Captain Jacowicz let me skip the admin hearing and duck stockade time?"

"Likely. But . . ."

That was it, then. Quit. Take my discharge, then take my chances with Judge March and prison or civilian life. "Okay. Just tell the captain I want out on a DD."

"Or . . . graduation is in two hours. You could make your own case to the captain in a hearing in one. Nothing to lose."

I shook my head and felt the cord around my neck. "Does the Drill Sergeant want his toothbrush back?" I wouldn't need it back in civilian life. I reached up to strip it off.

Ord cleared his throat. "I generally ask for it back after

graduation. Nobody I've given it to's ever . . . quit before. Maybe that was the real you that first day, after all. A no-guts joker."

The son of a bitch. Just when I thought he might care about me he had kicked me down a flight of stairs. I jammed the brush back inside my uniform blouse. The smart thing was to quit. My breath rattled short and quick. Ord made me so mad I didn't care about the smart thing. He didn't smile, but I thought maybe he nodded.

"Okay, dammit! You want guts? Jacowicz won't get rid of me without a fight. I want a hearing and I want it now!"

TWELVE

I SAT ON THE NAKED STEEL SPRINGS of what had been my bunk while I brushed down my Class-A uniform, then dressed and headed across the company street to my destiny.

Beyond the windows of Captain Jacowicz's outer office, summer at Indiantown Gap loomed as dark and cold as my future. An orderly sat behind a gray metal desk, his eyes staring blank at a flatscreen while he talked records into silicon chips.

There were empty chairs across from his desk, but I leaned against the wall so I didn't crease my uniform. I tugged up my trouser leg and polished a patent-leather low-cut on my sock. I plucked at lapel lint. It's not that I'd turned as gung ho as the captain. It's just that at the moment he held my life in his hands, so no amount of sucking up seemed like overkill. Frost framed the windows, but under my jacket I'd sweated through my uniform blouse already.

I'd read up on administrative punishment. It was pretty much what Ord had said. The accused threw himself on the mercy of his commanding officer instead of making his case with the so-called protections of the Uniform Code of Military Justice.

The theory was that you had a better chance to persuade one guy who knew you rather than a bunch of board-up-the-ass officers or noncoms. The trouble with administrative punishment was that if your CO threw the book at you, there was no Supreme Court to save you.

Jacowicz could slap me with a dishonorable discharge, stockade time, both, or I could just get extra duty out the ass or even just a chewing out. The last two seemed improbable.

"Soldier!"

If I hadn't already been standing, I would have popped up higher than burned toast. The orderly did.

Ord stepped in from outdoors and acted like he didn't see me. He said to the orderly, "I seem to have misplaced my training schedule. Print me one, Corporal."

While the corporal printed out a copy Ord looked over like he just saw me. He nodded. "Trainee Wander."

"Drill Sergeant."

Ord knew the training schedule like it was tattooed on his scrotum. It was flattering that he'd phonied up an excuse just to see me.

The corporal handed over the printout and returned to his work. Ord looked at me and elevated his jaw just a nudge.

I picked mine up, too. He nodded, then made a fist and pumped it back and forth an inch, like a piston.

I nodded back as he turned and walked out the door.

Something swelled up in my chest, and I almost smiled. That was about as close as Ord ever got to kissing somebody on both cheeks.

The intercom on the orderly's desk buzzed.

"Send in Trainee Wander!" Jacowicz's voice hinted of nothing.

I couldn't breathe, couldn't make my legs move. If I just stood here the worst couldn't happen.

The corporal jerked a thumb at the captain's office door. "Yo! Wander. You heard the man."

I shuffled forward, rapped on the doorjamb and the captain called back, "Come!"

The corporal whispered, "Good luck, man."

Jacowicz was in Class-A's, too. Graduation ceremony would follow booting my ass. He returned my salute and shuffled papers.

He looked up, put me at ease so I could sway and talk, but left me standing.

"Do I have to recount the facts, Wander?"

"No, sir. I can do it for you." I figured the best defense was a good offense. "I ingested a prohibited substance during duty hours. While under the influence a training accident occurred. A—"

The sight of Walter lying there wouldn't go away. I squeezed my eyes shut and swallowed.

"I know you and Lorenzen were close. That doesn't make your misconduct less serious."

"No, sir."

"Do you dispute the facts in any way?"

"No, sir."

"Do you have anything to offer in mitigation?"

I took a deep breath. "Sir, I believe the incident taught

me a lot. I believe it will make me a stronger soldier. I am strongly motivated to overcome the adverse impact of this event. I am willing to accept any administrative punishment that will allow me to continue to serve."

Jacowicz rubbed his jaw. "That's almost verbatim what your drill sergeant's recommendation says. I don't believe for one minute that he coached you. I think it is testament to his influence that you reached those conclusions independently. It speaks well for you, trainee."

My heart pounded. There was a chance.

He flipped a file page. "I'm looking at a copy of a letter I wrote. To Trainee Lorenzen's mother. It's the first such letter I have had to write."

I felt my eyes burn and blinked.

"Trainee Wander, my father was Infantry."

"Yes, sir. Sergeant Ord has spoken highly of General Jacowicz."

"He always said that letters like this one measured him as an officer as much as they measured the bravery of the soldiers he wrote about."

I nodded. I couldn't tell where this was going.

"I view this incident as a measure of my failure."

"Sir, the fault was mine."

"If I should allow you to remain in the service, you will be commanded by other officers."

"It would be my great privilege, sir."

"And if you faltered again, they would have to write more letters."

Oh no.

"That is a chance I am not prepared to take," he said.

"Sir—"

He grimaced. "Look, Wander. I gave this a lot of

thought before you got here. I'm not trying to ruin your life. If you had been a civilian, then taking those pills wouldn't have meant a damn thing. I am not going to impose administrative punishment of any sort. No forfeiture of pay and allowances, no letter of reprimand to your file. Your discharge will be general, not dishonorable. That's a lot better for you when you go to an employer in the civilian—"

"Sir, to stay in is the one thing I want!"

He stopped and stared, then turned his chair toward the window and looked away from me.

Seconds crawled by on his display-screen clock.

He turned back and looked up at me.

His eyes weren't cold, but they were hard. "I'm sorry, Wander. The one thing you want is the one thing I can't give you."

I heard myself breathing in hoarse gasps. I had known this was coming, but somehow I thought, somehow—

The orderly stuck his head in the door at the same moment he rapped on it. "Sir, there's someone here to see you."

"They can wait. You know I said—"

"Not they, sir. He. He insists."

The captain stood, balled his fists, and leaned on them across his desk. "Corporal, this is my company. Whoever it is will wait until this administrative proceeding is closed!"

THIRTEEN

"I DIDN'T COME ALL THIS WAY to watch some clerk talk to a computer!"

I turned and saw a gorilla-size silhouette darken Jacowicz's doorway.

Judge March bulled past the orderly and planted his feet in the middle of Jacowicz's office. The old boy wore a black suit with the sleeve pinned and a bow tie. I looked closer. The button-size fabric rosette in his lapel was pale blue with white stars. It was the first one I'd ever seen. The old boy was a Medal of Honor winner.

Jacowicz cocked his head. "Who the hell are you?" Then he stretched his neck forward toward Judge March's lapel and the Medal of Honor rosette. The only reward America's highest decoration actually brings you is that everybody up to the chairman of the Joint Chiefs of Staff owes you a salute.

Jacowicz straightened and snapped off a sharp one.

The judge returned it. "My name is March. Formerly Colonel March, Captain."

His Honor a full bird? Damn!

"Sir, what are you doing here?" Jacowicz asked.

"I'm here for Trainee Wander's graduation from Basic. With no goddam planes flying it took me thirty-six hours on a train."

Jacowicz and I looked at him like he'd grown fur.

"Jason sent me an invitation."

"I don't understand," said Jacowicz.

"Trainee Wander was once what you might call a customer of mine. I traded my rank for a judgeship years ago. But when I called for more information about the ceremony I heard about Jason's problems and about this upcoming hearing."

Ord. He had to have talked to Ord.

Jacowicz thrust out his jaw. "It's not upcoming. It's over."

"You know better, Captain. Whether the proceeding stays closed is entirely within your discretion."

Jacowicz stared at Judge March. "Why would I want to reopen the matter?"

"I'd like to speak on behalf of Trainee Wander."

"As a former field-grade officer, and a judge, you know he's not entitled to counsel."

"He's entitled to fair treatment! As an officer who served with your father, I know that!"

Jacowicz stiffened. "You're *Dickie* March?"

Judge March nodded. He reached his one hand across Jacowicz's desk and touched a framed picture angled toward us. A gray-haired man in fatigues who looked like Jacowicz smiled, a foot on the bumper of an old-fashioned Hummvee. "He was one hell of a soldier."

Jacowicz blinked. "Thank you, Colonel. Judge."

Jacowicz straightened the picture and cleared his throat. "What did you want to say?"

"Trainee Wander came to the Infantry as a result of events I set in motion. I thought it would be good for him. And he for it. I still do."

"He committed a grave offense."

"I understand Trainee Wander took a very normal dose of nonprescription, perfectly legal medication on a single occasion."

"And the regs are crystal-clear on the consequences of such behavior. Especially in light of aggravating circumstances. A trainee died. In combat it could have been far worse." Jacowicz shook his head.

"In combat we understood that even good soldiers make mistakes. And good soldiers are hard to find."

Jacowicz pressed his lips together.

"You know what your father and I did during the Siege of Kabul? When there was nothing to do all day but duck when enemy artillery came in?"

Jacowicz squinted while he nodded politely. So did I. The old fart was rambling.

"We sat around on cots and swapped stories. And we smoked a little grass."

My jaw dropped. Not because I couldn't understand him. "Grass" was old slang for marijuana. It was illegal back then.

Jacowicz seemed to know it, too, because he shook his head, slowly. "I find that incredible."

"I find it incredible that you think your father would

have told you everything he did in his off-duty hours. And that you think it made him a worse soldier. Do you think the army would have been well served to get rid of us if we'd gotten caught?"

Jacowicz pushed back from his desk, spun his chair, and looked out the window with his back to us.

Judge March looked at me and tapped a finger under his chin.

I nodded and raised mine.

In the distance Herc engines whined then died as a transport landed.

Jacowicz spoke without turning to us. "Come back in fifteen minutes."

Judge March and I stood in the company street. "Your Honor, thank you. Thank you so much! For coming. For everything."

Judge March turned to me and flicked his eyes to inspect my shoeshine. "You wear the uniform well. How have you been, Jason?"

"Not so great. Like you heard." It all seemed incredible. That Ord had taken my part. That the judge had come here. That he'd been a decorated, field-grade officer.

Judge March pointed at the mess hall, with its vacant horizontal ladders and that scrawny sapling shivering bare in the breeze. "You think an old soldier could scrounge a cup of coffee in there?"

Three minutes later Judge March and I hunched over coffee cups at an empty mess-hall table while the kitchen grunts clattered around in back burning evening chow.

He sipped. "You ever do any drugs besides that Prozac stuff?"

"Never. Swear to God, Your Honor."

He nodded. "If I ever hear different, I'll pin your ears back."

I wrinkled my brow. When the judge was young, body piercings were wick. But his tone now seemed punitive.

"Sir, why did you do this for me?"

He shrugged. "If you got discharged, you would have been back on my docket. I hate a messy docket."

"Oh."

He stared into his coffee, then looked up and grinned. "No. I just thought you were a kid with potential who needed a push in the right direction. I still do."

Just about now that was the nicest thing anybody ever said to me. I shook my head. "Sir, that is such a coincidence that you served with the captain's father. And that you and he, you know, smoked up."

The judge poured from the glass sugar shaker into his coffee with his remaining hand. He set down the shaker, picked up a spoon, and stirred. "Son, there's a saying among the criminal defendants who come before me. They think I don't know it."

"Sir?"

"If the truth won't set you free, lie your ass off."

He sipped coffee, shrugged, and watched my jaw drop. The mendacious old son of a bitch.

We sat and drank coffee for minutes.

The mess-hall door opened and Jacowicz's orderly poked his head in. "Wander! Captain's ready for you."

I squeezed my cup tighter.

"Move your ass, man!" The orderly pulled his head back and let the door slam. I must've jumped a foot.

When we got back, Jacowicz shooed the judge out.

The captain rocked in his chair and steepled his fingers

beneath his chin. "About that marijuana business. My father told me all about Colonel March. Dickie March was a good soldier but a rule-bender. They drank together but neither of them ever touched a joint."

My blood chilled. Jacowicz had caught my defender in a lie that slandered Jacowicz's dead father.

"Wander, do you know how Judge March won his Medal of Honor?"

I shook my head.

"During the Second Afghan War, my dad and Dickie March were the only survivors when a surface-to-air rocket knocked down a helicopter. My dad broke both legs. Major March's arm was crushed and pinned by wreckage. The wreck caught fire. Dickie March used an entrenching tool and hacked off the tissue threads that attached his own arm so he could drag my dad out before the wreck exploded. Then he evaded enemy patrols for three days, carrying my dad on his back, until they were rescued."

Jacowicz rocked back in his chair and fingered another frame, a holo of a pretty woman holding a baby. "I'd sacrifice anything for my wife and my son. But parents and children rarely actually have to make those sacrifices. Soldiers do. In combat, what we fight for isn't God or country or even the people we love back home. We fight for the GI next to us. They're more family to us than anyone else we'll ever know."

I swallowed. "Sir?"

"I owe Dickie March. My dad owed him. Dickie March is family. If Dickie March thinks you're worth lying for, that's enough for me. So don't think you're staying in the army because some naive West Pointer believed a lame lie. You're staying because somebody I care about believes you can make a difference."

Staying. My heart leapt.

"Sir, I'll be the best soldier—"

"Save it. I hear promises of life-changing experience daily. I'm sure the judge does in his court, too. If you stay in, this incident goes in your record jacket. You'll be denied every decent assignment in the army."

It couldn't be worse than Basic. I just drifted with the moment while my heart fluttered.

". . . make us both late for graduation, Wander. I said 'dismissed!' " He waved his hand.

I nearly forgot to salute as I spun an about-face. Basic was behind me! The worst mistake of my life was behind me!

Graduation was all the better because the judge stuck around and watched. Afterward, in the mess hall, we ate cookies and drank Beverage-Grape-Powdered and shook hands with everybody's mothers and fathers. I tried to buy the judge a steak dinner over in Hershey, Pennsylvania, but he got the tab. We both cried as I put him on the train back to Colorado.

We all got two weeks' leave after Basic. Most trainees had family to go home to. The closest person to me left on Earth was Metzger.

He flew out of Canaveral. With no commercial air, I had to deadhead a lift with a military truck convoy to Philadelphia, then hitch another lift with another convoy headed south.

The truck ride to Philly was bumpy and cold and gave me time to think. I thought about Walter, about the fate of the world, but mostly about what an idiot I had just been.

Jacowicz had said I could have walked away from the army.

Instead, I had fought my way back into a low-paying, dirty, dangerous job. A job where my screwups left me with no shot at advancing. Recruits like Druwan Parker, my broken-leg bunkmate with the high-ranking relative, might make a career in the army. Not me. The farther I got away from Indiantown Gap the more clearly I saw reality.

The freight depot in Philly was in a warehouse district. A big room with a supply sergeant behind a gray metal desk, vending machines on one wall, and a couple vinyl sofas, it smelled of wet cardboard. I had hours to kill before the southbound convoy left for Florida.

A couple civilians, guys near twenty, sat atop their luggage. Recruits, bound for Basic at Indiantown Gap with another convoy. Shaggy, unpressed, smart-ass. In short, me a few months ago.

I sprawled across a sofa and watched the supply sergeant run inventory on his screen. His olive skin was acne-pocked, and a scar twisted along his jawline.

"Where you from, Sarge?"

"The Bronx." His name tag read "Ochoa." Regular noncommissioned officers weren't like drills. Anybody could shoot the breeze with them.

"What you doin' there, Sarge?" I pointed at his screen.

"Entering paper goods inventory we got in this warehouse."

"Like what?"

"Toilet paper. Wrapping paper."

"Gotta keep 'em separate, huh?"

He shrugged. "This is the army. Paper is paper."

"You like your job?"

He shrugged. "I'm short."

As in short-time-until-discharge.

"Never figured I'd get to retire."

"Why not?"

"I've had my share of admins."

As in administrative-punishment hearings. A resource!

"What for?"

"Bar fights, mostly. I was stationed on a navy base." He spit tobacco juice into a bucket alongside his desk. "Who can drink with squids?"

Fair point.

"It didn't keep you from getting promoted."

"The army takes care of its own."

My chest swelled.

He shrugged. "Unless you got a drug incident in your record."

My heart sank.

"You dope, no hope."

"You mean coke addicts. What if somebody just did Prozac?"

He shook his head. "This is the army. Drugs is drugs."

I stared at my low-cuts. A fat lot of good it had done me to learn how to keep a shine on my shoes. This guy was me in twenty years, even if I *didn't* have a drug incident reported in my records.

I drifted outside the depot. Across the street a storefront church offered meals. A line of bundled men stretched from its door to the end of the block. They weren't homeless derelicts. They were responsible, respectable men from whom this war had stolen hope. I was made to melt into that line.

It would be easy just to disappear right now. Into the ranks of the homeless, the orphaned, the jobless. The army overflowed. Deserting would be a favor, making a spot for a new guy. The army couldn't spare resources to pursue deserters.

I had a couple months' pay on me and civvies in my duffel. I remember some comedian's epitaph had been "Better here than in Philadelphia." Philly was no prize, but it was big enough to get lost in.

I slipped back inside long enough to retrieve my duffel and hike it onto my shoulder. I'd find an alley down the block, change into civvies, and blend in.

Sergeant Ochoa looked up from his screen. "Your convoy to Canaveral rolls out at 0400. Don't get lost, Specialist!"

I already was.

I pushed my palm on the swinging door and the door pushed back. A black man in civvies came through, suitcase in one hand, steadying himself with an aluminum cane in the other.

I dodged around him.

"Wander!"

I turned. Druwan Parker, broken leg and all, grinned at me.

He dropped his bag and stuck out his hand. "Look at you! Sharp and rock-steady! You made it through Basic!" He looked me up and down while he pumped my hand.

"What are you doing here?" I managed.

"Second chance." He held out his arms and lifted his leg. "Pins came out a week ago. I'm getting recycled through Basic."

"Still Infantry? Can't your uncle get you a soft deal now that you got hurt?"

His grin faded. He looked at his feet. "I lied. I got one cousin who was an air force sergeant. I got no more life outside the army than you have. And this leg healed crooked. I'm probably gonna wash out of Basic, again. But you never know. My old man used to say 90 percent of life is just showing up."

I had only known Parker for one day before he broke his leg. Then he had been an optimist. Now he was a realist. But he was going to show up.

He looked at me. "So where you headed, now that Basic's over? You lucky son of a bitch."

Lucky. Maybe. I shrugged, dropped my duffel to the floor, and sat down to wait for the convoy. "Wherever the army sends me."

By the time I had wished Parker luck and ridden yet another diesel truck for a day and a half, my eyes were clogged with sleeplessness and the road grit of a half dozen states.

I tossed my duffel over the tailgate to the gray pavement skirting a warehouse complex. The buildings squatted at the edge of what was now known as United Nations Space Force Base Canaveral, Florida, USA. I followed my duffel and as my boots hit concrete, the earth shook.

FOURTEEN

THE EARTH KEPT SHAKING. Incoming Projectile? I looked around for something to cling to, then looked up. In the distance an Interceptor lifted off, slow, majestic, and rumbling. Perched on an orange flame pillar, it arrowed skyward from blooming white smoke.

Silhouetted against the smoke and fifty feet from me Metzger stood, arms folded and grinning, a regular recruiting poster. His Class-A's were blue and fancier than mine. He wore those plink flyboy ribbons on his chest. Okay, the Rocket Jocks were saving the world. He deserved them.

He walked toward me, silver captain's tracks on his shoulder boards. I saluted automatically, and he returned it, sloppy the way the Space Force does. Ord made us press our tattered fatigues like they were Armani tuxes. World War II pilots thought nothing of burning aviation gas, flying beer to thirty thousand feet to cool it. Maybe flyboy ribbons were plink after all.

He rested his hands on his hips, looked me up and down, and whistled. "You got in shape."

I shrugged. "Infantry runs for its life." I guess I could have punched his arm or hugged him or something.

I had my head tipped back, still gawking like a hick at a skyscraper.

He jerked a thumb at the Interceptor, now a speck atop a curving contrail, white against the cold, gray Florida sky. "Rocket Jocks fly from here, from Vandenberg on the West Coast and Lop Nor in China. Johannesburg covers the Southern Hemisphere alone. Not a lotta targets to protect south of the equator."

He reached across the space between us, took my duffel, and led me to his car. Vanity tags read ROKJOK on a Kia Hybrid.

I whistled. "These cost the brick!"

"She's fine on batteries, and she flies when she's on gasoline."

"You can get gasoline?"

"Rocket Jocks get everything." He tossed my bag in the back seat. "Get in. The girls are meeting us at the party."

"Oh." My social life since puberty consisted of doubling with every zit-faced, prude sidekick of every cheerleader who ached to lose her virginity to Metzger. Of course, my dates probably saw me the same way.

"No. Your date's cream. Honest." That was the nice thing about being with somebody you grew up with. You could talk without saying much.

We passed few cars. Nobody else got a Rocket Jock's fuel ration. The cars we saw drove lights on to penetrate the impact-dust twilight. We didn't even need our lights because Metzger's car had a night-vision heads-up display.

The perpetual overcast and the lack of traffic made the civilian world quieter. Or maybe it was the funerals.

Metzger's hands on the wheel seemed older, more surgical. He asked, "How'd you swing leave?"

I told him. The whole mess. Walter. The admin hearing.

"Oh."

I knew he meant it sounded bad.

I shrugged. "So, how's Large Ted and Bunny?" He wouldn't have brought up his parents because it sucked that my mom died just for taking a trip to Indianapolis. I had to ask about them.

He grinned. "Still living in Denver. Saw them last month. Large Ted still thinks you made a good choice with Infantry."

Metzger lived off post in Greater Orlando. Disney Universe had closed down for the duration, but the Orlando Metroplex was the closest thing to a playground left in the US. Temperatures still got up to sixty in Florida some days. We rolled past condo complexes fronted with palm-tree trunks hung with brown, drooping fronds.

"Metzger, you think we'll ever go after the bad guys? Really win this thing, instead of just slowing down the end of the world?"

"Maybe." He looked down and sideways. The last time he looked away from me like that was when a babe I idolized passed him a note that I had wolverine breath. But she made him swear not to tell me. He knew more than he could say.

"Oh." My reply told him I knew he knew something.

The party was in a gated community with dark streets. Well, all streets were dark, now.

The party house was more like a hotel, set behind vast

lawns with its own gate and a grumpy, tuxedoed bouncer out front. He leaned into the car, smiled at Metzger's uniform, shrugged at mine, and waved us in.

You could have played ball in the house's foyer, but we chased the live music through it and back outside to the pool deck. A couple hundred guests glittered poolside in sunshine.

Sunshine?

I looked up. From the still-green fronds of the palms that lined the deck shone man-made sunshine. Days ago in the suburbs of Pittsburgh, the survivors had been burning candles at noon. There was something about the sleek, bronzed crowd. Bronze. Since the war, the bare, Caucasian butts in barracks showers and the faces in Philadelphia bread lines were the color of risen dough. But these people afforded suntans.

My jaw dropped, and I grabbed Metzger's elbow and hissed. "Whose place *is* this?"

"Aaron Grodt's. The holo producer."

The band played an excellent cover on a Cannibal hit. I looked again. It *was* Cannibal. They finished and left the muted buzz of clinking crystal and laughter. Metzger and I were the only ones in uniform, and heads turned.

Our dates were already there, cocktail-dressed in spiderwebs of fabric that would have frozen them anywhere else on the planet. Metzger introduced me to his girl. Shelly had the most perfect face and the best shape I'd ever seen.

Until he introduced me to Crissy. She was blond and stood as tall as I did, on Everest-high heels. I smelled perfume when she pecked my cheek and as she bent forward other Himalayan comparisons leapt to mind. She drew back and ran her eyes up and down my uniform. Uh-oh. Ground-grunt green, not Rocket Jock blue.

Her eyes widened. "Metz says Infantrymen have incredible stamina. That absolutely makes my tummy flutter."

Mine, too.

"So, Crissy, what do *you* do?"

"Can't I just show you later?" She giggled. "Really, I model. Lingerie and swimwear. Not for the big weblogues. They say my breasts are too large."

Thank you, God.

The buffet would have been impressive *before* the war. Filet mignon so real they left it pink in the middle. Pyramids of roasted quail. Whole *bowls* of fresh fruit. Apples. Bananas. You name it.

As the four of us balanced our plates and looked for a table, I spotted a redhead, my age and as perfect and empty-looking as Crissy. She hung on a bearded, tuxedoed guy Ord's age but soft and round. They glided toward us, and the old guy took Metzger's hand in both of his. "Captain! Wonderful you could come!"

They say holos add twenty pounds but I did recognize him from the Oscars. It *was* Aaron Grodt.

He held his champagne flute above his head, then tinged it with a sterling fork. Everyone shut up and stared toward us.

"Here's the man who made our picture possible! Even if he wouldn't play himself."

I rolled my eyes. Hollywood was making a holo about Metzger while I was humping a machine gun through the woods. Story of my life.

Grodt kissed Metzger on both cheeks, then said to everyone, "We all owe so much . . ."

My stomach chilled, and my plate felt heavy. How could I be so stupid? These days, not even a Hollywood producer could throw a bomber like this without collecting a cover. Cannibal, alone, probably cost as much as a house. Between me and my date, I'd just blown a month's pay and allowances.

Grodt dragged me next to Metzger, an arm around each of us. Instead of whispering what the tab was, he said, "Where would we be without brave men like these?"

People applauded. One by one, they came up to us, shook our hands and thanked us for serving. It was nice, and nobody knew I was such a hick I'd thought I had to pay for the party.

I read in a history chip that during one of the ancient wars, Vietnam I think, some GI on leave was at a party like this. A flat-screen star came over and spit on him. And the other guests clapped for the movie star.

It just goes to show you can't believe everything that's burned on a chip. I mean, America could never have been *that* ass-backward.

For the next couple hours, Metzger danced with his date and got talked to by important-looking people. I drank too much free champagne, listened to the band, and watched Crissy giggle and nearly fall out of her dress.

Metzger had been visiting with our host, Aaron Grodt. Grodt came and sat between Crissy and me, in Metzger's empty chair. The producer laid his hand on my shoulder. "Captain Metzger tells me your military experience hasn't been good lately."

Experience? If the man could read a chest, he'd see the only thing on mine was the oft-awarded, seldom-earned

Expert Rifle badge and a ninety-day-service ribbon. I shrugged.

"We have a number of military-based projects in development. I need technical advisors." He raised his eyebrows.

"You mean I'd get assigned—"

He shook his head. "I need independent advice. I know people who could arrange your discharge."

I stiffened. Behind Grodt, Crissy's eyes were wide as she nodded rapidly and repeatedly.

Grodt squeezed my shoulder. "The pay would seem spectacular after the military."

"I—" How could I explain to someone who hadn't been there what it was to feel committed to service?

"Look, you seem like a nice kid. Captain Metzger thinks you deserve a break. The world is going down the toilet, and there's nothing anyone can do about it. You can spend the years you have left digging mud, or you can spend them like this." He spread his arm like he was sowing glitter on his guests.

"If you want the job, let me know before you leave. If not, there's a waiting list." He stood and smiled like nobody sane would turn him down.

After he left, Crissy squeezed my hand. "My God! Jason! Aaron *Grodt* just offered you a *job!*"

Committed? To what? Why? Two days before, I had been ready to desert rather than continue in the army. If Grodt was as connected as he seemed to be, he could not only get me out of the army legally, he probably could square my departure with Judge March, too. The opportunity of a lifetime spread before me. So why was I wondering what to do?

As I pondered, Crissy led me back into the house, upstairs and down a carpeted hallway that seemed as long as a company street. Moans and the sweet smell of dope, the illegal kind, leaked from behind closed doors.

"Aaron has, like, forty bedrooms. There's anything you want." At the moment, the one thing I wanted was to solve mysteries under her dress. She wobbled from the champagne as she opened a door and led me into a pink room with a canopy bed. She hopped on the bed, her Himalayas heaving, drained her champagne, and stretched to set the empty flute on a nightstand. Her hem rode halfway up her thigh, and she rolled on her back and patted the silk beside her. I sat and wondered why I doubted Grodt's job offer.

"Think about whatever it is tomorrow, Jason." She reached up and traced my ear with her finger.

I hadn't so much as smelled a woman in months. And the last one who had touched my ear was a doctor when I had an earache before I turned twelve. I breathed faster. Think about *what* tomorrow?

She breathed into my ear. "Very hard?"

"Huh?"

"Your training."

"It is. Was."

She scooted closer, slid up her dress, and snapped off tiny, pink lace undies with promising athleticism. I froze. If I moved, she might vanish.

She drew back and pouted. "'M I boring you?"

"No. God, no!" I shrugged. "It's just—I have responsibilities."

She fingered the ninety-day-service ribbon on my tunic. "Jason, get real! *Metzger's* got responsibilities. You're a grunt!"

Then she cocked her head. "Unless—Are you going for The Force?"

If The Force was anywhere between her knees and her collarbone, I surely was. "What?"

"Didn't you watch the news?"

Not in the back of a truck.

"It's on everywhere." She passed her palm above a remote, and Grodt's holo fired with no hint of dust-induced static. One more thing money *could* buy.

A newsreader stood on the carpet before us while the Holo News Network logo swirled around her.

"Already, volunteer applications for the UN's Ganymede Expeditionary Force are piling up. The world's best soldiers are clamoring to be selected. Officials conceded only today that plans for a massive spaceship to transport thousands of Infantry troops and carry the fight to Jupiter's largest moon are far advanced."

I shook my head and wished I wasn't so drunk.

The newsreader continued. "The ship's keel may be laid as soon as next spring, at a location undisclosed for security reasons. Speculation centers on the Arizona desert or the Sahara."

Her coanchor nodded from the corner of the room. "Any timetable?"

"Sources expect to embark trained Infantry troops within five years. Hopeful news."

The Vegas line was even money the human race would be extinct in four years. Hopeful, my ass.

Crissy waved off the holo. "You're upset, Jason."

My head spun as much from the news as from the champagne. Infantry. There was a chance for Infantry to make a difference in the world. There was a chance for me to make a difference. Or there had been until I screwed it up. Jacowicz had said I'd get crap assignments. The Ganymede Expeditionary Force was going to be the toughest ticket in military history. This was the Mother of All Screwings. I ground my teeth.

"Jason?"

"Huh?"

Crissy grasped my zipper between manicured fingers and slid it down. "Whatever it is, I can make it better."

No, she couldn't. The only thing that could was me getting assigned to the Ganymede Expeditionary Force, and that wasn't her department.

However, Little Jason was doing my thinking, and he had urgent ideas. I wrapped my arms around her waist and pulled her to me.

She giggled. "Izzat a pistol in your pocket, soldier?"

Her lines weren't original, but her attitude was flawless.

Rap! *Rap*!

The door knocks barely died before it swung open.

FIFTEEN

"SPECIALIST WANDER?" Two buck-sergeant MPs stepped through the doorway in black berets, shoulder bands with MP lettered in white, and plink white gloves.

Crap. Crap, crap, crap. Caught in an opium den, drunk and underage. My fake ID lay in Ord's personal-property envelope back at Indiantown Gap. And it had to be illegal to get lucky with a tanked woman this prime.

The MPs gaped at Chrissy while the first one said, "You gotta report back, Specialist."

I shook my head. "I'm on leave."

MP Number One waved old-fashioned paper, unsmiling. "Canceled."

Crissy pulled a sheet across herself and pouted.

"Report where?"

"Nearest post. Canaveral."

"When?"

"Now."

"Okay. Gimmee a few minutes." I jerked my head toward Crissy.

"*Now,* Specialist!" The MP hooked a thumb in his belt. He wore a sidearm.

I spread my arms, palms open. "Guys! I've been sleeping in a barracks with fifty hairy-butt privates for three months! Ten minutes—"

"The army doesn't care if you sleep with yaks. Move!" He stepped forward.

Quitting in wartime is desertion. The army can execute a GI summarily, ignoring trifles like the Bill of Rights. And I hadn't exactly built a reservoir of goodwill lately. I looked once more at his pistol, sighed, tucked in, and zipped up.

Crissy groaned and rolled on her side, facing the wall.

I stood. "How'd you find me?"

MP Number One tapped his chest with the index finger of one hand while he pointed skyward with the other. "Dogtag."

I nodded. At induction, every soldier gets an identity chip implanted beneath his or her breastbone. One purpose is graves registration. That's why the implant goes in the middle of the biggest piece of meat likely to be intact. The chip's also detectable by global-positioning satellites, just like everybody's car and bike. The Thirty-Eighth Amendment forbids satellite-tracking of natural persons, but it's just one more civil right GIs waive. I think they're called "dogtags" because the army tested the implants on canines. I heard another explanation, but it was stupid.

I glanced once more at Chrissy. She blew me a kiss, and my heart ached. Well, the ache was lower. The MPs flanked me, and three sets of clattering combat boots

echoed as we wound down marble stairs, across Aaron
Grodt's entry hall, and to their butt-ugly, government-
issue Chyota.

The door was open, and Metzger sat in the backseat,
head back, eyes closed. MP Number One put a hand on
my head as he tucked me in beside Metzger.

"You, too? Why?" I asked.

Metzger rolled his head my way and opened one eye.
"I get called back to alert every time they spot incoming.
I don't know why they want you."

"I thought it was for underage drinking." The words
sounded silly as they left my mouth.

Metzger closed his open eye. "Rest. Whatever it is will
be here too soon."

Like the end of my childhood.

The battery sedan retraced Metzger's route from Canaveral, but slower, so I dozed, numb from champagne, my
mind bubbling with questions.

I thought about Walter and Mom and a ship bound for
Jupiter without me.

At some point I realized how much I had changed.
The loss of a gorgeous woman wearing no pants scarcely
bothered me.

A few months ago I would have stewed for hours
about losing a quickie.

I wished Crissy and not Metzger was snoring next to
me, but all I *really* cared about was getting a berth on that
Jupiter ship, somehow.

The car crawled through Canaveral's main gate and
floodlights woke me. The notion that expensive wine
leaves no hangover is a lie as big as "Meals Ready to
Eat." I moaned.

The MPs stopped the car on a weedy, cracked-pavement apron in front of a windowless last-century building that stretched beyond the floodlights that lit its door.

Metzger jumped out, and I followed.

The Chyota whirred away as one MP slammed its door. I winced at the bang and stared at the building. "What's this?"

Metzger led me inside and into a room filled with banks of old-fashioned instrument consoles at which rows of shirt-sleeved men sat. Light came from the image on a screen covering the far wall. The men muttered into headset microphones straight out of a history holo.

"Captain Metzger! Jason!"

The voice I knew. I turned and saw the wrinkled geek Intelligence captain from Pittsburgh, Howard Hibble.

Hibble shook our hands, then led us into a glassed-in conference room. He sat us at a table, sat himself, and folded his hands in front of him. "We would have found you eventually, of course." He grinned at me. "But I didn't expect you close by, Jason."

A scrubs-clad medic stepped into the room carrying a vitals 'puter. Hibble nodded toward me. The medic wrapped my biceps with a blood-pressure cuff hooked to his little assistant and read its display. "Low-normal," he muttered.

I looked at Hibble. "I'm fine." Were they drug-testing?

The medic poked a temp-infection probe in my ear and grunted at the readout.

While the medic worked my knee joints, I looked back and forth at Metzger, then at Hibble. "What's with this museum?"

Metzger smirked. "Museum?"

I pointed through the glass conference-room panel at the wall screen. It showed a flat video of a NASA rocket. The old crate stood gleaming white in flood-lights, liquid-oxygen clouds boiling from its base. I used to collect spaceflight trading holos, mostly to get the gum. "That's a Saturn booster." I squinted at the nose. "With an Apollo module. Three hundred sixty feet tall. It launched manned missions to the moon in the 1960s." There was a certain sadness to the truth that the seventy-year-old Apollo program marked high tide for manned space exploration. I pointed. "Which mission was this?"

"That's a live image."

"You mean it was live when they videoed it."

Metzger broke in. "The old jigs and assembly equipment still existed, Jason. The frame and engines were rebuilt pretty much like the old design, with antique materials. But with updated computers, one pilot can fly it."

I looked closer at the vehicles crawling antlike around the Saturn's base. Electrovans. The first Electro hit pavement in 2032. My jaw dropped. We really had rebuilt an Apollo rocket! Just like we had demothballed Indiantown Gap and C-rations and the space shuttles Metzger and the other Rocket Jocks flew to intercept Projectiles.

I realized then how desperate the human race was, and my heart sank.

A century ago, in 1939, Polish horse cavalry attacked German tanks with lances. In the Insurrection of 2020, Tibetan rebels threw rocks at Chinese helicopter gunships.

Since the twenty-first century began, humanity had whipped AIDS, nurtured human rights, and back-burnered antimatter engines and death rays. Those had been dandy priorities. But they left us reduced to throwing a 360-foot-tall rock at our enemy.

Then it hit me. Humans had *big* rocks. For the first time, I was proud of us for inventing H-bombs. The Ganymede Expeditionary Force was a diversionary hoax. Why send Infantry into space when we could plaster the enemy with nuclear weapons?

Relief, hope, and a little disappointment, because Infantry wasn't going to lead the way after all, flooded me.

I smiled at Hibble. "I get it. That Saturn's going to carry a nuke big enough to crack Ganymede like a walnut!"

Hibble frowned. "I can understand why you'd think that. We probably could adapt a Saturn to launch an interplanetary payload. Logical enough mistake."

Mistake?

Metzger said, "The first nuclear warhead we fired to knock a Projectile off course didn't detonate. We thought it was a dud. Nobody's actually tested nukes since the late 1900s."

Hibble said, "The next four didn't explode, either. We tried conventional warheads. They worked. The enemy seems to be able to neutralize nuclear weapons. Our best guess is they permeate space with a subatomic particle that slows down neutrons. You can visualize how that would impede a chain reaction, of course."

"Of course." I had no earthly clue. Metzger, Hibble, and Einstein knew what that meant, but not me. Yet when I looked in their eyes I knew it was true. Humanity was screwed.

Hopelessness dripped through me as I realized that for some reason those MPs had dragged Metzger and me here like North America's Most Wanted.

I pointed again at the oversized antique fueling up on the wall screen. "So why us? Why the rocket ship?"

Hibble looked up at the medic, who had run out of body parts to abuse. The medic wrapped wires around his machine as he walked out. "He's good to go, Captain Hibble."

"Go where?" I asked.

Howard waited until the door closed behind the medic, then unlocked a drawer in the table and pulled out a paper book. Actually, it was bigger than the books I had read in the day room, the dimensions of an old laptop computer, or more accurately, a stack of them.

Yellow letters across its top read TOP SECRET. Howard let it thud on the tabletop, grunted, then laid his palm over the letters. "This notebook details every artifact we've recovered from Projectile detonation sites worldwide. Learning what we're fighting might turn the war. This book doesn't tell us enough. We've mostly recovered cinders the size of rutabagas."

I'd never seen a rutabaga, but I gathered it wasn't very big. I shook my head. "So? Why me?"

Howard batoned an unlit cigarette with bony, yellowed fingers. "What science can't explain, it calls luck or coincidence. Historically, certain humans have displayed a knack for attracting alien contact. I never had the knack. But in Pittsburgh you beelined to the single most significant alien artifact ever found. I don't understand why that happened. I expect you don't know either. But I flagged your records in our database. You're attached temporary duty to my platoon for the next two weeks."

Me an Intel weenie? Still, my chest swelled. I was the Chosen One. But chosen for what?

"So I'm an artifact bloodhound?" Hair stood on my neck.

Howard shrugged. "That's my hunch. Besides . . ."

"Besides, what?"

Howard looked at his hands. "The scientist who trained for the slot you're taking was tracking fragments in Nigeria when she came down with dysentery."

"Oh." I had been chosen by the runs. "What do you expect me to find?"

"Nothing. We already found it. A Projectile crashed, largely intact, four days ago. You've already signed the requisite secrecy paperwork—"

My heart skipped. "You want me to go with you to the wreck!" I was going to make history. This was almost better than going to Jupiter. My head spun. I saw myself hacking through jungle with a machete, leading Howard to his prize, vine-smothered like a ruined temple. But something was wrong with my picture.

The conference-room door opened again and a corporal wearing well-cut utilities with Quartermaster Branch collar brass came in. Hibble nodded at me again.

A yellow tape measure hung around the corporal's neck. He made me stand and wrapped the tape around my chest while I talked.

"Okay. I'm the second-string artifact bloodhound." I jerked my thumb at Metzger. "But why's he here?"

Hibble paused while the Quartermaster corporal held out my arm and taped it, then my inseam, speaking measurements into a wrist 'puter. He left.

Howard answered. "Captain Metzger is one of two

pilots checked out to fly the Apollo *Mark II.* The other guy's on alert at Lop Nor in China."

"Pilot?" A knot grew in my stomach. "To where?"

"The Projectile crash-landed at ten degrees, two minutes south latitude and fifty-five degrees, forty minutes east longitude—"

"That's in—" I wrinkled my forehead, visualizing a globe.

"The middle of Mare Fecunditatis." Howard looked at his watch. "At ten tomorrow morning, we three leave for the moon."

SIXTEEN

A DAY LATER, they walked us three out on the gantry in baggy, white space suits. The one I'd been measured for actually fit. We carried little air-conditioner suitcases, just like old movies. Real old. They hadn't used Canaveral's launchpads since satellites went private. I shouldn't have been surprised at the rusty girders. I shook. I hate heights. The narrow bridge to the capsule was latticed steel, so when I looked down between my feet the ground was 350 feet away.

In three days the ground would be 250,000 *miles* away. I stared ahead at the open capsule hatch, squeezed the bridge rail harder with shaking hands, and shuffled toward the capsule.

The Apollo capsule itself had just been built so it smelled like a new car inside. But it looked as old-fashioned as a laptop computer. I lay there flat on my back while technicians snapped fishbowl helmets over our heads, Howard on my right and Metzger on my left.

A tech patted my head, shot me a thumbs-up, then ducked back outside and sealed the hatch. Gray sky shone through the little capsule window. I scrunched my shoulders, hands at my sides, and tried to remember all the things I'd been taught over the last twenty-four hours, mostly what not to touch. The trip to the moon would last three days, but they had crammed me with three months' training since yesterday. I had been nervous about learning my flight duties until they explained that I had none.

My trainer assured me, "The first American astronaut was just a monkey. He did fine." Then my trainer eyeballed the Infantry tab on my file. "A really dumb monkey."

My trainer taught me that the monkey wore a little space vest and diapers. My trainer never taught me how to pee in space.

Metzger's voice and the ground controller's rang inside my helmet. We had more room in the capsule than the old pioneers had because the old-fashioned instruments that had filled much of the capsule had been replaced by a wireless 'puter Metzger held. It was not much bigger than a Playstation Model-40.

I sat atop history's biggest conventional bomb. This spaceship was strictly forties, according to the briefings I'd sat through yesterday. But its ancestors had a few problems. Out of less than twenty Apollos, one incinerated its crew on the ground and another blew apart on its way to the moon and limped home. The space-shuttle airframes that had been revived to make Interceptors like Metzger flew exploded one trip every fifty. No wonder we started years ago to send robots to space instead of people.

My heart rattled like a stick dragged along a picket fence.

Metzger glanced over and raised his white-gloved thumb at me.

Pumps rumbled hundreds of feet below me and jostled my couch.

In my helmet, somebody said, "Ignition!"

SEVENTEEN

I FIGURED IT WOULD BE LOUD. And I expected the G-forces, like a piano on my chest. But the vibration nearly had me screaming in my helmet. I'd read that these tubs shook like crazy.

I gripped the seat so hard I was afraid my fingers would puncture my pressure suit. I tried to relax my hands but couldn't. I saw blue sky, really dark blue, for the first time in months. Then the palsied view ahead was blackness and stars.

When the engines cut off, the silence was as deafening as the roller coaster had been.

Metzger was saying something about attitude and roll, then he looked over and winked behind his visor. The view changed as he rolled the ship onto its back. It didn't feel like that, of course. There's no up or down you can feel. I just mean we were upside down, relative to Earth. Once he rolled us, Earth was over my head, not at my feet.

The planet a hundred miles below filled the little windshield. Or whatever you called the front window up here where there was no wind.

Until that moment all the pictures from space I had ever seen were the burnished, blue planet with the wispy white cloud streaks.

The dirty gray ball we've gotten used to since the Projectiles and their dust made me cry.

I tried to wipe my nose and bumped my hand against my helmet faceplate while Metzger and Ground Control rattled back and forth. He didn't sound excited, exactly. Just a notch higher voice pitch, like he always sounded before an exam.

He held a Voiceboard in a gloved hand and studied its readouts, then let go of it. It hung there, weightless just like the holos show it.

"Metzger, can I undo my helmet?"

"No."

"Just to wipe my nose—"

"This thing's brand-new. If it develops even a pinhole leak, we could be dead."

We were drifting a quarter million miles through vacuum. I'd seen all those holos where the guy in the space suit has a bad heater and he freezes solid. Or his head explodes when his suit rips. Or he just floats off into space sobbing into his radio. I always thought that last would be the worst. I licked my lip and tried to forget the snot.

There was no sound except the three of us breathing into our helmet mikes.

The Apollo looked like a big rifle cartridge. The three of us sat in the cone-shaped capsule that formed the "bullet" on Apollo's front. The cylindrical "cartridge" behind us stored the spider-legged Lunar Excursion Module. It was the part of Apollo that would drop to the lunar surface, slowed by retro-rockets, then land on its unfolded legs. Later the LEM would rocket us back to dock with the "bullet" capsule orbiting the moon. Then we would crawl back into the bullet and ride it back to Earth.

Over the next day, Metzger and Canaveral decided the capsule wasn't going to spring a leak, so we got to take off our helmets and pressure suits. Metzger jettisoned the skin that encircled the LEM, then detached the "bullet" capsule we were riding in and reversed it so it traveled fat end forward. That let him dock the hatch on the capsule's pointy end with the LEM's hatch.

Once we popped the two hatches, we created a narrow tunnel between the two vessels. After hours shoehorned in the Apollo capsule, the extra space felt like we had finished off our attached garage.

Moving around in zero gravity is like swimming, except that every movement's consequences are exaggerated. I got the hang fast, but Howard bounced around the Apollo like a golf ball hit in a shower stall.

Metzger and I finally strapped him back into his seat, and he explained our gear to me, panting. He held up a plasteel box the size of a kitten. "Mass spectrometer. Touch the probe to any part of the Projectile hull, and we'll read chemical composition in a nanosecond."

The next item I knew. "Palm holocam."

He nodded. As we ticked off each item it went in a rucksack that soon bulged like Santa's bag before his first stop.

I pointed at it. "Who carries that?"

"On the moon it weighs one-sixth what it does on Earth."

"Meaning I carry that?"

He nodded. "And this." He drew a pistol from floating wrappings, an old, nine-millimeter Browning automatic. He held it between fingers like it was rotten fruit. "I hate these things."

I could tell the weapon was clear because the slide was back, and the magazine floated next to it.

He held up a plasti of ammunition. "The shells are loaded with less powder to reduce recoil in lunar gravity. Guns work fine in vacuum. Their combustion oxygen is stored in the powder grains—"

"Howard, why do I need a gun? It's just a broken machine."

He shrugged. "Precaution."

"There's something alive in that thing?"

He shrugged again. "Who knows? Be better if there is."

"Better for who?"

He just shrugged.

Howard and Metzger kept busy in the LEM. Metzger checked the LEM's systems, Howard the sensors and recorders he would use to examine the alien wreck.

My job was to check the low-tech part of the lunar-excursion equipment Howard wasn't checking. I had a day to do it, and I thought while I worked.

We were actually going to walk on the moon in white, extravehicular-activity suits with gold visors, just like the old pioneers. The suit sleeves still had fifty-star American flag patches.

Until I unpacked the EVA suits I didn't know how "just like." While the suits had been updated, they had actually been built and used for training decades ago, during the Apollo program.

This mission was so tacked-together that our EVA suits hadn't even been laundered or checked since last century. Those old pioneers had trained hard enough to sweat plenty. I unzipped the first suit and ammonia reek slapped my nose like a gym locker of old jocks opened after seventy years. I breathed through my mouth to filter the stink as I worked.

I dug in a cargo net behind the suit that had been altered to fit me and found a fat-barreled signal-flare pistol and a yellowed pamphlet, copyright 1972, titled *Surviving in the Pacific.*

The capsules used to parachute into the ocean. I made a mental note to remind Howard and Metzger that they had forgotten to brief me whatsoever on return-flight procedure and tucked the leftovers into my suit's thigh pocket.

I also found a packet of orange powder called Tang. I dissolved a little in a water squirt bottle and tasted it. Tang is to orange juice as MREs are to food.

It brought home to me how hardy the old-time space pioneers must have been. They crossed space in this tiny coffin, like a rice grain tossed on the Pacific, living on acidic swill. Many died. Not from the Tang. It wasn't that bad.

But they didn't even have 'puters. They did math with wooden rulers.

The history chips say they came in peace for all mankind.

If that had been true, they wouldn't have quit coming. Those old sleeve flag patches weren't United Nations, and they sure weren't Russian. The Cold War drove mankind to the moon. When America won that war, we stopped coming.

Since the first Neanderthal figured out he could poke his rival better with a stick than a finger, quantum technology leaps have been war-driven. From the chariots and long bows of antiquity to jets and nuclear fission last century to coagulant bandages and Brain-Link Robotics in this century, the sad truth is that war is to human innovation as manure is to marigolds.

Peace lets us meander. So, seventy years of peaceful meander after man landed on the moon we were making the crossing in this same primitive pod.

By day three, the moon's white glow filled the viewport.

Metzger pointed at a gleaming flat to our lower right. "Mare Fecunditatis. The Sea of Fertility. It's just a couple hundred miles from the dark side."

"Why did it crash there?"

"Wouldn't we like to know?" said Metzger. "That's one question we want answered. No Projectile's so much as sputtered on the way in before."

I turned to Howard. He was unwrapping nicotine gum. This might be a tobacco-days spacecraft, but this flight was *all* nonsmoking.

"Howard, what's the terrain like?" This question made me proud. A good Infantryman always knows METT— mission, enemy, terrain, and time.

"Flat. A lava flow covered in dust of unknowable thickness. We guess a few inches thick from the skid mark the Projectile cut on impact. It crash-landed oblique. That's why it's still in one piece." Howard angled one palm above the other.

I'd already asked about the presumably nonexistent enemy, and I knew the mission was to poke our collective nose into this wreck. But I hadn't asked about time. "How long do we have down there?" I didn't know the answer, but I knew blasting off from the moon to rendezvous with the capsule was a critical, sophisticated game, even with forties 'puters.

Howard shifted his gaze to Metzger.

Metzger shrugged. "Long enough."

They knew more than they were telling me. I looked from one to the other. Metzger looked away.

Before I could get pissy with them over the secrecy, it was time to struggle into our extravehicular-activity suits while Metzger inserted Apollo into lunar orbit.

My EVA suit still reeked of ammonia inside. You'd think if they send you to save the world, they wouldn't make you wear somebody's stinking pajamas.

Metzger's voice crackled inside my new helmet as he closed the hatch between us three, stuffed in the LEM, and the now-uninhabited Apollo. "Disengaging LEM."

A faint thump disconnected us from our way home. Tang ate at my stomach lining.

The descent to the moon was slow. Since we had now strapped bouncing Howard to the LEM wall, I got to stand at the window and watch the Sea of Fertility rush up to greet us.

Flat as the sea looked from space, it spread cobblestrewn and undulating. We closed in, and I realized the cobbles were as big as Dumpsters. The last fifty feet our engine kicked up dust, so I saw nothing. Obviously, Metzger couldn't, either. If we roosted on a boulder, the LEM could topple, tear out its insides, or just break something vital to us getting home. I clutched a stanchion and gritted my teeth.

Thump.

Just like that, we were down. Metzger made it seem cake.

Metzger ran system checks while Howard and I waited in a two-man line. Metzger had to operate the ship, and Howard was never the first to do anything physical. So I would be the first human to touch the moon since the days when major-league baseball used wooden bats.

As I waited I thought of something. "Metzger? How do we pee?"

"Use the little condom thingy in the leg. You hooked it up, didn't you?"

Air bled from the lock.

"What thingy?"

"Sorry. Should've told you. Just hold it."

He opened the hatch.

Before me another world, as dead and white as bones, stretched to a black horizon. I turned around, felt for the descent ladder's first rung, then stepped into airless nothing cold enough to freeze helium.

I hopped off the bottom rung into the Sea of Fertility's dust, then focused my vision on the object a half mile away.

Peeing my pants was the least of my worries.

EIGHTEEN

HOWARD LOWERED MY GEAR RUCKSACK on a synlon rope. I shuffled aside, tripped on a rock, and nearly fell.

I yelped. Falling would kill me if a rock punctured my suit. My coordination sucked after three weightless days, and, even with suit and gear, I only weighed forty pounds.

Howard's knees wobbled as he backed down the ladder, and I steadied him as he planted his feet in moondust.

"My God. Missus Hibble's geek is an astronaut."

So was Missus Wander's.

I spent ten seconds in mental back-patting while I looked up at the LEM, jumbled boxes papered in gold foil. My escape from the moon depended on discarded Christmas wrap on legs.

I pointed past the LEM's spider leg. Howard's mirrored helmet faceplate turned where I pointed.

A hundred yards from us ran the brink of a shallow canyon as wide as a shopping mall. Its edge was strewn with jagged boulders like plowed-up refrigerators. The canyon ended a half mile away. At least, that's what the distance looked like to me. The moon's smaller than Earth. The horizon's closer. They briefed me that the curvature distorts perception. Whatever the distance, my heart pounded.

At the canyon's end the Projectile rose. We couldn't know how much of it had burrowed beneath the surface. What we saw was a blue-black dome bigger than a football stadium. Spiral whorls creased its surface like a metallic snail shell.

Howard examined it through binoculars fitted with a rubber hood that fit against his faceplate. "It skidded in here at ten thousand miles an hour, but it seems intact. I was counting on a hull rupture to get you in."

"In? In*side*?" I pointed at the Projectile.

He lifted the rucksack and strapped it to my back.

Metzger's voice came from aboard the LEM. "Take care, Jason."

Howard and I skirted the canyon the Projectile plowed when it skidded in. There was no telling how unstable the disturbed lunar surface could be.

My brief Earthside lessons in moon shuffling at one-sixth my weight clicked in after a hundred fumbling yards. Still, sweat soaked my long johns in minutes.

Howard clumped and bounded, his hoarse panting roaring in my earpiece. "Flex your knees before you land, Howard. Like jumping rope."

"I never jumped rope. Worst mistake of my life."

I looked at the sky. Earth hung before me, blue streaked with gray soot clouds and a quarter million miles away. Was this the worst mistake of *my* life?

Waiting for Howard took forever. We wound around
bus-size boulders just as craggy and uneroded in three
billion airless, waterless years as the ones the Projectile
had gouged from the substrate days ago. Howard kept
stopping and thrusting his faceplate against boulders,
muttering about vesicles and rhyolite. On one such de-
tour, he stepped on a smooth spot that turned out to be a
dust-filled pothole and sank to his chest. After I hoisted
him out, I leashed him to me with synlon cord around our
waists so he had to follow my footsteps.

Finally, we stopped and looked up at the derelict fifty
yards in front of us. The exposed part of the Projectile rising above us could have been a domed stadium, skinned
iridescent blue-black. That it had moved seemed incredible, but spiral scratches scored its flanks. It had been ro-
tating like a passed football when it hit, scraped but
barely torn by a ten-thousand-mile-per-hour crash. I
whistled.

Howard breathed. "Holy Moly."

As soon as we got off this rock I was giving Howard
expletive lessons.

Something keened in my ears, a repeating whine,
high-pitched, then low.

"Howard, I hear sound. But there's no air to carry the
waves."

He stomped the ground. "The sound's conducted
through rock. The Projectile's making noise."

"It was supposed to be dead."

He turned me, pulled the palm holo from the rucksack
on my back, and held it against his suit. "Now we're
recording the sound."

He dug the spectrometer out of the rucksack and clambered over gouged-up rubble toward the Projectile. He tugged me at the end of the cord that connected us like he was a poodle chasing a squirrel.

Pressing the spectrometer's probe against the Projectile hull, he hummed along with the rhythmic, conducted sound, "Wah-aah, wah-aah."

While he worked, I looked up. Forty feet above us, just a fraction of the thing's height, I saw a circular, silver opening.

"Howard!" I pointed. "A maneuvering nozzle! Just like we found in Pittsburgh!"

He stopped humming and backed away from the hull. Standing beside me, he pointed, too. "Better. Look closer."

I shaded my eyes with a gloved hand held above my visor. A spiral scratch crossed the nozzle and widened into a man-sized gash.

"Weakened hull section ruptured. There's your way in, Jason."

"Uh-uh." I shook my head, the gesture invisible inside my helmet.

He just reached for my rucksack again.

I shook my whole body. "Howard, I hate heights. I hate tight, dark places worse."

"Jason, if I could climb, I'd do it. It's the chance of a lifetime."

"Or the end of a lifetime!"

"But what a way to go!"

Four days ago I was feeling sorry for myself because I couldn't make a difference. The human race had shipped me a quarter million miles so I could make a difference. I couldn't say no. I eyed forty feet of slick metal wall that separated me from the goal Howard had chosen and sighed. "I can't climb that." Pointing out impossibility wasn't saying no.

Howard pulled from my rucksack two rubbery, black discs with looped cords on their backs. "Put these on over your gloves."

"Howard, suction cups work on air-pressure differential. We're in vacuum." I was pretty proud I thought of that, even if it was an excuse to wuss.

"These are Attagrips. All-temperature temporary adhesive. You only weigh forty pounds. You'll climb like a fly on a wall."

"Oh." I sighed and pressed one pad to the surface, then the other, forearms quivering. A thumb push released the right-hand pad so I could move it up the wall. Another push refastened the pad. Then I moved the left-hand pad. Howard was right. I scaled the Projectile like a holotoon superhero. Jason Wander, secret identity of Attaboy.

"Howard, what do I do when I get to the opening?"

"First, get inside. Then I'll tell you what to get out of the rucksack and what to do with it."

Howard couldn't plan a coffee break. The other half of his team never finished high school. "Howard, is the human race just making this war up as we go?"

"We do our best work that way."

The rip's edge loomed a foot above my helmet visor. I looked down. Howard was only forty feet below, but he looked as small as a cake decoration. I took a deep breath, then another, and levered myself above the brink.

The ripped Projectile skin was two inches thick and the same blue-black color all the way through. I waited as my eyes adjusted to the dark opening. Below the skin, a

six-foot lattice of metal as asymmetrical as drool strings
made a sandwich filling that separated the outer skin
from a second one. The inner skin wasn't torn. I described
it to Howard.

"It's a pressure hull," he said.

"What now?"

"Is there a door, a hatch?"

I shook my head.

"Jason? You okay?" Howard's voice rose an octave.

Any fool who shakes his head at a microphone should
be euthanized. "Howard, I don't see—" Through the dim-
ness I made out indented lines on the inner hull, a parasol
pattern. "Wait. There's something."

"It's a repair hatch. You're in!"

"Forgot my key."

"Oh." He paused. "You may not need one. Crawl up to
the hatch. It may fail-safe open to motion. So the repairman isn't stranded in space in an emergency."

What if the repairman was waiting for me on the other
side of the hatch? My heart raced.

I pulled myself, all forty pounds, over the torn outer
skin, careful not to snag my suit. The skin tear was three
feet high. The rucksack and I were four feet thick. I
pulled back outside and slipped the sack off. Then I rolled
my body into the space between the hulls, dragging the
sack behind me in one hand. Lying there, I felt the Projectile's up-and-down sound vibrating through my thighs
and belly.

I waved my free hand toward the parasol. Nothing.
"Howard? The hatch didn't open."

"—whole body."

"You're breaking up." Part of me hoped he'd say, well,

then, come on back down. Good try. Let's go back to the LEM and fly home. But I knew what he meant. I wormed my whole body closer to the parasol, like low-crawling under barbed wire on the infiltration course.

The parasol moved.

Its panels shot back into its rim, like a dilating camera iris.

"Howard, you were right. It opened."

"Jas . . . hull interferes . . ."

The open hatch yawned dark and wide enough to admit me or the rucksack but not both at once. Six feet farther inside a closed door like the first sealed the tube. An air lock. I'd either have to crawl headfirst, pushing the rucksack ahead of me, or back in and drag the sack behind me. If I backed in I could see whether the outer door closed behind me. I'd be pointed the right direction to get the hell out. The inner hatch *should* open automatically in response to me, like the outer hatch had. Space beyond the air lock would surely be wide enough for me to turn around.

Feetfirst it was.

I got shoulder deep through the hatch, dragging the rucksack with instruments, survival gear, and the pistol, and spoke once more. "Howard? I'm going in."

Only a crackle came back over the radio. It joined with the oddly familiar up-and-down whoop I had been listening to for the last half hour. The passage was inches wider than my space-suited shoulders. I could barely move my arms. At least backing in like this I would be able to see the light at the end of the tunnel, the way back outside. Headfirst into darkness would have terrified me.

I wrestled the rucksack past the outer hatch, and it snapped shut.

I shrank back into the passage and felt with my boots. The inner hatch had opened. I wormed backward, over the inner-hatch lip, then tugged the rucksack toward me. I gathered myself on knees and elbows and let go of the rucksack straps.

In the instant my hands drew back inside the hatch lip, the inner hatch snapped closed and sealed me in the dark.

NINETEEN

I COULDN'T SEE. All I could hear was my own breathing and the unceasing, rising and falling whoop. I pressed my hands on the hatch. It didn't budge. I pounded, as hard as I dared without risking rupturing my suit. I ran my hands over the walls around me. No doorknob. No lever. "Howard? I'm stuck in here!"

Not even static came back. The Projectile hull was not only tough, it was radioproof.

The rucksack lay a foot away, separated from me by a sealed hatch. In the sack lay a flashlight, a gun, food and water that could be taken through a helmet nipple, and all the equipment that was supposed to let me gather intelligence and bring it back. Those things might as well have been back on Earth.

This was like waking blind in a coffin. Another sound joined the Projectile's familiar whoop. More rapid, wheezing.

It was me, panting and buried alive. I couldn't move,

and I couldn't see. Claustrophobic panic boiled up in my brain.

I forced myself to think. The visor. The mirrored sunglass layer could be slid up. I moved it and could see again. My breathing slowed.

The tube I lay in wasn't completely dark.

It was circular and crenellated like a drainage culvert. I could see, barely, because it was suffused in purple light that glowed from the walls. The light pulsed in time to the whooping. I twisted to look over my shoulder. My purple sewer pipe corkscrewed out of sight fifty feet ahead, but it was no wider than the air lock.

I had two options. Wait here and hope Howard or fate would open the hatch. Until my oxygen generator quit or I died of thirst or starved. Option two was I could wriggle, feetfirst, deeper into the Projectile. I might find wide spaces, useful information and a way out. Or I might blunder into something that would kill me.

I never could sit still.

The tube's featureless walls were cut every fifty feet or so with slots maybe three feet tall and two fingers wide. Ventilation ducts? Ventilating what? There must be atmosphere in here. After all, there was an air lock. That meant something had been alive in here to breathe it. Or was still breathing. I wanted that pistol from the rucksack.

The second set of ventilating ducts caught my thigh for the second time. I worked my hand down to my thigh and felt a lump in my suit. The thigh pocket. I peeled back the Velcro flap and felt the object inside. The flare pistol! My heart leapt. I was armed, sort of.

I worked my hand up alongside my body until I held the flare gun in front of me. This meant I could shoot anything that tried to sneak up behind me, but anything ahead of me could slink up and bite my feet off before I knew it.

I backed another hundred feet down the tube, keeping my fingers out of the air-conditioning vents.

My feet seemed suddenly freer. I wriggled onward. Six feet later, my torso entered a right-angle intersection with a larger-diameter tube. The intersection allowed me room to turn headfirst. And to realize that I could crawl or duckwalk along the bigger tube.

I sat up in the intersection while purple light pulsed in time to the incessant whooping. I took stock. I was stranded in a labyrinth. The old suits had been retrofitted with up-to-date oxygen generators so I could breathe, indefinitely. I had no food. I had no water. That last wasn't all bad, as my bladder kept reminding me. My only weapon was a seventy-year-old flare pistol with one big, fat, slow bullet. My mission depended on measuring things, but my measuring equipment sat back outside the hatch that had trapped me in here. This vessel was as big as Dubuque. It surely had more than one door. I'd just keep crawling until I found another one, or I figured out how to open the one where I came in.

As I traveled, if I couldn't measure what was in here, maybe I could take samples. I reversed the flare gun in my gloved hand like a geologist's pick and hammered the curved wall.

The gun butt bounced back like a tennis ball off concrete.

I shrugged. I'd just have to remember what I saw.

The wide tube was more likely to lead somewhere important, so I changed course.

I made better time in the big tube, which I thought of

as Broadway. Twenty minutes of crawling and griping to myself about the state of my bladder later, Broadway widened into an oval room as tall and wide as a garage. Times Square. Its walls were studded with glowing ovals, green, not purple, and twiggy lumps that could be controls.

Hair stood on my neck. Somehow, I felt that I wasn't the only living thing in here.

I froze in the doorway and squinted as my eyes adjusted. Doorway was as good a word as any.

Across the room a shadow twitched.

I should have been terrified. But the enormity of this moment of contact overwhelmed me. My skin tingled.

The shape was a banana, colored like a new one, green. But five feet long and maybe two feet across the middle. It was as featureless as a banana. No eyes, just white bulges on its head end, no mouth.

It squirmed, twisted into a question mark, on an oval pedestal that rose out of the floor. Its skin rippled, from the elevated end of its question-mark body to the tail end, like a toothpaste tube squeezing itself. Black goo oozed from the tail into the pedestal.

For a thousand millennia humankind had wondered whether we were alone in the universe. For countless generations we had imagined and longed. Now, at this moment, the first representatives of intelligent species made physical contact across the cosmos.

And one of us was on the crapper.

Inside my helmet, I cleared my throat.

TWENTY

I POINTED THE FLARE PISTOL. "Hands up!" Well, what was I supposed to say? Maybe it would get the message from my tone.

Sluggo—just one look named him for me—curled his head end my way.

We both froze while my heart pounded.

A row of the green wall lights flashed. His head end wagged slowly, like a cobra coiling up out of a basket.

He could be saying hello. He could be hypnotizing me.

I thumbed back the flare pistol's hammer.

He slid off his toilet and circled to my left. He squirmed along, just like a garden snail, but fast. I circled, too, the pistol quivering in my hand.

I was on his turf. For all I knew, my next step could put me on top of a trapdoor that he could open and flush me into boiling oil.

Thup.

I flicked my eyes down. My foot drum-thumped a

black, shiny hollow thing as big as Sluggo and shaped like him. It rocked on the floor.

He jumped at me, I dodged backward, and we ended up ten feet apart.

"So you don't like me near your clothes."

A bulge grew sideways from his midriff, became an octopus tentacle, and slunk toward a curved, metallic rod lying on the floor next to his outerwear. A gun?

I poked my gun at Sluggo and tightened my finger on the trigger. "Hold it!"

He stopped.

"Good boy." I nodded.

His tentacle shot out toward the rod.

I dived for it. My glove got there first, and the rod skidded beyond Sluggo's reach.

Dragging myself off the floor, I planted my body between him and his weapon. I trained the flare pistol on him, then stepped toward him. He retreated. Another step, another backward squirm. The room had no corners, really, but one rounded end narrowed. I herded him back there and trapped him.

He weaved back and forth. I had him, and he knew it.

Sluggo collapsed like a punctured balloon.

I counted ten heartbeats.

Sluggo didn't move.

His color faded.

More black goo dribbled from his tail.

"Jeez. You killed yourself." I stepped back and listened to my breath wheeze inside my helmet.

Maybe he wasn't dead. The flare gun dangled from my fingers. I uncocked the hammer, then lobbed the gun and hit him amidships. He didn't flinch.

I inched to him, repocketed the flare pistol, and toed him with a boot. It was like kicking Jell-O. He was dead, alright.

Howard had said a Projectile might have a kamikaze pilot. Sluggo was already dead in his own mind, so swallowing some kind of snail poison pill probably hadn't fazed him. He had died for God and country, if he had either, rather than be taken alive. I guess that made him a good soldier.

"Howard?" My radio was deader than Sluggo.

Then hair stood on my neck like it had when I had come into Sluggo's presence. Again, I felt I wasn't alone.

Something hissed, then something else.

I turned.

The doorway I'd entered through boiled with Slugs. They thrashed and wriggled toward me like maggots out of a week-old carp.

I jumped back, snatched up Sluggo's metallic rod. Some of the Slugs had them, too, and they seemed to hold them in tentacles they grew from their bodies whenever and wherever they chose. One pointed his gun—that's how I thought of the metal rods, now—at me and tightened his tentacle around a ring near one end. Trigger! I pointed my rod at him and squeezed the ring on mine.

Something shot from the tip of my weapon and arrowed through his middle before he could fire at me. He dropped like a hundred pounds of wet liver.

There must have been forty Slugs behind him. They fanned out from the doorway, and some aimed their guns in my direction.

I snatched Sluggo from the floor at my feet for a shield and backed toward the doorway at the room's opposite end.

The Slugs held their fire. I backed into the tunnel, dragging Sluggo's carcass.

Two of them rushed me. The curved weapons had swordlike edges. The Slugs slashed at me with them. I flinched and retreated. If they slashed my suit, I couldn't cross vacuum back to the LEM if I ever got out of here. And if the atmosphere inside leaked into my suit, it could poison me.

Before they got closer, I dropped them with a shot apiece from my newfound weapon, then lunged forward and dragged their bodies into the doorway, forming a slimy, green barricade.

I grabbed my prisoner around his dead middle, hefted him over my shoulder like a flour sack, and scrambled down the passageway. I made good time and managed to avoid snagging either Sluggo or myself in an air-conditioning slot. I rounded a bend and found a Slug posse ahead, but with forty Slugs behind me somewhere, I couldn't retreat.

I blazed away with my stolen weapon and dived through the posse. I have no idea how long or how far I scrambled with them on my heels and Sluggo across my shoulders, or how often they just seemed to materialize in front of me, like they had walked through walls. I'd shoot a couple, dive through, and keep going.

Sluggo and I didn't weigh much, but I was sucking wind and sweating buckets. Worse, I was slowing down, and my Slug weapon had stopped firing. Whether I was out of ammunition or I'd broken it I didn't know.

Finally, I realized they weren't back there anymore, and they had stopped popping up in front of me.

I stopped at an intersection, slid Sluggo to the floor,

and sat for a breather, back to the wall and looking in all directions at once.

Where had the Slugs gone? I'd seen easily forty, killed maybe ten. The lights pulsed, and the alarm kept whooping.

Alarm. *That* was the pattern of the whoop and the lights. Alarms said "Beat it!" "Abandon ship!"

Of course. Sluggo dropped dead to avoid capture. His buddies were just as ready to blow this Projectile, and themselves and me, too, into rutabagas to prevent capture. No wonder they had stopped chasing me.

How long did I have?

I looked down the narrower, intersecting tube that made this junction. A white rectangle lay on its floor. I crawled to the object and read the words *Surviving in the Pacific.*

My travels had brought me full circle, back to the intersection of Broadway and the tube back to the outside hatch. This pamphlet had fallen from my unfastened thigh pocket as I tugged out the flare pistol.

The whoop shifted up an octave and pulsed faster. So did the lights.

The Projectile had entered the final countdown to its death.

I looked down the narrow connecting tube. One hundred feet away lay the hatch that had imprisoned me. If it would open to motion to let a repair-Slug back in, maybe it would now open to inside motion since the Projectile was near self-destructing. Or maybe the hatch would sense a Slug's presence and open if Sluggo were near it. Sketchy, but I had no alternative. I pushed Sluggo into the smaller tube, ahead of me, like a laundry bag.

The narrow tube had been long and slow on the way in. Now it seemed unending, the pulsing and whooping sounds so close together now they seemed nearly constant.

At last I saw the tube's end. The hatch remained closed. My heart sank, but I pushed Sluggo forward.

I got him within ten feet of the inner hatch. Nothing. I wiggled him around like an oversized puppet. Nothing.

How much longer until this thing blew? Minutes? Seconds?

If I had accepted that Hollywood job on the spot, Aaron Grodt might not have let the MPs take me. I might be lying by a pool under artificial sunlight right now contemplating Chrissy's monokini and feeling no pain.

When this thing blew, would I feel anything, or would I disintegrate before my nerve endings could register pain to my brain?

I rubbed Sluggo headfirst against the hatch. Nothing.

In an Aaron Grodt holo, a trapped hero would shoot off the door lock and escape.

The flare pistol still bulged in my thigh pocket. I drew it, backed off ten feet. Using Sluggo as a shield, I reached around him, aimed at the hatch, then closed my eyes and pulled the trigger.

Nothing. I squeezed the trigger again, so hard my hand shook. Nothing. My last hope was a seventy-year-old dud.

I felt the swell in my closed eyes as tears started. I would die here for no reason.

I opened my eyes. In the purple light I saw my hand wrapping the pistol butt and the uncocked hammer above my thumb.

I could squeeze the trigger until the moon turned to

cheese, and the pistol wouldn't fire if I didn't cock it, first!

My thumb trembled as it pulled back the hammer.

If the seventy-year-old flare fired, would it do any good? What if it ricocheted in close quarters and holed my suit?

I didn't know prayers, so I just said, "Oh, please."

I increased force on the trigger an ounce at a time until I felt the sear release. The hammer seemed to arc forward as though moving through molasses. It struck the cartridge primer.

TWENTY-ONE

THE HATCH REMAINED CLOSED. Then the flare pistol flashed, kicked in my hand, and the flare rocketed ahead and struck the hatch dead center. Nothing budged.

The flare ricocheted back at me, a red streak, and I dodged. The flare glanced off my helmet then bounced against an oval on the tube wall.

The hatch flower-petaled open again as the flare skittered in front of me, slow in the tepid gravity, then died. I looked at the oval on the tube wall. The Slug doorknob had been there all the time.

Black sky, more inviting than any blue summer day, shone beyond the hatch. The flare had not only punched the button that opened the inner door, it had broken either the air lock outer door or the mechanism that controlled it. Both ends of the air lock stood open. The only things holding apart the Projectile's pressurized atmosphere and vacuum were Sluggo and me.

Explosive decompression spit us through the air lock

like champagne corks. We shot out into sunlit vacuum, forty feet above the moon. Sluggo led, I followed, flailing and screaming like Superman chasing a rocket-boosted zucchini.

We arced toward the surface. At our projected impact point, two hundred feet from the air lock, Howard bent, back to us, scooping rocks into sample bags.

Sluggo's shadow flashed across Howard, and he turned, too late.

I screamed, "Howard! Watch out!"

Sluggo slammed Howard like a ton of suet and flattened him. I spun a municipal pool–quality somersault, hit Sluggo feetfirst and trampolined ten yards. I had that cushion, and I weighed no more than a suitcase, but I sprained an ankle during my second landing.

I lay on my back, waited for explosive decompression from a suit puncture, and saw the Milky Way smeared across the black lunar sky. Whooping vibrated through my shoulder blades. I rolled to my hands and knees. Ten yards away, Howard lay spread-eagled and still, bombed by a giant gherkin. Sluggo lay alongside him.

I crawled to them. "Howard?"

No answer. He didn't stir, and the only thing visible in his gold faceplate was my reflection.

No Projectile hull interfered between us, now. Maybe the impacts had knocked out one or both of our radios. If sound carried through rock, it should carry through helmets. I leaned forward and laid mine against his. "Howard?"

"Jason? What happened? What hit me?" His voice echoed like it came from a fishbowl. Which it did.

I shouted, "The Projectile's booby-trapped! We've got to move! You okay?"

He sat up, then I dragged him to his feet and pointed him toward the LEM. "Run!"

He bent toward Sluggo, then reached to touch him. "What—?" I shoved him and gathered Sluggo under one arm. "*Run*, goddammit!"

How long had it been since I entered the Projectile? How much longer did we have?

Beneath my arm as I lunar-bounded, Sluggo flopped like a salami. Pain spiked through my ankle every step. Ahead of me, Howard had mastered the lunar shuffle and bounded fifteen feet at a pace. I was making thirty. Give the moon that. If I have to run for my life, I want to do it where I cover thirty feet per step.

What was a safe distance from the Projectile? How big would the explosion be? I glanced back over my shoulder. We'd put a hundred yards between us and the Projectile. The whooping had faded, again.

It changed from a pulse to a solid tone, and my heart skipped.

I caught Howard in midleap and dragged him behind a mag-train-size boulder as the flash blinded me. I hadn't dropped my sun visor when I came back out of the Projectile.

The blast sound and shock seemed to lift the moon, itself, but as soon as I bounced loose from the ground, the sound vanished. I landed on Howard. Exploded pieces swarmed above us and ricocheted off the boulder that sheltered us, though they made no sound in vacuum.

I lay facedown across Howard while baseball-size chunks and smaller bits that had been blown sky-high rained down on us for what seemed like minutes.

Finally, stillness returned to the Sea of Fertility.

I touched helmets with Howard.

"Wow!" he said.

We got to our feet and bits of Slug Projectile cascaded off us and plopped into the lunar dust. Sluggo lay at our feet, none the worse for wear. Howard knelt beside him. "Is this—?"

"The Projectile was crawling with them. They tried to shoot me and cut me to pieces. It was dark and terrifying."

"God, I envy you, Jason!"

I sighed, then stepped around our shielding boulder and looked back. Where the Projectile had been was nothing. Moon boulders had been swept away for a hundred-yard radius around what had to be one big-ass crater, though I couldn't see it from this angle. Across that swept surface, and beyond, the moon's gray and white was sprinkled with black Projectile fragments as thick as poppy seeds on a bun.

A watermelon-size rock near us, but beyond the big boulder, lay split in two by a whizzing fragment. That could have been my head, or Howard's.

The blast radius spanned easily two-thirds of a mile. We hadn't come close to clearing it. We survived only by sheltering behind the boulder. I felt smart until I realized that I had not only failed to bring back information, I had blown the biggest Intelligence coup in world history into rutabagas.

Howard tapped my shoulder, then leaned his helmet against mine. "We need to get the alien out of vacuum."

I lifted my chin. I had brought back something, after all. Mankind's first prisoner in the Slug War. Even if he was currently frozen as stiff as a cucumber.

Howard pointed at Sluggo. "Let's get him back to the LEM."

The LEM! Metzger and the LEM had been a half mile from ground zero! I spun toward where they had been, but house-size boulders blocked my view. "Metzger?"

No telling if I was radioing or if he was transmitting to me. Metzger wouldn't have known the explosion was coming, not that he could have done much about it.

My heart raced. I stepped back, got a skipping start, and jumped ten feet on top of a flattopped boulder. I nearly overshot it, then caught my balance.

Scanning the horizon, I couldn't find the LEM. Maybe my radio worked up here. "Metzger?" I yelled it. Nothing.

Then I glimpsed the LEM's gold-foil sparkle, half-obscured by a boulder field. My heart leapt.

Something seemed different. Maybe from this angle— I looked closer.

One of the LEM's four legs lay alongside it. The Module tilted like a cocked hat. A dish antenna dangled where it should have stood straight.

Even as I jumped from the boulder to the surface and gathered Sluggo, my heart sank. The LEM was primitive, but it was no Conestoga wagon we could lash together with rope. It was going nowhere. Howard had said that this was the only Saturn that had been reconstructed. Canaveral had no lifeboat to send. Howard and I would die slowly here. It almost didn't matter if Metzger was alive inside the LEM.

Still, I was already bounding toward the crippled spacecraft, waving Howard to follow. "Metzger?" I yelled at the apogee of each bounce, but got no reply.

I reached the LEM before Howard and dropped Sluggo in the dust. The damage was worse up close. The main-engine nozzle lay beneath the crew cabin, collapsed like a stomped Dixie cup.

I picked my way up the bent ladder, touched my faceplate to the LEM window, and hollered, "Metzger?"

Combined tinting of my helmet visor and the window blackened the LEM's interior.

"Jason?" Metzger's voice. I jumped.

"You okay?"

"Bruised. You two?"

"Fine. The Projectile was booby-trapped."

"Gone?"

"Cinders."

"Oh." I heard disappointment in his tin echo.

"But we took a prisoner. Sort of. He's dead."

Twenty minutes later the three of us huddled in the LEM, EVA suits hung on the wall, sucking synthetic chocolate milk.

I told Metzger, "It's like a jellyfish. Or a slug. Banana-shaped and green."

"You're kidding. I expected, you know, bug eyes, fingers. We're losing to snails?"

Howard unwrapped a foil food tube. "We need to get the alien out of vacuum."

I scrunched my face. "Bring him in here?"

Howard shrugged. "I suppose he could rot if we warm him. He lived at zero Fahrenheit."

My EVA suit hung on the wall. Howard pointed. "Would he fit in there?"

"I guess. He's like five-five, 150 pounds."

There was an extra suit, but it hadn't been unpacked.

Metzger and Howard suited up, went down the ladder, and wrestled Sluggo into my suit while I unpacked the new one.

They stuffed him into the suit, his butt end down one leg, his head end just peeping up inside the helmet, behind the visor like . . . let's just say the word "dickhead" will never be the same for me. They left him lying on the moon, frozen but protected, and came back inside.

I addressed the burning question. "There's no way to repair the LEM."

Metzger shook his head. "Dead as your green friend outside."

They both avoided my eyes.

Did they think it was my fault that the Projectile had blown up? That I had marooned them here, to die? Neither of them knew Slugs like I did. Nobody in *world history* knew Slugs like I did! The little worms were going to blow themselves to pieces, regardless. I had fought my way out of that snake pit dragging a dead Slug! I hadn't asked to die this way, either.

I opened my mouth to snap at them, then turned away and looked out the viewport at Sluggo. He lay inside my misshapen EVA suit, dead on a harsh and lifeless world far from home, as I would be, soon. Had he died an orphan, as I would? Were the other Slugs whose ashes lay scattered across the Sea of Fertility *his* family?

I looked beyond him, beyond the boulder fields, unchanged for three billion years, to the distant hills, pale against the black sky. Within days I would starve, then freeze, then lie here as still as those hills for another billion years.

On the horizon, something moved.

TWENTY-TWO

I COULDN'T SPEAK, so I grabbed Metzger's hair, pulled his face to the viewport next to mine, and pointed. One speck crawled down a slope toward us, then another and another. The Slugs must have sent out patrols. They were returning. We would be very unpopular.

I turned from the viewport, squeezed past Howard, and reached into a wall-mounted cargo net. We had one more pistol.

Howard shook his head.

I dug in the cargo net for an ammunition magazine. "I'm not just quitting!"

Metzger tuned from the viewport. "No, Jason. It's okay."

I knew from Metzger's tone, after a lifetime together, that it *was* okay.

Metzger peeled the rubber eye shield from Howard's binoculars and held them in front of my eyes. I toggled the focus lever and saw a powder blue rectangle. A UN flag on an EVA suit sleeve. I widened the view field. A half dozen lunar dune buggies bounced toward us, filled with EVA-suited humans.

"What—?"

Howard said, "We couldn't tell you. If you had been captured, you could have talked."

My head spun. "We aren't going to die?"

"Not from being stranded on the moon." Howard pried the pistol from my fingers and slipped it back in the cargo net.

I pointed at the bouncing buggies. "What are they?"

"Gravity-optimized all-terrain vehicles." Howard turned to Metzger. "What do we need to take with us? Those GOATs will be here in two minutes."

I grabbed Howard's elbow. "How did they get here?"

Metzger stuffed one foot into his EVA suit. "Just the Slug and any instrument readouts you picked up."

Howard nodded, then turned to me. "Four days overland. We were afraid it would take even longer. GOATs weren't designed to travel long distances. That's why I gambled our only Saturn to get us here earlier. Good gamble, too. If we hadn't gotten here early, those guys"— he pointed out the viewport—"would just be picking up Projectile pieces, like you and I did in Pittsburgh."

My head spun. "I mean—there are other people on the moon?"

"Long story. We built a base on the dark side of the moon."

My jaw dropped.

"You'll see it. That's where those guys are going to take us."

An hour later I sat strapped into the front passenger's

seat of a GOAT, jerking slowly toward the dark side of the moon. The GOAT's tires were springy, porous screen, its frame metal tubes as delicate as a racing bike. Its roof was a solar-cell panel. It might have weighed as much as a car on Earth, but here a man could lift it by one corner like a bed frame.

I looked at my driver. By the chevrons on his sleeve he was a master sergeant. I couldn't ask him much, except during stops when we could touch helmets. This suit also had a bum radio. It made me wonder how we ever reached the moon in ancient times until I remembered that this suit was seventy years old.

We led the little parade. Howard rode in GOAT two, behind us, with Sluggo strapped across the backseat.

The trip gave time to think. Foremost, I was glad to be alive. I was mad at Howard and Metzger for letting me think, even for minutes, that we were stranded on the moon. I was even madder that Howard probably had guessed before we ever left Earth that the Slugs would blow themselves up. In fact, he said as much when he told me why he used up mankind's one and only Saturn V to get here early. Knowing that, he had let me go inside a ticking bomb.

As a soldier, I knew it was all necessary and sound operational security. But I was still pissed.

Over the next four days, with nobody to talk to, my mood drooped from pissed to depressed. Somebody had to take the blame for wasting a zillion-dollar rocket ship and blowing up the greatest intelligence find in history, with nothing to show for it but a hyperthyroid amoeba frozen as stiff as a cucumber.

Howard was in charge of intelligence that would shape

the war. He was safe. Metzger was a hero. In all the years I'd known him, he always skated past blame.

That left me.

It promised to be a long four days. At least this time I had hooked up my bladder-relief tube.

The journey turned uncomfortable and boring after two hours. The terrain soon became monotonous, even after we crossed to the dark side after two days. Plains and hills and boulders gave way to plains and hills and boulders. All blindingly bright but as black-and-white as an art-gallery holo.

Blindingly bright wasn't what I expected of the "dark side," one of history's great misnomers. The moon doesn't rotate on its own axis but always keeps one face toward Earth. When that face is sunlit, we see the moon. When the moon swings between Earth and the sun, the side toward Earth is dark and the "dark" side is lit.

During our trip, the moon swung so the front side we landed on darkened and sunshine "dawned" on the dark side. Sad to say, the moon is the moon. I'd sooner drive across Kansas.

There was little more to the trip until we crawled up a jagged hill range on the fourth day. A crater rim, as it turned out, then paused at its crest and looked down on Luna Base.

I shielded my eyes with my hand and stared across row after row of round-roofed white buildings. Vehicles crawled antlike between them. The place sprawled for miles, a town, not a base.

The bright sunshine faded, and I dropped my hand from my forehead. A cloud must be crossing the sun.

Cloud? There was no atmosphere here.

I swiveled my head and looked up. Above us loomed a gray metal skeleton frame that had to be a mile long and a quarter mile wide. I pointed and tugged my driver's sleeve.

He leaned across and touched helmets. "Relax. That's the ship. United Nations Spaceship *Hope*."

Miles above us, the frame drifted slowly past us. Fireflies twinkled and zoomed all around it. "*The* ship? The one that we were going to build five years from now? The one that's going to Jupiter?"

I understood. She would be ready in months, not years. The biggest sucker punch in history.

I looked again. The hundred fireflies must be supply barges, construction-crew transports, tugs. It was the greatest show on Earth. Well, not on Earth. I touched helmets. "Why build it up here?"

"*Hope*'s transplanetary. She's strong enough to travel between here and Jupiter but if we set her down on Earth, or even here on the moon, gravity would collapse her. *Hope* was born in vacuum. Someday she'll die there. Her orbit's calculated so the moon or Earth is always between her and Ganymede. Any observer out there won't know she exists."

If nobody on Earth knew she existed, no spy—and no captured Spec Four—could give her away.

In orbit, *Hope* dwindled to a speck above the lunar horizon.

We zigzagged as we dropped toward the flat crater floor while another object grew against the moon's black sky. A shuttle craft, looking much like the ones I had seen at Canaveral, powered down to the surface, its wings useless in vacuum.

A hundred yards away the UN flag stood stiff, framed to keep it flying in the nonbreeze.

We rolled past building after building. The building we stopped at was like every other building there, a white half tube you could fit a football field under, with a man-sized air lock sticking out one side. Two sergeants wrestled Sluggo loose as Metzger and Howard climbed down from their GOATs.

My driver grasped my elbow, holding me in my seat. Crap. They were separating the Bad Boy from the heroes.

Three buildings farther the GOAT halted. Stenciled on the building's air lock door was "Detention." Whether it was Judge March or Captain Jacowicz or the Grand Poobah of the Dark Side of the Moon everybody wanted me in the slammer.

My cell was a windowless room eight feet on a side with a bunk, sink, and toilet. They gave me fresh coveralls, a shaving kit, and freeze-dried rations no worse than Meals-Ready-to-Eat.

I planted my palms against the wall, hung my head, and shook it. I lay on the bunk and wondered why.

The door clanked; an MP in coveralls like mine stepped in and waved me out of the cell with a white-gloved hand.

He led me down into the tunnel system that linked Luna Base's buildings. Our footsteps echoed down the rock tube. I asked him, "How'd they make the tunnels?"

"Melted with lasers."

We walked for ten minutes, stopping at intersections to let electric trams pass. They shook the floor and bounced me in lunar gravity.

Cargos of hull plates flexed and rumbled toward the shuttles that would lift them to orbit.

Returning trams bore off-shift welders and riveters,

swaying shoulder on shoulder and sound asleep with lunch therms in laps.

I smirked. "Union labor, huh?"

The MP glared at me. "Sixteen-hour shifts. Twenty-eight days every month. Quarter million miles from home."

One thing you had to say for war, it got people off their butts. A century ago, humans flew in canvas-covered air-planes. World War II started, and six desperate years later humanity had jets, radar, and nuclear power. The Slug War had pushed humanity farther into space in months than all the idealism of the post–Cold War had in fifty years.

Finally, another MP at a desk looked over papers the first one gave him, then at me. He buzzed me in through a steel door behind him.

I stepped into an operating room, all stainless steel, bright light, and white sheeting. Chill enough that I saw my breath. The lights brightened a pedestal operating table in the room's center, and a couple rows of am-phitheater seating rose behind the table.

On the table was strapped my slimy sparring partner, Sluggo. He looked none the worse for wear after we'd dragged him from Mare Fecunditatis. Still short, green, and tapered.

A guy stood behind him, skinny, bald, and beetle-browed. Civilian, because a last-century soul patch smudged his chin. He wore a white lab coat and a hands-free headset with a mike that cherry-stemmed around his cheek. His headset was wired to a Chipman that stuck from his coat's breast pocket among a cluster of pens.

He nodded at the Slug. "You did this?"

I stuck out my chest. "Yeah."

"Tragic." He snapped on latex gloves as he circled the operating table. "Our first meeting with extraterrestrial intelligence ends in violent death."

I nearly laughed. The Slugs had killed how many million people, and he wept for this one?

He bent and sidestepped alongside the slab, lifting, then plopping down the carcass like a gob of liver. "You killed it?"

"He committed suicide."

He sneered. "An alien psychologist. Did it leave a note?" He stabbed his finger like a cross-examiner at the carcass. "This body bears bootprint bruises!"

"He died before I made those."

His eyes narrowed.

"We both got shot out of a cannon. I dropped on him."

He snorted. "This is no joke."

"Neither was that. We landed on a commissioned officer."

He pouted at me, then spoke into the mike. "*Reported* cause of death, self-inflicted."

"You think I killed a POW? Did you talk to Howard Hibble?"

"I'll ask the questions." He adjusted his glasses, then sniffed. His eyebrows flew up, and he bent and sniffed the length of the carcass. He pulled his mike to his lips and his voice quivered. "Subject emits an unmistakable odor of urine! This suggests Earthlike excretory system and metabolism! An unexpected phenomenon!"

"It's mine."

"Don't worry. You'll get credit for your kill!" He snorted.

"The urine. It's mine. We zipped the body inside my EVA suit for the trip from Mare Fecunditatis. I kind of had an accident in the suit, before that."

"Oh." He grumbled, then pressed the erase button on the Chipman in his pocket. "Anything else you haven't shared with me?"

"If you're really interested in how it excretes, I think it was on the toilet when I first saw it."

He sneered. "Don't tax your brain, killer. I'll analyze behaviors."

I shrugged. "Just a hunch."

"Well then, let's have a look, shall we?" He lifted the corpse's tail end, peeked underneath, plopped it back, and smirked. "Nothing. And I know an anus when I see one."

I stared at him. "Me too."

The MP marched me back to detention after that.

TWENTY-THREE

THE MP LEANED AGAINST MY CELL doorframe while I sat, elbows on knees, on the side of the bunk. He was as bored as any GI. I told him I didn't kill Sluggo.

He shrugged. "It was a preliminary inquiry with a cryptozoologist, I'm guessing. And you wised off, I'm guessing."

"You guess. I guess. Is everything here secret?"

"Not once you're here. Nobody's going anywhere. Unless we win the war."

"How the hell did this get here? How can they keep it secret?"

He shrugged and sighed. "The impact dust Earthside *is* bad for jets, but the reason commercial air is grounded is most of the aircraft mechanics and aviation machine tools on Earth got diverted to build modified space shuttles to ferry stuff to the moon. Six weeks after the first Projectile hit, the first ship landed here. There are thirteen thousand people here now." That was one thousand times as

many people as had set foot on the moon during the
course of human history before the war started.

"Imminent genocide lit a fire under the human race."
He nodded.

I snapped my fingers. "Static in the holos? It's not
Projectile dust." We had diverted every communications-
satellite repair and launch vehicle to hauling material and
workers up here. Nobody found disappearing loved ones
unusual. Not with millions of people missing.

He nodded.

I nodded back. "But still, you can't cover up a project
this massive completely. So we announce we're building
a ship, alright, but it's going to be built on Earth and take
five years. That way we can train troops openly."

He shrugged. "The spooks say that a good lie has a
basis in truth."

Sun Tzu wrote, "All warfare is based on deception."
He could have continued that it *has* to be if your side's
too weak to kick ass. I sat on my bunk, pressing into my
mattress with one-sixth my normal weight and wondered
what would come next.

I knew history's biggest secret. So did thirteen thousand others, at least. But the thirteen thousand were se-
questered on the moon, where they couldn't blab.

It seemed like overkill. Especially now that we knew
that a Slug couldn't exactly slap on a false mustache and
spy around Earth undetected.

But there were other ways to spy. Eavesdrop on radio
or holo or video. Look down with high-powered imagery
systems. Remote-sensing intel was the one area of the
military that had advanced in this century while weapons
rusted. Even Infantry units, real ones, not training menag-

eries like I had endured through Basic, had little observation drones that hovered above the battlefield like giant bugs.

We had to assume the Slugs knew whatever the human media knew. So since I knew about the massive deception of this base and this ship, they would lock me away here for the duration. If they didn't just court-martial me and shoot me. My success in bringing back a dead Slug evidently was overshadowed by my failure to bring back a live one, not to mention that they thought I blew up his ship.

I slept poorly.

The next morning, the MP led me back to the floodlit operating room. Sluggo still lay on his table, but the amphitheater seats were filled with twelve silhouettes.

I shaded my eyes to confront my jury.

They wore officer's uniforms of a half dozen armed forces. All theater-grade brass by their shoulder boards. Mr. I-know-an-asshole was absent. This crowd was way above his pay grade. Except one scrawny silhouette. That one stood.

My heart pounded.

Was he the jury foreman, about to sentence me to life imprisonment on the moon?

The foreman stepped down to the operating-room floor and walked toward me, squinting. Unlike his spit-and-polish cronies, his boots looked like he shined them with a Hershey bar.

"Jason? Did they feed you?"

Howard Hibble pumped my hand. He now wore major's oak leaves on his collar.

"Howard? You need to tell them! I didn't kick that Slug to death!"

"That investigation? Bureaucratic humbug! It's over and done."

He raised his hands in front of his chest.

And applauded. The rest stood and clapped, too. Within ten minutes, I had been congratulated by generals from four nations.

They and a panel of experts donned surgical masks and gowns, filed back into the seats, and oohed and ahhed while other experts sliced Sluggo up and asked me questions.

During a break in the autopsy, Howard sidled up to me. He hacked a smoker's cough, his fist to his surgical mask.

"We never had a chance to talk. What was it like in there? How did they move? Did they display individualized characteristics?"

"They oozed at me like green spaghetti. I ran for my life. I was so scared I wet my pants."

"I bet that was terrific!"

Six hours later, the brain trust had decided that the Slugs see with the white patches near their heads, even though they don't have what we'd call eyes. They don't see visible light but infrared. They are cloned, not born. The hollow thing I tripped over was probably artificial body armor. They communicate with sound, but maybe they can project vague feelings, too. They have outsized neural ganglia but little cerebral capacity for independent thought. They stink to high heaven if you don't keep dead ones frozen. And the experts agreed with me about the toilet.

After my brain was picked as clean as Sluggo's body, they filed out. Howard stayed. "You did say your family was killed at Indianapolis?"

"My mom. She was all there was."

"The Ganymede Expeditionary Force will be orga-
nized like a light-infantry division. Ten thousand of the
best, most experienced soldiers in the world. The volunteer lists were overwhelming. The UN decided to take
only those who had lost their entire family to the Slugs."

What was Howard saying? "I'm a war orphan. But I'm
not experienced."

"The hell! You're the only human who's ever seen
Slugs alive!"

"Huh?"

"The Headquarters Battalion will have my Intelligence
company attached. Our job is to tell the commander what
to expect from the enemy. I told them I need your ex-
pertise."

"I'm no scientist. I barely passed precalc."

Howard waved his hand. "I handled that. Your records
say you can shoot. I got you assigned to the commanding
general's personal security detachment."

I swallowed. "PSD have the shortest combat life expectancy of any military operational specialty!"

He shrugged. "Take a bullet for the team. Mostly
you'll be a resource for me. That ship you saw, above us?
You're going to be on it!"

My head spun. I'd gone from court-martial to the one
thing I wanted more than anything in the world.

Later, a Military Police corporal escorted me not to my
cell but to the bachelor officers' quarters.

I entered the dark room and stumbled. Metzger waved
the lights on and levered himself off his bunk on one
elbow. "What happened?"

I cocked my head. "Everything."

Metzger, Howard, and I left the moon the next morning. The Luna Base Shuttles landed at Canaveral at night, one after another, so no one would know there was all this traffic going into space and coming back. The crew let Metzger bring our shuttle in. A one-hundred-ton glider screaming down to a pitch-dark runway with landing lights off. What a rush.

A day later, I left to report. Even though my Slug battle was secret, and I had signed another secrecy agreement to prove it, my GEF billet meant no more military hitchhiking for me. I rode for two days in a Space Force blue bus with reclining seats. An orderly brought me sandwiches, I caught up on months of sleep, and I watched rural America pass.

Closed businesses squatted alongside deserted highways as we headed northwest across gray, cold Oklahoma. There was no agriculture left to speak of, so roadside businesses had no customers.

I slumped in my seat and watched flat Oklahoma dirt turn to flat Colorado dirt by Act of Congress. On my previous car trips from back East, the Rockies usually rose on the horizon while we were well out on the plains.

This time, the mountains never came into sight through the twilight. Humanity didn't have much time. The ship couldn't be ready too soon. Neither could the division I was about to join.

In Denver, I boarded a helicopter headed deep into the Front Range.

And I thought the moon was cold.

TWENTY-FOUR

THE SLUGS WERE REMAKING GANYMEDE just the way they liked it. That meant they had so far warmed it to zero Fahrenheit in the twilight that passed for day way out there. The atmosphere they breathed was 2 percent oxygen, not 16 percent like Earth. Gases trapped in Sluggo's tissues confirmed remote spectroscopy. Ganymede's artificial atmosphere was also as thin as the air miles above sea level.

So when the UN looked for a place to train the Infantry division that was going to fight on Ganymede, it needed a place where the air was cold and thin but that had enough infrastructure to move troops in and out and house ten thousand of them plus trainers and alternates.

Camp Hale, Colorado, was old, like Indiantown Gap. It sat two miles above sea level on the western slope of the Rockies, six miles north of the old silver-mining town of Leadville. Built during World War II to train and house ski troops, it had been knocked down to nothing but foundations in the snow.

But you wouldn't have known that as the helicopter drifted over the base carrying me and a dozen other GEF selectees.

Luna Base had been built from nothing a quarter million miles from Earth in short months. Camp Hale's snowy foundations were closer to home, but the sprawled prefab structures, roads, and bustling troops and vehicles were equally startling.

Mountains around Camp Hale thrust up another half mile higher, the peaks above tree line as gaunt as ax blades.

As an early arrival, I drew modern gear and humped it all to my billet, which was a double room in the barracks complex that housed Headquarters Battalion of GEF. I had stowed my gear in my locker when my roomie arrived.

He rapped on the doorjamb. "You Wander?" He stuck out his hand. "Ari Klein."

He wore civvies, but I knew already that my roomie was part of Howard Hibble's Military Intelligence company. Ari Klein was rostered as our TOT-Wrangler, so I expected weird.

Ari's black hair reached such unmilitary length that it curled like wool. Over it perched a knit *yarmulke*. His eyes were dark beneath bushy brows, but his smile was broad. The TOT-Wrangler scars showed faint at each temple. "Howdy."

He wore a plaid shirt, jeans, and ostrich-skin boots. Intelligence Branch. My roommate was a Jewish cowboy.

"Don't let the outfit fool you. I'm not a real cowboy. I'm from North Dallas."

Ari was a surprise, but his duffel was astonishing. It wriggled. He set it on his bunk, unsnapped it, and stood back while I stared.

A six-legged, black velvet football wriggled out and stared back at me with eyes the size of gray Oreos.

"Jason, meet Jeeb."

Everybody has heard about Tactical Observation Transports, but few people have been as close to a TOT as I was to Jeeb.

Theoretically, a TOT's just a sophisticated version of the police surveillance drones seen over every American neighborhood day in and day out. Except that a drone has a four-foot wingspan and costs a couple hundred thousand. Ari's tin friend cost as much as a tank battalion. So even division-size units like GEF only got one.

A TOT, even with wings spread, can fly through the average window with six inches to spare. It can crawl on six legs faster than a cheetah can run, has a velvet-texture skin invisible to radar and infrared, can change color to blend with its surroundings like a chameleon. Its ultra-tanium chassis is hardened against small-arms rounds, fire, water, and the electromagnetic pulse of a nuclear blast.

Ari clucked, and his robot alter ego hopped onto his shoulder, still watching me. "He's a J-series. He's the second one, 'B,' of six. So, Jeeb."

Jeeb twisted his head to take in the room. He imaged visible light, infrared, ultraviolet, and radar. He heard sound from five to fifty thousand hertz and soft as a rat fart, plus all bands of radio.

"Is he looking for his bunk?" I asked.

Ari shook his head. "He's programmed to scan for eaves-dropping sensors. He makes you nervous, doesn't he?"

"Nah." Of course he did. I was sleeping with a mechanical cockroach as big as a Thanksgiving turkey.

Jeeb hopped from Ari's shoulder to the windowsill, worked the latch with one arm while perched on the other five, and threw up the sash. The covering on his back split, telescoped into wings, and Jeeb flew away.

Ari grinned as he began unpacking the inanimate parts of his gear. "The Swedish troops are landing. Half women. Babefest!"

Ari was seeing them as he spoke, through Jeeb's eyes. A TOT displayed holo images on a suitcase-size viewer for analysis, but its input also beamed directly into the Wrangler's brain, through surgical implants.

TOTs are just metal-and-plastic machines. They respond to the thoughts of their Wranglers and to no other input, immune to jamming. They have enough artificial intelligence to function when out of range of their Wranglers, but no personality, theoretically. But I read that Wranglers and TOTs are closer than the old K-9 dogs and trainers.

Ari laughed. "The Swedes are catching hell from the drills, blonde or not."

GEF was technically a UN operation. But after a century as the world's policeman, the US military, sad as it was, functioned light-years ahead of the rest of the world's. Most of GEF's troops were American. Most of GEF's equipment was American. Most of GEF's trainers were American.

So experienced soldiers arriving from other countries were being subjected to American boot-camp indoctrination just to get them up to speed with the likes of me.

Ari consulted his wrist 'puter. "Hour 'til chow. Let's go down to the airstrip so you can see it, too."

By the time we arrived the decorative Swedes had moved out for a jolly double-time around the post.

A Herc disgorged a sorry-looking bunch of male and female soldiers.

"Egyptians." Ari was getting input from Jeeb. I shaded my eyes with my hand and squinted at the low clouds. I knew Jeeb hovered up there, but still I couldn't find him, his belly chameleoned gray to match the clouds.

"They're bitching about the cold." Jeeb also translated languages, dialects, codes, and ciphers in real time as he sent his eavesdroppings back into Ari's head.

The Egyptians formed up and stood more or less at attention. Frigid wind off the peaks ruffed the fleece halos on our parka hoods. The poor Egyptians wore just desert fatigues and shivered on the runway, especially the small or skinny ones.

A voice echoed across the runway.

"Sir? Commissioned officers are addressed as 'Sir'! I am Division Sergeant Major Ord and am so addressed!"

Even though the words weren't addressed to me, I shivered.

Ord! It hadn't occurred to me that Pittsburgh had made Ord a war orphan, eligible for GEF, just like me. But with his qualifications he didn't need to capture a Slug to get in, like I had.

As divison sergeant major, he ruled my HQ Battalion with an iron fist. Oh joy.

We sidled up to the formation.

The object of Ord's affection was a young, female soldier, who wore the uniform of an Egyptian army lieutenant. In GEF, we all gave up our rank pending final assignment. She was just another grunt.

She stood maybe four-ten, so Ord had to bend at the waist to get nose to nose with her.

When he finally drew back, I saw her face and nearly stopped breathing.

Her skin was olive and flawless, her eyes wide and dark, and her features perfect. Fatigues don't reveal much about a woman's shape, but hers looked promising.

As Ari and I watched, arms folded and smirking, Ord ended his welcome spiel. He commanded, "Dis-*missed*!"

The Egyptians spun stunned about-faces, picked up their gear, and jogged toward trucks that would haul them to the quartermaster building.

I jogged alongside the little officer, whose head hung a millimeter. "Don't let Ord bother you."

She raised her head. Her eyes were prettier up close.

"He picks on soldiers he likes. He did it to me when I was in Basic."

"And you are?" Her English was perfect but accented. I could watch her lips move all day.

"Wander. Jason. US Army. Specialist fourth class. Or I was. Now I'm just another GEF grunt."

She nodded and extended her hand. "Munshara. Sharia. Egyptian Army. Formerly lieutenant, Specialist." She raised her chin a notch.

"Yes, ma'am." Erased rank or not, military courtesy was a hard habit to break.

Her duffel slipped from her shoulder. The canvas bag was as big as she was, and I reached to steady it. She jerked away and struggled not to puff in the thin, two-mile-high air.

How do you pick up another soldier, especially one who outranks you?

"I'm a machine gunner."

"I also. Perhaps we will compete."

Not exactly a date, but the door hung ajar for further contact.

She reached the truck and hefted her duffel in. I thought about offering her a hand up. Maybe a push on the fanny. She shot me a look, and I dropped the thought.

She had to hop twice to get herself up and into the truck. I looked away.

"Thank you for the American welcome, Jason." She smiled down at me. I watched the truck lurch away as my heart fluttered.

"Nice." Ari stood beside me. "But not my type."

"Huh?"

"Israel and the Arabs made peace twenty years ago but Mom wouldn't have been ready for me to bring home a nice Egyptian girl." He blinked at the mention of his mother.

"Oh."

Dallas had been an early hit and one of the worst. Every soldier in GEF had lived some variation of the same tragic story. Etiquette developed quickly. You never asked about anyone's family, directly. Unless the other soldier brought it up, first. "Lose anyone else?"

Ari nodded. "My father was a haberdasher. We had three stores. North Dallas has good rag trade. Had."

He couldn't ask, so I said, "My mother was in Indianapolis."

The other part of the ritual was to change subjects once basic information was exchanged.

Jeeb fluttered down and perched, one wing brushing Ari's curls. Four talons gripped Ari's shoulder, two talons wiped antennae as they retracted into Jeeb's anterior. Jeeb was a J-series, so he not only observed things, he hacked into any known database and cross-referenced anything he found.

Ari pointed at the shrinking truck. "Lieutenant Munchkin, there? Her father was a colonel in the Egyptian Air Force. She lost her parents and six sisters to the Cairo Projectile. She can shoot the eyes out of the jacks in a card deck at six hundred meters with an M-60. She's single and straight. She wears thong underwear."

"That's some nosy bug you got there, Ari."

Ari adjusted his *yarmulke*. "His grandma *was* Jewish."

Her truck turned and disappeared behind a row of parked Hercs. Jeeb had to be exaggerating. I was the best shot I knew with an M-60, and I couldn't *see* a deck of cards at six hundred meters. But I hoped he was right about the thong.

The next morning everyone at Camp Hale but support staff assembled in a rock bowl at the foot of the peaks. In its center, the Combat Engineer Battalion had erected a stage and loudspeakers. Earmarked for personal security, I sat up front with HQ Battalion, below the stage, with frigid rock searing my butt through insulated trousers and frigid wind searing my bare nose.

Major General Nathan Cobb mounted the stage in the same fatigue parka the rest of us wore, but with two stars on each shoulder. Our commanding officer flipped back his hood. Better him than me.

Completely gray and rail-thin, he wore old-fashioned glasses. He pushed them back on a red nose and drew a paper from his pocket. Wind whipped it in his fingers.

He looked out over fifteen thousand faces. Ten thousand would form the division, the rest were alternates. What that said about expected training casualties knotted my stomach.

Nat Cobb adjusted his microphone. "Cold enough for you?" I'd read up on the man for whom I might take a bullet. He came from a small, plain town in Maine and talked like it.

"No, sir!" Fifteen thousand voices roared back.

"Maybe we can warm things up for the Slugs."

Bigger roar. Nat Cobb wiped snot off his nose with his mitten and smiled at his soldiers. Most generals come with papers like a pedigreed poodle. West Point. Family history. Embassy and Washington liaison assignments.

Nat Cobb was a mutt. He'd enlisted at eighteen, got a field promotion and fought his way into Officer Candidate School. Over the years, he'd earned a master's in international relations and kicked ass at the Command and General Staff College. He spurned Pentagon career-builder assignments to stay close to troops in the field. They said he didn't know which fork to use at White House dinners and didn't care. Fortunately for Cobb's career, the current occupant of that address didn't care either, and she was the commander in chief.

He cleared his throat, and the vast audience fell silent. "I'm not going to bullshit you or motivate you. We've all had plenty of both lately. Each of us has the most important, hardest job ahead of us any human being has ever had. Most of us will die trying to do that job. All I can offer you is my promise that I will bring you home alive even if it costs my own life. But if I must choose saving you or saving home, my choice is clear. I know each of you will make the same choice."

He paused. The wind died, and I heard breath in fifteen thousand throats.

"You've already listened to me beat gums too long. Let's get to work." He turned and stepped down, to dead silence.

I suppose we expected fist-pumping oratory or a detailed outline or something. General Patton telling us to make the other son of a bitch die for his country. General Marshall laying out the master plan.

Ari leaned toward me. "Gets to the point, doesn't he?"

"Wait 'til you meet his division sergeant major."

The next weeks flew. The good news was we slept an honest six hours daily, had staff to pull KP and the like, and got almost-edible meals. Nat Cobb was a GI's general. It was usual to find him in a mess hall, at a table with privates, eating off a tray like a regular grunt. And woe betide the mess sergeant who burned the bacon at that meal.

The bad news was every minute that we didn't spend on bullshit we spent humping up mountains or cleaning weapons. Basic was a vacation by comparison. And the cold hung around each of us morning and night like an icy rag.

Which brings me to temperature endurance testing and back to Munchkin.

TWENTY-FIVE

TEMPERATURE ENDURANCE TESTING involved freezing your ass off. Every moment at Camp Hale involved freezing your ass off, but TET had it as a specific objective.

The brains had figured out early that humans would freeze to death on Ganymede without battery-heated fatigues. So they invented Smart Clothes. Very forties. A chip calculates your body's need for heat against available battery power. You stay alive, if not comfortable.

If you're wondering why battery depletion was an issue, remember that the Eternad system wasn't perfected at first. In case you've been living in a cave the last few years, Eternad's a system of flexible bands and levers built into clothing that stores body-motion energy in rechargeable batteries. Just like the alternators on internal-combustion cars recharged the battery by harnessing engine motion. Simply breathing keeps you juiced.

But at that time, the batteries were conventional. A GI with hardy metabolism could last a day under field conditions without a new battery. Another might popsicle inside twelve hours because his chip calculated he needed more warmth. The twelve-hour troops simply couldn't be sent to Ganymede.

TET consisted of two GIs just sitting in one foxhole in a line of foxholes dug along a wind-scoured ridge at twelve thousand feet. Chill factor was equivalent to eighty below zero, Fahrenheit. You stayed in your hole for a solid day while your fatigues kept you right on the edge of misery. It was the one test you couldn't retake, except in case of verifiable mechanical breakdown. If you made the day, you stayed in. If you were cold-sensitive and sucked off your battery juice in twelve hours, you went hypothermic and washed out of GEF permanently. Simple, pragmatic, and a bitch.

Each GI wore a finger clip so the instructor could test body-core temperature periodically. If a soldier went hypothermic, the soldier washed out but lived.

As they trucked us up to the ridge, my soon-to-be foxhole mate swayed against me. She shrank away, as she had a week ago.

If I had harbored romantic notions about Munchkin, as Ari had called her, they died a week before. We were at the range, testing to rank machine gunners for division assignments. Munchkin and I tied for top score. We would both be assigned to HQ Battalion, which I was, already. But we had to have a shoot-off to determine who would be gunner and who would be loader. Gunner was not only boss, gunner humped the gun, not the heavier ammo load.

The rest of the failed competitors stood behind us. She, in turn, stood behind the gun, tight-lipped and shaking tension from her fingers as she gazed downrange at the targets six hundred meters out.

"Good luck," I had said, as she wriggled down prone behind the gun and adjusted the sights.

"I won't need it."

And I didn't need a snotty Egyptian Princess. Maybe she was just covering her nervousness. I wanted to say something diplomatic to former Lieutenant Munshara. I really did. Not something personal that might upset her concentration. But what actually spewed out was, "What you need is a spanking, Munchkin."

Somebody laughed, then somebody else. It was the kind of nickname that stuck. Especially if the nicknamed hated it.

She turned as red as a café-au-lait complexion can turn, and fixed me with a stare as cold as Camp Hale. Then she laid her cheek alongside the gunstock, and the range went silent.

Never, ever piss off a shrimp. The competition was over before it started.

Munchkin nailed every target, then begged another ammo belt and drilled a batch of leftover tank-gun targets a thousand meters out.

I didn't even bother shooting.

So a week ago she had stood and brushed off her fatigues. "How's that for a spanking, Wander?" She had waved her hand at the gun on the ground. "Clean that up, Wander!"

"Wander!" The voice snapped me back to the present as the TET truck squealed to a stop. My still-pissed gunner jolted against me again.

"I said first pair out now. Wander and Munchkin." Mr.

Wire, the chief of this exercise, was a US Navy SEAL. As old as Ord and of equivalent noncommissioned rank, a master chief petty officer. He screamed to be heard over the wind.

Thirty seconds later the woman I had forever dubbed "Munchkin" and I stood together on a gale-swept ridge. The truck disappeared as wind needled snow into the bits of skin that our face masks didn't cover.

I tapped my mitten on her padded shoulder, pointed at our snow-swirled hole, and screamed, "Out of this wind!"

She nodded. By the time we wedged ourselves in she shook so hard her voice trembled. "God tests me."

"Yeah. It's cold."

"I mean putting me together with you."

"The feeling's mutual." Not really. If you have to freeze your butt off better to do it with a babe. "Look, I was just kidding the other day."

"You were just arrogant!" She hugged her torso and turned her face to the rock wall.

"Attitude won't keep you warmer. Take it from a Coloradan. Neither will the fact that they dropped us off first. We'll be out here longer than anybody else. Bad luck."

"No. Not luck. For this single thing I apologize to you, Wander. It's my fault. We are placed near the command post so the instructors can watch me closer."

"Huh?"

"I'm the smallest person in the entire Ganymede Expeditionary Force. Their charts say it is physically impossible for me to retain adequate body heat. They already asked me to withdraw, voluntarily."

"The weather isn't that bad." Actually, it was horrible. I was freezing my ass off already, batteries or no.

"It isn't the cold. It's the unknown. I've never been cold. In Egypt it never even approaches zero degrees."

"Zero's damn cold."

"Zero Centigrade. Where water freezes. Egypt never even gets close to *that*. This is beyond imagination."

"And I suppose having to go through it all with me makes it worse?" I'd read all the propaganda about superior female judgment and endurance and the sheer justice of including female soldiers in this Force. But here I was having a prom-night spat in a foxhole.

She twisted to look at me as I pulled my face mask up and blew my nose into my mitten.

She rolled her eyes and turned away again.

I peeled my mitten down and looked at my 'puter. "Only twenty-three hours and fifty minutes to go. As the cold-weather expert in this team I have a suggestion. Huddle together for warmth. I think they expect us to do that." I spread my arms. "Come to Papa."

"God willing, I shall freeze to death first."

I shrugged. "Suit yourself."

It felt like she sat with her face to the foxhole wall for hours. My 'puter insisted it was thirty minutes. I alligator-clipped my finger. Body temperature 98.6, battery draw-down 4 percent. I was chilled, but I'd make it through with juice to spare.

"Okay, Munchkin. Time for your physical."

"Fuck off."

I uncoiled the wire for the fingertip sensor from the monitor box. "It's not gynecology. Hold out your finger."

She grumbled but extended her hand back to me, poking her trigger finger out through the firing slit in her right mitten.

I slipped the alligator clip on. Her hand was as delicate as a child's. And shaking.

"Well?"

"It's 98.5. So far so good. But your battery dropped 9 percent in the first hour. You'll be cold meat in ten hours."

She didn't say a word. She just turned and hugged herself to me, burying her face against my chest.

After a couple minutes, she said, "Don't think I'm enjoying this."

"Me either. This sucks." I thought it was a credible lie. She smelled wonderful.

Four hours after we were dropped off, Mr. Wire emerged from swirling snow and squatted alongside our hole, wind whipping fur parka trim around his bare face. He was just an instructor, not part of GEF, which meant he had the bad fortune to have a living family. SEALS drew this duty because being cold was their business. Well, okay, much as it pains me to admit it about squids, they're also probably the world's best troops.

He motioned us to hold up fingers and took his own readings on each of us. "Mr. Wander, you seem just dandy."

"Hooya, Mr. Wire." The SEALs may be good, but they are as full of crap as any unit. They insisted we say "Hooya" in place of "yes." It built esprit de corps. They thought.

Wire turned to the Munchkin. "Ma'am, I'm not gonna bullshit you. Your body temp's sketchy, and it looks like you're gonna run out of battery juice sometime middle of tonight. I can't make you drop out, but I really don't see the point in your continuing this exercise. No reflection on you personally. It's just physics. You sure you want to hang in?"

"Hooya!" Her voice quavered already, and we had twenty hours to go.

He slapped palms on his thighs and stood. "Hooya, ma'am. Carry on." He turned to me. "Wander, you keep an eye on her. Hypothermia's nothing to screw with." He disappeared into a gauze of snow.

Munchkin pounded fists against the rocks.

"Look, I know you want this. We all do. Bad. But Wire knows what he's talking about."

"He plays games of the mind with me. He wishes me to quit. I will not quit."

She knew better. We all did. Neither the SEALs nor anyone else played mind games with the future of humanity at stake. The only reason to wash out a soldier from GEF was to protect the mission. The human race had too much invested in each of us to wash out a single one for laughs or prejudice. But there were going to be training accidents, changes of heart, performance failures. There was a shadow force training in parallel. If a soldier stumbled, five thousand stood ready to replace her.

"Why do you want this so bad?"

"Eight reasons. My mother, my father, my six sisters." Her voice caught.

I pulled her against me again while I watched the sky. The sun was weak these days, but I could tell it was going down.

Wire visited us two more times that miserable night during his rounds of the foxhole line.

Each time Munchkin's battery was drawn down farther than schedule. Each time she shivered and seemed to shrink even smaller before my eyes. Each time Wire asked her if she insisted on continuing. Each time she snapped out a faded "Hooya."

I finger-clipped her again. The needle on the battery meter didn't move. I thumbed the readout button to show her body temperature. It was down a half degree since last check.

I felt like crap. But Munchkin was dying. "Munchkin, what's four times three?"

She stared through me and her lips quivered, but she said nothing. A first symptom of hypothermia was the inability to answer simple questions.

"That's it. Let's go to the command post. You're done, Munchkin."

She might have been on the edge of hypothermia, but through her fog she understood.

"N-no!"

"We still have six hours to go. Wire will pull the plug on you next time he comes by if I don't."

I grabbed her under the arms and heaved her up.

"No, you bastar'!" Slurred speech, too. Another symptom. She pushed out her arms and legs against the foxhole walls, wedging herself in like a cork.

"I'm not a bastard! I'm trying to save your life!"

Weak as she was, she thrashed and kicked. My frozen shin burned where her boot toe thwacked it.

"What life, Wander? This is all I have left. Think what it would be like if you didn't have something, somebody."

I thought about it every day. Until now I believed I was the only one.

I stopped tugging at her and thought. What if roles

were reversed? If I was going to lose my spot in the Force? There had to be a solution.

I finger-clipped myself. I had 40 percent juice left in my battery, and my body was humming at a toasty 98.6. "Turn around."

"Wha?"

I slung her like a flour sack, unzipped the battery compartment on her fatigues, and snapped her dead battery out of the socket.

I pretzeled my arm to pop my own battery out, plugged it into her socket and popped her dead one into mine.

"Whaju do, Wander?"

"Nothing. Snuggle up, Munchkin." I wondered whether I could feel more miserable.

Three hours later I knew I could.

I shook inside my field gear so hard that I thought I would rattle Munchkin's teeth loose. The wind had picked up and howled as it drove snow in the darkness. But her body temperature had risen a hair.

Wire's flashlight bobbed toward us through the night.

"Hooya, troops! Anyone for a cold beer?"

"F-fuck you, Mr. Wire!"

"Yes, ma'am!" He squinted at her. "Don't we sound perky all of a sudden."

He finger-clipped Munchkin, read his meter, then shook it and read it again. He looked at her, then at me.

"Munchkin, what's three times two?"

She didn't shake as she looked him in the eye. "Six."

He finger-clipped me. "My, my. Wander, you have been busy. Your battery is stone-dead. And your body temperature is falling. It's gonna be close, but I think you will barely make it to End-of-Test. And with 40 percent juice left, Munchkin will, too. How fortunate for both of you."

Wire paused and rubbed his fleece face mask. "Wander, please step out of your hole and join me over here."

He cupped a mittened wave as he walked out of Munchkin's earshot.

Crap. Crap, crap, crap. Why did I always get caught? Metzger never got caught.

Wire turned and faced me. The snow blew so hard I couldn't even see our foxhole. He shouted over the gale. "Wander, did you swap batteries with Munchkin?"

Judge March said that if the truth wouldn't set you free, lie your ass off. "Negative, Mr. Wire!"

"I'm not asking for the bullshit teamwork answer. Did you?"

"Negative, Mr. Wire."

He looked down and scuffed snow with his boot toe. "If she sucks batteries like that in combat, she can't function. She'll die. People in her unit will die when she doesn't do her job. Worse, she will jeopardize the mission. This exercise isn't hazing."

"This exercise is bullshit. When we get Eternad batteries—"

"*If* you get 'em! If you get 'em, maybe they'll change this exercise and she can get reassigned to GEF."

"You know anybody that falls behind will never catch up."

He looked away. "It isn't up to you or me to decide who stays and who goes. Look, I know you people stick together, and I'm not saying I want to trade places."

He surely did want to trade places. SEALs trained a lifetime hoping to be part of a mission like GEF's. They were the best soldiers on the planet. SEALs like Wire had the bad luck to have live families. So the politicians had pulled the rug from under them in favor of neophyte orphans like me and Munchkin. Life's a bitch.

"We're in the places we're in, Mr. Wire. For better or worse, Munchkin's my family. She wants to stay in."

He nodded. "So. You're already soldier enough to know that in combat we don't fight for duty and honor and country. We fight for the soldier next to us. That's admirable. But there's no room for chivalry or for covering up a buddy's weakness. If Munchkin's not mission-capable, she should be dropped."

"When we get better batteries she'll be mission-capable."

He sighed. "You can cover for her now. I can't prove you swapped batteries. But you can't cover for the whole training cycle. Protecting her now just prolongs the agony for her and endangers your unit. I respect your reasons for your decision. But I'll watch you and Munchkin with special interest for the duration of this cycle. Are we clear?"

"Hooya, Mr. Wire."

"This is the stupidest abortion of a training stunt I've ever seen! Just to give a stubborn half-pint a chance to get her ass shot off!" He paused, then shook his head. "A SEAL would do that."

That was about as big a compliment as Wire was capable of to a non-SEAL.

"So. Because I do respect you people—and that's no bilge—the additional physical training you'll do to make up for what you missed during our little philosophical discussion here will be reduced. Push out one hundred for me."

If somebody had pulled on me the stunt I'd just pulled on Wire, I'd have made 'em do a *thousand* push-ups.

After the TET exercise ended, Munchkin and I limped stiff into the mess hall. We sat across from one another, shivering, and wrapped our fingers around coffee cups that couldn't be too hot. We didn't even think about taking off our parkas.

"Thank you," she said.

I shrugged and spread my fingers. "No frostbite."

"Not just for taking the cold. I know Wire must have interrogated you. You must have lied for me. They might have thrown you out."

Shit. I hadn't thought of that.

"I will never forget what you did. No brother could have done more."

Brother? I was hoping for sexually irresistible bedmate.

She reached across the table, peeled my fingers off my cup and rubbed them, to bring back circulation. Like a sister.

It was then I knew that Munchkin and I would love each other, but we would never be lovers. We had grown too close for that, as combat soldiers do.

We trained for two more weeks. Munchkin and I grew closer, as soldiers and as friends. Then Metzger showed up.

TWENTY-SIX

METZGER GRINNED AS HE LEANED against the frame of my barracks-room door. I dropped the manual I was studying as I jumped up from my bunk.

Before I could ask, he said, "I'm on leave." That explained his civvies. "I've been down in Denver, visiting Large Ted and Bunny. They send their love." He looked around the room and focused on Ari.

"You're Metzger. I've seen your picture." *Everybody* had seen Metzger's picture, even Munchkin. Ari stood and shook his hand. Jeeb, on Ari's shoulder, held out a forelimb, and Metzger tweezed it between finger and thumb like he was handling a worm.

Nobody from General Cobb on down got time off from GEF training. But when you're a war hero, not only can you get a weekend pass, you get a weekend pass for your buddies. Metzger had passes for me and my roommate. He also had a car and a condo with hot tub reserved over in Aspen. Ari declined on grounds that taking Jeeb off post was a security risk. I suspected he really just wanted more sleep. Metzger got Ari's pass transferred to Munchkin, and we picked her up twenty minutes later at the women's barracks.

Metzger and I leaned against the rental car's fender so long we nearly wore out the plasteel. Finally, Munchkin came to the car carrying an overnight bag, coat over her arm. She wore a clingy red dress, the first time I'd seen her in one, high heels, and her hair down, framing her face. My jaw dropped. A *girl* would freeze her ass off to look good, but this was my Munchkin.

I introduced Metzger, but she knew him from his pictures, just like Ari had. They just stood there shaking hands like two dopes and smiling at each other.

Finally, we all started shivering, especially Munchkin. I punched Metzger's arm. "Let's go, huh?"

The rest of the weekend was great. I had the hot tub to myself. Inexplicably, Metzger and Munchkin sat in the condo living room and talked by the hour. More beer for me.

Metzger barely got us back by lights on Sunday night.

Three days later I was cleaning weapons in the armory when an orderly stuck his head in the door. "Wander! You got a holo. They're *holding*!"

Camp Hale's quarters may have been thrown together, but they were up-to-date. The day room had a brand-new bumper-pool table, on which I taught Munchkin the game's angles and thereafter got whipped daily. It also had two AT&T holobooths as well as a big-tank holo with all the premium channels and massage recliners from which to enjoy same. A cold cabinet was stocked with free soft drinks and even nonconcentrate fruit juice. Real upscale treatment, at last.

Up-to-date didn't change basic economics, though. At holo rates, nobody went on *hold* except maybe the president. It couldn't be good news. My heart pounded. I double-timed down the corridor, crossed the day room in two strides, found the booth with the blinking light, and popped the door.

Inside, Metzger leaned against the wall wearing sky-blue Space Force flight coveralls. My heart skipped. He flickered just a little.

"Hey."

"Hey. What is it?" I looked him up and down. No wounds.

He shrugged. "I figured they'd pull you off most any detail if I holoed. I get a thousand free, donated minutes every month."

A *thousand*? Free day-room Coke plummeted down my list of upscale perquisites.

"So you're okay?"

"Never better. I go up in an hour. How's GEF?"

"Cold."

"So I heard. I got the Aspen condo again for this weekend. I can get passes. You wanna come over and we'll veg? Free beer. And the Broncos are on."

"I'm there."

He shifted his weight. It was already dark at Canaveral and his Interceptor stood floodlit behind him. "Y'know, it's a shame to waste that third bedroom. Why don't you ask your gunner, whatzername, if she wants to come?"

Whatzername? I'd seen Metzger study the periodic

table of the elements for four minutes before a quiz, then recite it backward with his eyes closed. "You remember her name. Munchkin doesn't drink, and she thinks American football is barbaric, so why . . ."

He bit his lip and fidgeted.

"Oh my God!" Ever since Metzger and I had figured out that girls weren't just guys who couldn't throw a spiral, he had been the aloof, pursued stud. I flitted from one unrequited crush to the next while Metzger fended off women with a pole. I let my grin spread. "You've got a thing for Munchkin."

He purpled. "I do not! I just thought—"

I poked his belly, or the air where the image of his belly flickered. "You've got it so bad that you're too shy to ask her yourself!" I puckered up and made a kissing noise.

"Grow up, Jason!" He sighed. "Did she, you know, say anything about me?" He raised his eyebrows.

"You mean like carve your initials in her homeroom desk?"

"Don't be a dick, Jason."

No chance of that after all those years of watching the women of my fantasies throw themselves at Mr. Indifferent.

"She said you were an arrogant blue-suit fruit."

His face fell so far that my glee vanished.

"Okay. Truth is I haven't said two words to her since you left."

"But you could ask her to come this weekend?"

"Maybe."

"Jason!" He whined.

"Okay."

"And, you know, put in a word for me?"

The man was a genius with a holostar's looks and money. He had a chestful of medals and a smile that made women mail him their panties. He needed a word from me like a tuxedo needed a toad. "Sure."

A tech knocked on the clear door of Metzger's booth in Florida. The fog of liquid-oxygen boil-off swirled in the darkness.

"Gotta fly, Jason."

"Be careful up there."

An hour later I found Munchkin sitting at a desk in the women's barracks day room. We studied there together, evenings. I read military history. She mostly studied the training schedule. She could be anal about what she had to do next.

She pointed at her screen. "We're supposed to have twenty weeks of individual and small-unit training, yes?"

I nodded.

She pointed at the screen. "And they always post six weeks in advance. But now it goes blank four weeks from now."

I shrugged. "Maybe they're revising."

"I don't like it."

"You don't like changes."

She wrinkled her nose at me and stretched. "So. Tell me about your Rocket Jock friend, whatzisname."

Whatzisname. Munchkin was no more amnesiac than Metzger.

I let the silence thicken.

"You hot for Metzger?"

"I just think he's got an interesting job."

"I just think you want to peel off his shirt and lick his chest like a Popsicle."

She turned pink.

Oboy. Metzger and Munchkin smitten with one another. I licked my lips. This was the triple-hot-fudge sundae of harassment opportunities.

"He holoed me today," I said.

She turned toward me, then tried to look away.

"He's got more passes for this weekend. And that condo. Don't suppose you'd want to come along?"

She studied her boot toe and shrugged. "Maybe. I wouldn't mind spending time with Major Metzger if the chance should arouse." She squeezed her eyes shut and glowed red. "Arise."

I grinned. "Munchkin Metzger. *Such* a nice name. You writing it inside your Chip-pad covers, already? Your new in-laws' names will be Ted and Bunny."

She threw a chair cushion at me.

None of us three ever saw the Aspen condo again. The next morning at 6:08 Mountain Time the Denver Projectile hit. We used the passes to attend the memorial service for Metzger's parents.

TWENTY-SEVEN

"TONY, DID YOU GET THAT PEACH COBBLER RECIPE?"

I flexed my knees as I stood in the conference room corner at ease and listened to General Cobb run the GEF daily staff meeting.

It had been two weeks since the Slugs had killed Metzger's family and the rest of Denver. Judge March had been out of town; so had my brief foster family, the Ryans.

GEF's business continued. Permanent assignments were being made. Munchkin and I were the crew-served-weapons team of the Headquarters Battalion personal security detachment. That meant one of us attended each staff meeting in case a Slug wandered in to knife the general.

Even though I was just wallpaper, it was interesting.

General Cobb stared across his conference table at his logistics officer.

"Distributed the recipe to every mess in camp, sir."

"Finest damn cobbler I ever tasted."

When I was a civilian, about a million years ago, I would have thought that a general spending staff meeting time on dessert recipes was insane. But Napoleon—who knew a thing or two about soldiering—said an army travels on its stomach.

General Cobb spun his chair toward me. "What do you think, Jason?"

"Sir?" My spine stiffened and adrenaline spiked through me. General Cobb knew the first name of every one of the ten thousand soldiers in GEF and called each of us by it. Or so the legend went.

"Well?"

"It's beats ham and limas, sir."

"How'd you know about ham and limas, son?"

"We ate C-rations in Basic, General."

"I'll be damned! Well, they didn't kill either of us, did they?"

"Not yet, sir."

The commander of the Ganymede Expeditionary Force nodded, grunted, and turned his attention back to saving the human race.

Howard Hibble sat at the table's far end, and General Cobb nodded for him to report.

In the smoke-free room, while he licked a Tootsie Pop, Howard reported a 2 percent probability that the Slugs would incinerate us on landing.

What strategy and tactics we had sprouted from the loopy crania of Howard's spooks. From wreckage and Sluggo's anatomy and my experience they tacked together our battle plan. What to take, what to leave on Earth; how we would travel on Ganymede, how we would shelter; most of all, how to win. Ganymede was

300 million miles distant, but the answer to that last question seemed even farther away.

As division sergeant major, Ord sat in, too. He didn't say much, either. But it comforted me to know his infallible self was part of the team.

"Space Force choose us a ship captain yet?" General Cobb looked at the Space Force liaison officer, a light colonel.

She screwed up her face. "They've trained several. There are political considerations. It's down to a field of three."

"It better be down to a field of one by next week."

We weren't scheduled to embark for months. For *years,* as far as the public, and hopefully the Slugs, knew. We needed every minute of the time to train.

But Munchkin had noticed that the training schedule cut off next week. General Cobb wanted a pilot for the big ship being built out in lunar orbit, the ship that nobody knew existed, also by next week. My adrenaline spiked again.

TWENTY-EIGHT

TWO DAYS LATER they packed us all into the auditorium building. MPs stood guard at every door, weapons locked and loaded. That was new.

General Cobb strode to the stage, fatigues crisp and eyes clear. "You know we have six weeks of training to complete here. And more before we embark."

Years more, theoretically. And we needed it all.

He nodded toward the MPs. "What I say next remains here. No outgoing holos, no letters, nothing."

Feet shuffled.

"The ship is ready."

Silence became more silent. Officially, the GEF soldiers knew no more than the published cover story. Embarkation was five years away. Unofficially, most suspected it would be sooner, maybe after only a couple years.

"The ship's waiting in orbit around the moon. We leave for the moon next week and transfer to the ship there. We'll complete training during the six hundred days en route to Ganymede."

A hiss of fifteen thousand drawn breaths echoed through the room. General Cobb couldn't have surprised his troops more if he had shown up in clown shoes and a red rubber nose.

He looked to the back of the auditorium and nodded. An MP turned and opened the double doors.

"Her name is United Nations Spaceship *Hope*. UNSS *Hope* is one mile long, and she will carry us 300 million miles. And back, God willing. I'll let her skipper tell you more. Most of you know him, by reputation, at least."

The commodore commanding the biggest vessel in human history walked down the auditorium's center aisle to the stage as troops stood on tiptoe for a look. Resplendent in Space Force dress blues, he looked old beyond his years, weary. Like a man who had been orphaned two weeks before.

Metzger reached the stage, and General Cobb walked over and handed him up.

I didn't hear much of what Metzger said. I just watched him while my ears rang. I think it was mostly details of how they would pack ten thousand of us into Interceptor cargo bays like cordwood to fly us to the moon.

Afterward, Metzger, Munchkin, and I sat in the Officers' Club and talked over beers.

"You could have told me."

"It wasn't final until two days ago."

Metzger twirled his beer bottle. "The psych people needed to check me out. See if I was stable after the loss."

"And are you?" I tried to see behind his eyes. I knew what ate him. Metzger had wangled a weekend pass to chase a girl when he could have been on duty, intercepting the Projectile that killed his parents and one million others. No guilt could attach to him, personally, any more than to the patrolling pilots who were up there, in crates too old and slow to stop every Projectile. But guilt is as personal as a thumbprint, and as indelible.

Such guilt and sorrow would have crippled most people. Metzger wasn't most people. He could firewall those emotions from the calculating part of his brain that was going to exact revenge.

His voice echoed from behind the firewall. "I'm coping."

"But why you, anyway? *Hope*'s an ocean liner. You drive speedboats."

He shrugged. "It's not like anybody else has experience at this. And there's politics."

Of course. There were lots of pilots. Few of them were heroes. None of them were war orphans. Until two weeks ago.

War never made sense. But the idea that losing your family passed for luck was hard to swallow.

I shook my head. "Even if *you're* ready, we're half-trained."

He shrugged. "And the ship's barely flyable. But the Slugs will expect us to embark so that we intercept Jupiter when it's closest to Earth. That means departure in two years. Going now may surprise them, even though we fly farther." His face darkened. "And Earth is running out of time faster than we knew. Ambient–temperature drops will freeze most harbors permanently within a year. The climate of Kansas is already Alaskan. Three years from now wheat won't grow at the equator. We go half-ready or we may as well stay home and die."

Two days later, after dark, a stream of Hercs landed without lights to fly ten thousand of us to Canaveral.

The five thousand alternate troops would remain at Camp Hale and impersonate fifteen thousand people, to keep the Slugs from knowing we were on the way. They had inflatable, fake vehicles to park where ours had been, and banks of radio and holo transmitters to send out tons of voice and coded traffic like we were all still here. They would go into Leadville for haircuts twice as often, so civilian businesses would see no drop-off. Since none of us had family to wonder where we were, the deception would be easier.

The Allies pulled off a similar trick before they invaded Europe in World War II. General Patton commanded a phony army in England. The Axis believed it was the main force for weeks after D-day.

Those who remained behind turned out on the runway to watch us go.

Headquarters Battalion formed up on the frozen tarmac, all of us navigating using our night-vision goggles. I saw Wire, the old SEAL, striding up the line, inspecting gear. He gigged a soldier who had a pocket unbuttoned, and the guy said, "Yes, Sergeant Major."

Odd. Ord was the division sergeant major.

I glanced at the stay-behinds lining the runway. Ord stood among them, arms folded. He had been designated a mere decoy. My stomach knotted. I was about to fly 300 million miles to fight a desperate battle. Now I had to do it without Ord.

Wire, our new division sergeant major, faced us right,

and we marched to our Herc's rear ramp in the green darkness of a night-vision world. I snuck a glance at Wire. He
had aged years in the last days. Losing family does that.
Would the next year shock *me* as gray as Uncle Sam?

Engines whined, and the smell of burned kerosene
filled the wind. My boots hit the aluminum ramp, and I
scanned the crowd until I picked out Ord again.

He snapped off a salute in our direction.

It was intended for me. That was impossible, of
course, since I was an enlisted man, and one among thousands, at that. But I returned it, as a lump swelled in my
throat.

I don't remember much of our trip from Canaveral to
Hope. They sedated us all to slow our metabolisms, made
us wear diapers, then tucked us into individual, coffinlike
tubes. The tubes got stacked inside Interceptor cabins and
cargo bays like cordwood, one hundred per Interceptor.
That meant a hundred ships had to fly to the moon. If we
had all ridden up like airline coach passengers, it would
have taken a thousand ships.

I understood why we had to travel that way. Still, I
awoke three days later hungover, weightless, a quarter
million miles from home, and needing a diaper change. I
was among the few who awoke so early.

My travel tube had been loaded in the forward cabin of
my transport. I popped the end off and wriggled out.
Drifting forward, I anchored myself with two fingers on
the pilot's seat back. I peered out the windscreen, over the
pilot's shoulder.

Hope hung regally above the moon's white curve, gray
against space's blackness, even bigger than my memory
of her as an orbiting skeleton. Though she was built to

move faster than any manned object in history, she needed no streamlining. She most resembled a mile-long beer can, with an open parasol attached to her front.

We drifted toward *Hope* while our pilot stretched arms above her helmeted head.

"Automatic pilot?" I asked.

She nodded. "For a couple more minutes."

I pointed ahead at *Hope*. "What's the parasol?"

"Solar-wind sail. Photons headed out from the sun bombard it and boost her speed. But her conventional engines do most of the work."

"What happens when she gets to running as fast as the photons?"

"Photons move at light speed. *Hope* wouldn't get going that fast if she accelerated on out past Pluto!" She snorted.

Well, pardon my dumb-grunt command of physics.

It occurred to me that I didn't want another round of extravehicular activity like the one that nearly killed me on my last trip to the moon.

"How do we get aboard?"

She pointed at a belt of indentations that circled the big ship's midsection. "Docking bays. There's twenty. They're really for those dropships that fly you from Ganymede orbit to the surface."

A tawny-gray wedge shape drifted behind each docking bay, at the end of a slender tether. Actually, the dropships themselves were so small compared to *Hope,* and almost the same color, that what I saw were the black shadows they threw on the mother ship's massive hull.

"They disengaged the dropships and hung them out on their umbilicals so we could deliver you guys."

I squinted at the dropships and remembered my trading-holo pictures. "They're Lockheed-Martin Venture Stars. NASA cancelled that project in 2000."

She half-glanced my way. "2001. You're smarter than I thought. The dropships are unpowered airframes. The troop-transport bays are 767-airliner fuselages stuffed in where the fuel tanks would have been in the old space plane."

My jaw dropped. "We fly through space in antique airplanes?"

"The fuselages are reinforced. But they're really just souped-up gliders."

I swallowed and wished I hadn't read so much military history. "Every major glider-borne assault in the history of warfare ended in catastrophe."

"That's because they didn't have the world's best pilot flying lead."

"And that would be . . . ?"

"Me."

I pulled myself forward to see what the only human cockier than Metzger looked like, but her helmet visor covered her face. Her coverall name tag read HART.

I was close enough that I heard a faint voice squawk inside Hart's helmet. She jerked her thumb aft. "Get back there and strap in. I'm flying, here."

Hart was a captain so I did as I was told, but I left the end of my tube open and watched. One by one, our hundred-foot-long transports drifted close, then stabbed their disembarkation tubes against *Hope*'s docking-bay air locks, like a mosquito swarm attacking a rhino.

Up close, the dropships drifted in vacuum like titanic

bats, a graceful, new generation dwarfing these old space shuttle–based crates.

Metzger's maneuvering of the LEM when he landed us on the moon had been impressive. But Hart slid us up to *Hope*'s air lock as smoothly as a falling snowflake.

Hope was a mile long and three hundred yards in diameter, but that didn't mean we had elbow room. Fuel and munitions packed much of her. We did, however, share semiprivate cabins for the nearly two-year crossing to Jupiter. Her decks were concentric, so the floor of the lowermost deck was the outer hull. The inhabited decks formed rings around a tubular core that was fuel, mechanicals, and storage. *Hope* rotated just fast enough to create centrifugal gravity equivalent to Ganymede's. The decks, in turn, were stacked like cake layers.

The embarked division lived in the aft layers, the Space Force crew forward. Headquarters Battalion bunked forward, right at the Space Force boundary. Each deck was further divided into male and female territories, which were closed to the opposite sex except for the hour after evening chow.

Ari and I drew a cabin two hundred feet from Munchkin's.

The three of us ate our first meal aboard together, then Ari went to recalibrate Jeeb to reduced gravity while I walked back with Munchkin to see her cabin. We had to sidestep down the narrow corridors, a maneuver soon dubbed the "*Hope* Shuffle," because food and munitions palettes packed every corridor to the low ceilings. In six hundred days, the excess would be consumed, and there would be room to play hockey in the corridors if we chose.

Munchkin's cabin was identical to ours, spartan bunks, wall lockers, and two tiny, built-in desks with wall screens. She waved her arm at the unpainted bulkheads. "I think pale yellow."

I shrugged. "I wonder what else didn't get finished before we left."

The uniforms hung in the other wall locker were sky-blue. "Who's your roomie?"

"The numbers came out odd. I drew a Space Force pilot. An officer."

"Hey." The voice was female and familiar.

I turned and saw in the cabin's hatchway a Space Force captain not much taller than Munchkin. Her hair was silky, brown, and short, framing a round face with cheeks like peaches. She wasn't slim like Munchkin, but to me she filled her coverall perfectly.

It was her eyes that made my heart skip. Big and brown, with long lashes.

She extended her hand. "You Wander?"

"Yes, ma'am."

"Pooh."

"Ma'am?"

"Forget the ma'am. It's gonna be a long trip. Call me Pooh. Short for Priscilla Olivia Hart." She poked an index finger into each cheek and grinned. "These were even chubbier when I was little. My brother said I looked like Winnie the Pooh. He used to read me the book. I loved that book." She blinked as her grin faded. Every grin on this ship faded when the subject turned to family.

She was cute and vulnerable, and I melted. Then I recognized the name. The cocky transport pilot. Cute, vulnerable, but also sassy. My meltdown turned permanent.

A Klaxon sounded, and I jumped.

Munchkin said, "Hours. See you in the morning, Jason."

Pooh Hart smiled. "Tomorrow night you can read to me."

The gravity seemed even lighter as I crossed the bulk-head back into male territory.

The next morning we awoke to metallic clatter in the corridor. I opened our hatch to find Space Force enlisted men dropping off paint cans and old-fashioned brushes at each cabin. They said spray painters would have over-loaded the ventilators. I think the army just wanted to keep us busy.

The first weeks of the voyage we all painted, sanded, bolted, and welded everything the exhausted workers on the moon had been unable to finish before they passed *Hope* to us like God's own relay baton.

As for Munchkin's dream of a pale yellow cabin, the army supplied one color. UNSS *Hope* soon became known as UNSS *Taupe*.

While we kept busy with the brushes, Metzger and his crew steered a course that kept either Earth or the moon between *Hope* and Ganymede. The idea was to hide us until we were a few million miles from Earth. Space is a big place, so when *Hope* emerged, naked in space, any Slug watching wouldn't notice one more mile-long aster-oid. Theoretically.

It was no more audacious than Doolittle's raiding Tokyo with one naked aircraft carrier during World War II. And the Pacific's a smaller place to hide than the Solar System.

You have no idea how many brushstrokes it takes to

paint a vessel the size of a couple dozen aircraft carriers. I occupied my mind during the painting day thinking up excuses to drop by Munchkin's cabin during social hour, on the chance Pooh Hart would be there.

After social hour, I spent any spare time chipping out every military-science entry in the ship's library. One midnight I was sitting at my desk reading. Ari, face to the wall in his bunk, moaned. "You actually care whether the Byzantines adopted Roman combat-engineer practices?"

Jeeb never slept, so he perched on my chair back, reading over my shoulder. What Jeeb saw, Ari saw, too, in his head.

"I dunno."

"You bucking for Officer Candidate School?"

Until he said it, I'd never thought of it. "You need a college degree."

Ari wrapped his pillow around his ears. "You need a lobotomy. Go to sleep."

Besides sleep, our routine included PT, of course, to keep us at Earth-normal strength and fitness levels, even as our coordination adjusted to Ganymede-level gravity. We would be strong enough to perform as human soldiers never had.

We also got periodic lectures from Hibble's spooks on what to expect.

On the sixty-third day out, we sat in the forward mess, which doubled as a lecture hall, and listened to an astro-climatologist, a Nepali.

The scientist aimed a laser pointer at an on-screen out-line. "The atmosphere will be as thin as Earth's at Mount Everest's summit. Colder—2 percent oxygen compared to Earth air's 16 percent."

That meant no air support. Jets, prop planes, and heli-
copters needed oxygen to combust their fuel. Jeeb, who
ran on Eternad batteries, would be our only flying vehicle. Ditto tanks and trucks. A handful of battery-powered
GOATs, adapted from lunar service, would be flown
down in the first dropship, but Ganymede was going to
put the foot back in foot soldier.

A soldier raised her hand. "Will the Slugs have air capability?"

Howard Hibble stood at the side of the room. "We're
betting no. This is one of the most important things we
learned from inspecting that crashed Projectile. Slugs are
anatomically similar to cephalopods and jellyfish. No
skeletons. The only Earth phyla that have evolved flight
capacity are vertebrates and arthropods. An animal needs
rigidity to fly. Our flying machines mimic animals with
hard parts." He shrugged. "The Slugs shouldn't have figured out flight."

"They figured out interstellar travel."

Howard said, "Moving through vacuum doesn't in-
volve aerodynamics. It's a human conceit that since we
built spaceflight technology up from atmospheric-flight
technology that another intelligence had to do the same."

The climatologist broke in, "If they were so smart,
they would have stabilized Ganymede's climate better.
Like Earth's moon, Ganymede keeps one face to Jupiter.
Its sidereal period—one revolution around Jupiter—takes
just over seven days. Sunshine, such as it is, for eighty-
four hours, then an eighty-four-hour night. In the night
cycle, contraction of the atmosphere due to cooling cre-
ates windstorms."

So we had heard. Rather than tents, we would shelter

the stormy nights in fiberglass huts, which the combat engineers would glue together with an epoxy that sprayed out as liquid but set up instantaneously even at zero Fahrenheit.

The army being the army, somebody in supply had loaded a thousand extra palettes of epoxy in place of a thousand of dried and fresh fruit. Anyone aboard would kill for strawberries, but we had enough epoxy to glue together the city of Tallahassee. Logistics were a bitch, as Lee found out during the American Civil War when he tried to invade the North.

Mistakes in feeding his troops drove General Cobb nuts. He even had communications cobble together a cook-to-cook radio net to improve meal quality.

That evening after chow Pooh had duty, so Munchkin visited *our* cabin. She flopped on my lower bunk and tap-danced her boots on Ari's mattress above, where he propped on one elbow, reading. She had to stretch her legs all the way out to reach. If I joked about it, she'd be hurt.

"I can obtain freeze-dried peaches. My friend in Delta Company came in to a boxful. She says she sweet-talked a mess sergeant in a battalion back aft. Personally, I think she sucked his dick for them."

Munchkin relished things sexual. Just not between us.

Ari poked his head over his bunk edge. "You can earn a can of real ones in syrup I was saving for my birthday."

"You? For a single can of peaches?" She wrinkled her nose.

"I call this progress. Now we're just haggling over price."

The contemplated activity was entirely hypothetical.

Romance aboard *Hope* violated regs, even between fellow noncommissioned personnel like Munchkin and Ari.

"But I know your heart belongs to the unobtainable commissioned officer, Commodore Metzger." Ari sighed and hung his head in mock dejection. Jeeb, dangling batlike from a bunk rail, couldn't sigh; but he mimicked his Wrangler's action.

Metzger took meals with us when his enormous duties allowed, he and Munchkin mooning at one another across a table two feet across, but separated by nonfraternization regulations as wide as the Asteroid Belt.

It would have been laughable, but I felt the same ache whenever I saw Pooh Hart.

Other than eating chow, sleeping, sponge bathing, reading, and speculating on the deviant behavior of others, for the next five hundred days we cleaned weapons, broke them apart, and cleaned them again until we were afraid we'd rub them down into useless metal slivers.

We did calisthenics in the training bays. We double-timed laps around the outer-perimeter corridors like hamsters in an interplanetary wheel. We moved crates and keyed letters into Chipboards that we hoped someone would read someday. We maneuvered in units small and large. We took target practice on virtual and live-fire ranges.

And all the while we tried to forget what we were preparing for.

One of those attempts to forget became my third court-martial offense.

TWENTY-NINE

IT BEGAN INNOCENTLY. Everyone, except General Cobb who spent his so-called off hours prowling the ship in search of ways to make his troops' lives better, got one day off duty out of every ten. You might wonder why bother, sealed up with the same ten thousand others in a taupe-walled tin can.

But that free day became the cherry on everybody's sundae. First, you could wear civvies. Everyone had been permitted to bring one change of civilian clothing. Second, you could sleep until noon if you chose. Third, you could play. Some soldiers formed bands, mixing everything from bagpipes to balalaikas. Others went to the holos. One of the teaching classrooms had a killer setup and it was given over to recreation half of every day. The cooks even took turns making free popcorn, theater-style.

I always went to the holos. Not for the shows, though the ship had every title imaginable. I begged Munchkin to clue me when the world's best dropship pilot scheduled her free

days, then I bartered desserts and extra duty like a rug mer-
chant until my schedule matched Pooh's. Pooh loved holos.
At least, she was always there when I turned up.

It took me weeks to figure out that Pooh and
Munchkin planned Pooh's schedule to match mine, anyway. Women think men are idiots. They're right.

Pooh hailed from western Wyoming. Her civvies were
a plaid shirt and jeans that fit either too tight or just tight
enough, depending on one's perspective.

No nonfraternization reg restricted one's perspective,
nor how good an officer could smell. On that day Pooh's
jeans fit indecently, and she smelled of lilac.

"I've seen this one already. I'm skipping." She pointed
at the bulkhead holo poster.

I had been aching to see it for weeks. "Me too."

She ducked her head toward her popcorn bag and
plucked a kernel out with her moist tongue tip. "Gravity's
less in the storage bays at the ship's axis. I thought I
might go try it."

"Want company?"

"C'mon." She waved her hand as I followed her jeans
to the elevator tube.

The munitions bays were always populated as the
Space Force armorers checked and rechecked the millions of pounds of precision-guided munitions that *Hope*
would rain down from her orbit around Ganymede to
support us. Similarly active were the vehicle bays where
mechanics maintained the GOATs.

Deepest inside were stored the upships. They were
packed away because they would only fetch us back up to
Hope from Ganymede if and when we had won. Rumor
had it they only held five thousand, total. That meant the

planners calculated that one of every two of us would buy the farm on Ganymede. I preferred to calculate the perfection of Pooh's jeans.

The provisions-storage areas were dimly lit and deserted.

Hope's core rotated more slowly than the inhabited, perimeter decks. The resultant reduced gravity caused my first step to bounce me off the deck as I stepped from the elevator into a freight-palette maze. I read a label. One of our zillion palettes of epoxy that had displaced fresh fruit.

Ahead of me, Pooh hopped and touched fingers to the twelve-foot ceiling. Her giggle echoed in the emptiness. She lost her balance on the way down, spun to face me, and I caught her at the waist.

The right thing was to set her down and let her go. Fraternization was a court-martial offense in combat, and we had begun drawing combat pay when the first booster lit at Canaveral.

Her lips and mine were eight inches apart, and the warmth of her breath feathered my cheek. She closed her eyes, and I forgot about the right thing.

The most wonderful thirty minutes of my life later, the roar of my own breath in my ears was interrupted.

"Jason? What are you *doing*?" The words exploded an electric shock up my spine. I knew General Cobb's voice without opening my eyes, even here where no one should be. The best commanders inspect what the troops ignore.

What to answer? Practicing mouth-to-mouth? Pooh's mouth was in no position to improve my respiration.

I opened one eye and saw General Cobb standing hands on hips, jaw hung open. I tried to straighten to attention and screen Pooh from view but tripped on my pants. I tried to salute but tangled my hand in her bra.

General Cobb averted his eyes. "Don't answer. I'm old, but I remember what you're doing."

Pooh and I tucked ourselves back into our clothing, then he turned and faced us. I knew he would recognize Pooh as an officer. As Number One Dropship pilot, his life and that of all of us in Headquarters Battalion would be in her hands. Which, at the moment, she was wiping on her jeans to obscure certain evidence.

I squeezed one eye shut. "Sir—"

General Cobb held up his palm and sighed. "You two aren't the first." He shook his head. "Stuff ten thousand kids with maybe two years to live in a steel tube. Then pretend they aren't human. Sex won't kill us, but time wasted hiding it might."

He turned away. "Carry on."

The next day regs changed. Cabin hatches could be closed during social hour with no questions asked. Rumors spread that even marriage might not be questioned.

One hatch that closed immediately was to the commodore's cabin. I never saw Metzger or Munchkin anymore except when I guarded a staff meeting he attended and when Munchkin and I trained together.

At sixty DTD, or days-to-drop, we had an early-morning University-of-Hibble class in Slug biology. Munchkin and I sat together as gunner and her loader.

The lecturer, Dr. Zhou, held captain rank, but she was just a cryp. Short for cryptozoologist. "Pseudocephalopod physical construction is barely more complex than the amoebae under your high-school-biology microscope. The lone specimen lacked neural structures consistent with independent thought. Socially, Slug society may resemble a single organism."

On a high-school-science trip into the Rockies, I saw the world's largest single living thing, an aspen grove that looked like a thousand separate trees. It was centuries old when the Slugs killed it.

Howard Hibble chimed in. "Expect perfect coordination among individual enemy soldiers, directed by a hive intelligence."

Someone asked, "What will that intelligence tell them to do?"

Howard shrugged. "To behave like perfect soldiers. We'll learn as we go."

I swallowed. Sixty days remained before school would be in. Lots of us would learn only how to die. The day before, somebody leaked onto the ship's net a Pentagon study made before we left. It ranked GEF military-occupational-specialty categories for combat survivability in the coming action. The release infuriated the chain of command, and the study quickly became known as "The Numbers."

Hope's stay-in-orbit crew had the longest life expectancy, followed by the dropship pilots like Pooh. The flyers would stay at arm's length from the fight.

Projected lifetimes for other MOS shrank after that. Shortest were the commanding general's personal security detachment. Not only did the theater commander in chief have an invisible bull's-eye painted on his butt, the soldiers assigned to protect him were expected to throw themselves in front of it to save him. According to the Earthside computers, once a firefight started, Munchkin and I each had eleven seconds to live.

She seemed untroubled, though. I had watched Munchkin's hands on our gun for nearly two years. They shook when she was happy, steadied as she got serious and deadly. This morning they positively trembled.

She leaned close, and whispered, "Jason, last night Metzger asked me to marry him."

She could have just slapped me with a dead trout. I knew Metzger was busy, but this highlighted the gulf that had opened between us. Munchkin had displaced me. Metzger's world now revolved around her like Ganymede around Jupiter. "That's great."

"We want you to be our best man."

I felt less left out and smiled a little. "When we get home?"

"Next week."

For the next hour I watched the instructor pace the stage, but I heard little. I thought, then I thought some more.

Since the fraternization policy change, Ari had hooked up with a demolitions expert. A nice girl from Tel Aviv who drooled at his accent but couldn't tell a west-of-the-Pecos cowpuncher from a north-of-the-LBJ-Freeway haberdasher. After all, his MOS *was* Wrangler. Jeeb, his Wrangl-ee, got exiled to the corridor during Ari's social-hour trysts with her in our cabin. Still, doing it with a guy whose brain was coupled to an electric roach smacked of *menage a trois* to me.

Ari and I now alternated closed-door rights to our cabin for social hour. That evening was my turn. When I got there, Pooh's coverall already hung folded over my chair back while she lay on my bunk with the blanket pulled up to her nose.

"In a hurry?" I asked.

Her eyes twinkled. "Just horny."

I pulled my chair next to the bed, straddled it, and laid my chin on its back, where I could smell the sweetness of her in the fabric of her coverall. "I've been thinking."

"Me too. Climb in, and I'll prove it."

"No. I mean thinking. About us."

A shadow crossed her face.

I unbuttoned my bulging uniform-blouse pocket. There was a ship's store aft. The jewelry section was small potatoes, but the clerk said it was the thought that counted. I fished in the pocket and my fingers touched the velvet box.

Her hand pressed mine. "Don't."

"Don't what? You don't even know—"

She shook her head and her eyes glistened. "We can't. I can't."

The human heart is physically anchored in the chest by tissue and cartilage and blood vessels. Mine sank into my gut like a cannonball. "What?"

She sat up, the blanket still clutched to her chin, and brushed her fingers on my cheek. "It's nothing wrong with you. There could never be anything wrong with you."

"Then what?"

She turned away and whispered into the bulkhead. "You saw The Numbers."

"I'll beat The Numbers."

"You'll do something noble and stupid and die!"

We sat still, and I listened to her breathe.

She turned to me, her eyes swollen. "I'm already an orphan. I won't become a widow in eleven seconds." She squeezed the blanket with both fists while her breath came in gasps. Then her hands trembled, and she sobbed, huge and soft.

I grasped her bare shoulders, turned her to me, and held her while she shook and wept.

An hour later, the Klaxon sounded, she dressed and left without a word.

We didn't speak about it again, but in the remaining days we made love like each moment counted for a lifetime, while the DTD clock rushed toward zero.

The Metzger-Munchkin nuptials were strange, not just because they were the first in human history held beyond the moon.

Hope's only window was the Navigation Blister, a forty-foot crystal dome that jutted from the bow. A platform extended into it like a wide diving board. There an astrogator peering through an ancient, manual alidade could navigate by the stars, and even steer the ship from the blister if the computers went down. They went down frequently, for hours at a time, but since *Hope* was tracking toward Jupiter like a bowling ball between rails, the blister never got used.

Metzger was ship's captain but couldn't officiate the civil ceremony for his own wedding. However, Metzger's crew numbered five hundred, and GEF was ten thousand. So the embarked-division commander was really in charge, and everybody knew it. General Cobb stood at the far end of the diving board in full-dress uniform, the civil-ceremony book resting in his white gloves. Above his head and beneath his feet space's still, black velvet stretched. Sprinkled stars seemed to swirl as *Hope* rotated on her axis. Metzger stood beside the general, every inch the military groom, down to his sash and saber.

We had adjusted roles. Pooh served as maid of honor, Ari stood in as best man, and I gave the bride away, like a brother.

First down the aisle trundled Jeeb, history's first six-legged ring bearer.

Pooh stood beside Munchkin and me, waiting her cue. Jeeb waddled ahead, his radar-absorbent coat gleaming in starlight, a velvet pillow balanced in his forelimbs.

Pooh touched her bouquet to her nose, then turned and pecked my cheek. "Someday, I want white roses, too. You're the best."

My chest swelled. My weeks of bartering for duty time to match Pooh's schedule had taught me *Hope*'s black-market structure. *Hope* had an agriculture lab, the idea being that after we took Ganymede we would try to grow stuff to feed ourselves. For a month's pay plus a Crackerjack ring I no longer needed, I had scrounged the rarest commodity in outer space, flowers, from an ag-lab technician.

Munchkin's bouquet trembled, and I felt her arm shake as it threaded through mine. She wore dress whites, with a veil and a train added. A uniform may not sound like much of a wedding gown, but Munchkin was the loveliest bride I'd ever seen.

I had a little speech ready, to tell her how perfect it was that the two most important people in my life were going to be together forever.

I bent to her ear to whisper.

"Don't speak, Jason." She gulped. "Or I'll lose it."

Fair enough. Tears blurred my own vision, already.

The bride and I literally flew down the aisle in the

tiny center-axis gravity, Munchkin's train drifting behind like a cloud. At the ceremony's end, Ari pulled out a lightbulb wrapped in a napkin and had Metzger stomp it. Jeeb reared back in horror at the murder of his fellow electrical appliance. Munchkin taught Pooh a tongue-wagging Arab yodel, which, I learned, only women do, and the newlyweds exited to her ululations while bag-pipes keened.

The event was supposed to be private, but when the wedding party emerged from the Navigation Blister, Metzger's cheering crew waited with a raucous reception that broke more regs.

Another thing the agriculture lab manufactured ille-gally was potato vodka. It curled my toes and made Pooh hornier than usual.

I was almost tired of getting laid by the next morning when, on flight day 602, *Hope* intersected the orbit of Jupiter.

Silly me.

THIRTY

"MANY OF US WILL DIE IN THIS PLACE." GEF's Operations officer stared down at the boxing ring–size holo image of Ganymede Landing Zone Alpha at his feet. Ten thousand of us peeked over his shoulder from temporary bleachers that ringed the big training bay for predrop briefing. We'd heard it all a hundred times, but we hung on every word.

The day-old holo had been broadcast back from a deep-space drone, Jeeb's dumb, muscular cousin. *Hope* had launched the speedier DSD weeks before.

Ganymede, like Earth's moon, was barren, crater-pocked rock and ice. Astronomers debated whether its core was molten or cold or liquid water, but its surface was as dead as headstones.

LZ Alpha was a crater floor. The army didn't care whether some astronomer had named it, it was a landing zone. Hibble's geologists had lectured us how the three-thousand-foot mountain in the astroblem's center resulted from rebound of the planetary fabric after a meteorite impact. The flat crater floor was cooled lava that had oozed from the impact perforation eons earlier.

The resulting topography formed a perfect defensive position: high ground centered in a circular plain, sixty miles across, with billiard-table-flat fields of fire and observation. That plain also provided miles of smooth runway for the dropships that Pooh led, which would glide in at two hundred miles per hour with no brakes.

The Ops officer waggled a red laser pointer's tip at a spot on the plain a couple miles from the mountain. "The dropships will overfly the crater rim here, touch down, then roll to a stop here." He slid the red beam to the mountain. "The Force will assemble, then advance to and occupy this prominent terrain feature. There we will set our operational base."

Cakewalk. Assuming the Slugs were deaf, dumb, and blind. Boots scuffed bleachers in restless disbelief.

He looked up. "The DSD detected no Slug sign at the LZ. The drone wasn't acquired by radar or any other active-imaging medium during its flyby. We're ready for a hot LZ, but we don't expect one."

Munchkin leaned against me, and whispered, "If we know that's the flattest spot on Ganymede, next to the best natural fort, so do the Slugs."

I looked across the big chamber at Pooh. The pilots sat in a row at ringside, in the order their dropships would land. Pooh flew Dropship Number One, carrying General Cobb and all of us in Headquarters Battalion, but physically she sat second-in-line. First down would be the mech ship, loaded with all the GOATs and heavy weapons, to give the engineers extra minutes to drive them off the dropship and reassemble them. I smiled as she pouted, arms crossed. It burned her ass that she had to fly second position and watch a lesser pilot become the first human ever to land beyond the moon.

After briefing we lined *Hope*'s corridors, hunched under basic loads of ammunition, grenades, rations, water, and clothing that no Sherpa on Earth could have budged.

My gear had evolved as far from my old Basic equipment as the 300 million miles that separated me from Indiantown Gap, Pennsylvania.

My M-20 handled just like an ancient M-16. All the weight the rifle itself lost, through zoomy neoplast construction, came back in the extra ammo held by the M-20's bigger magazine. Ganymede cartridges packed less powder so recoil and muzzle velocity would replicate Earth-normal, but a hundred of them still weighed the brick.

We *had* gotten the Eternad fatigues that weren't perfected when I cheated Munchkin through temperature-endurance testing back at Camp Hale. Most people think the hard shell is strictly body armor. In fact, the rigidity aligns the joints so the bands and levers that move with the wearer crank kinetic energy into the batteries. We looked as clumsy as medieval knights, but Eternads weighed a third what a turn-of-the-century football uniform did. And those old suits didn't heat, cool, and stop bullets.

We looked more like halfbacks than infantrymen, too, because the armor's iron-oxide, mercury-sulphide coating was as red as an old fire engine. Howard's Spooks thought it would diffuse our infrared-visible signature so the Slugs could hardly see us. Maybe.

My helmet was no trainee's Kevlar pot. Like Eternads, it weighed less than old football equipment. But packed into its bulges and ridges were flip-down passive–night vision goggles, a multinet radio, and electronics supporting the heads-up display and laser designator. The soldier sees the HUD and LD display in the battlefield awareness monocle. The BAM is that retractable gizmo that makes recruiting-holo Infantrymen look like one-eyed pirates.

Underneath it all I was still just scared blood and bones.

Metzger and General Cobb walked the lines, inspecting and wishing luck. Metzger stopped in front of us and stepped over our machine gun to stand close to his wife. "Nice makeup."

Munchkin stared at him through a mask of gray-black camouflage insulated-paint stripes. The theory was that the thermal-insulated gray paint and uninsulated black would create cool and warm stripes, breaking up our facial outline to an infrared-seeing Slug. A tube curled like transparent spaghetti from each nostril along her cheek toward her oxygen generator. "Nice honeymoon." She stretched her lips over her teeth, imitating a smile.

As he bent and hugged her, he tucked something in her hand. A white rose from her bridal bouquet. "Love you."

"Me too."

Then he was gone down the line, her hand reaching after him until he vanished in a sea of soldiers. One rose petal drifted to the deck.

Pooh was already at our dropship's controls, so we had no good-byes to say.

General Cobb hobbled past us and into the air lock, struggling under the same basic load he demanded of his far-younger troops. Munchkin and I fell in behind him, then sat at his left.

I squatted to dip my pack under the top air lock lip, then I stepped outside my home of six hundred days. The Ganymede-normal zero-Fahrenheit air of the dropship cabin slapped my face. I watched my breath and shivered until my fatigue batteries kicked on.

It wasn't until Munchkin and I lumbered to our places on the sidelining benches, sat, and strapped in, that I realized something was missing. I patted my web harness. Grenades. First aid–dressing packet. Entrenching tool. Insulated canteens. I felt for the night-vision goggles pushed up on my helmet and found them right where I'd left them.

Finally, I got it. No vibration. For nearly two years, I had lived within *Hope*'s always-rumbling womb. The stillness in this cabin was, I supposed, like being born again at twenty-one.

Munchkin, beside me, sat closer to General Cobb and eavesdropped on his half of command-net conversation.

After three hours by my wrist 'puter, she leaned to me and whispered, "Two females in Dropship Number Three tripped in the air lock. Dislocated elbow and hip. One damaged an air lock seal."

I expelled a breath too loudly. I'll fight next to any female soldier proudly, present company of the Munchkin being Exhibit A. But when society in its collective wisdom decides to send someone to break things and hurt people, men are the gender of choice.

The next delay resulted when a male soldier in Dropship Number Sixteen suffered an epileptic seizure and kicked an air lock seal loose. It took Metzger's crew three hours to repair. So much for the gender of choice.

I hoped Hibble guessed right about the Slugs' lack of air-warfare capability, because if he was wrong, these delays gave time to scramble flocks of interceptors down below. He couldn't have been that sure, or these dropships wouldn't have been equipped with electronic countermeasures.

All the while the dropships undulated at the end of their air lock tubes as *Hope* spun slowly in orbit, provoking mass motion sickness.

From up front, Pooh serenaded us over the intercom with century-old show tunes.

Ari faced us across the aisle, Jeeb hibernating in his pack. Ari rolled his eyes. "I can take the puke smell, but make her stop."

At last the air lock rasped shut, and the cabin lights dimmed and reddened, to allow us to build night vision.

Pooh stopped singing long enough to tell us she knew we had a choice of airlines today, and she appreciated our business. Then she told us to remember that when we landed we had completed the safest part of our journey.

We were about to drop a hundred miles in ancient aluminum eggshells, then crash them under control at two hundred knots. But she was telling the truth.

Intercoms crackled. "Begin drop sequence on my mark . . . Now."

THIRTY-ONE

WE FELL TOWARD GANYMEDE a hundred miles below. The dropship's acceleration pressed me sideways against Munchkin's shoulder. At first, we seemed to ride a fast-descending elevator. Then atmospheric friction against the hull behind me soaked heat through my backpack.

The first bump nearly sent me through the ceiling plates, harness or not. The hull creaked as the explosive stress of internal atmospheric pressure against vacuum reversed. Now Ganymede's artificial atmospheric pressure squeezed the dropship.

Pooh's voice dripped casual through the speakers. "Skin temp eight-five-zero. Ablation pattern nominal."

Cookies bake at three-five-zero.

The buffeting pounded all four hundred of us against the hull and against one another.

Munchkin panted like a horny Chihuahua. "They test-dropped these hulls from Earth orbit, didn't they?"

"Yeah." But nobody had tested them after they had

been hauled across 300 million miles of vacuum at close to absolute zero for two years.

"Skin temp one-zero-zero-zero."

Pooh's reports ceased, and there was only the roar of Ganymede's atmosphere against our hull and the crash of loose equipment as she and her copilot fought the bucking dropship.

Munchkin stared at me, her eyes so wide that the whites looked like hard-boiled eggs against her camo paint.

My heart pounded. "We're okay. We're okay, Munch."

Like hell. If she got out her Muslim beads again, I'd pray with them myself.

The troop cabin's only window was a half-foot-thick porthole in the emergency hatch across from me. Gobbets of flame flashed by it as the ceramic coating on the dropship's leading edges burned away. Ablation was supposed to happen. They said.

I looked across the cabin at Wire, the old SEAL who had usurped Ord's division sergeant major job. Wire should have been crapping bricks. But he just sat limp, eyes closed, body rolling with the bumps, conserving energy for when it would matter. Experience would carry him through this. Would inexperience kill the rest of us?

Buffeting slammed heads against hull plates.

How much vibration and temperature these dropships would really take nobody knew. We had been up to a thousand degrees on the nose when Pooh stopped her play-by-play reports. Thirteen hundred degrees was predicted. As for vibration, the ship groaned and bucked so violently that I thought I could see it flex. It seemed like the lines where hull plates joined grew wider as I watched. We could only have seconds left.

Ahead of us streaked the mech ship. Strung out behind and above us at six-mile intervals flew thousands more troops in eighteen other dropships.

I squeezed my eyes shut and counted my heartbeats as the pounding compressed my vertebrae together, then stretched them apart.

My count reached eighty, and I realized I was still alive.

Whump!

The jolt was different. Bigger yet smoother.

Pooh's voice crackled over static. "For you in back, the ECM pods just redeployed. Our skin temp is nine-zero-zero and dropping. Airspeed's below a thousand knots. Just a slow float from here down."

I looked at Munchkin and nodded. "Told ya we were okay."

"Bite me." She had her prayer beads out.

The flight smoothed out to something equivalent to parachuting through a thunderstorm.

After five minutes Pooh came back on. "Ladies and gentlemen, we have begun our final approach to Ganymede. Local time is oh-dark-thirty, and the ground temperature is a brisk ten below zero."

Nobody laughed.

Her voice was a tone higher when she spoke again. "We're twenty-five miles high and two hundred miles off the LZ. ETA seven minutes. Ganymede looks just like the holo sims so far. We're busy up here, so 'bye for now. We're comin' in a tad hotter than plan, so strap in tight."

Pooh, queen of understatement, said "a tad" only once before. We'd made love, and she lay gasping, as limp as a beached jellyfish, her bangs sweat-plastered to her fore-head. "That was a tad tiring, Jason." Hair rose on my neck.

The plan was to touch down at two hundred miles per hour. Whispers drifted back along the rows. "Two-fifty!"

I adjusted my web gear and felt for magazines in my ammo pouches. I checked the safety on my rifle and ran my eyes along our machine gun, lashed snug to the floor plates beyond my boots and Munchkin's. I turned to her, and we repeated the routine on each other. Gear clattered throughout the cabin as other pairs did the same.

"One minute."

Thump.

A soft one. Landing skids lowered. The engineers said tires were too risky on the crater floor's lava rock, so our dropships' skids would be the first man-made objects to touch Ganymede.

Our battle fatigues' torsos were armored against shrap-nel and small-arms rounds and proof against liquid flame, radiation, and chemical-biological agents. We could breathe indefinitely in an oxygen-free atmosphere, live at thirty below, and see in the dark, passively and actively. We each held a rifle with a cyclic-fire rate of eight hun-dred rounds per minute, and we each carried two thou-sand rounds in the light gravity. We carried grenades by the dozen and more plasma packets, atropine syringes, and coagulant dressings than a clinic. Each pair of troops was deadlier than a whole Korean War platoon. Our com-manders were radio-linked and could pinpoint each sol-dier's location on a global positioning system tied into a satellite network sown in orbit earlier today by *Hope*. We packed laser designators that would allow *Hope* to rain down from orbit everything from one-ton smart bombs to burrowing bunker-busters, and bull's-eye targets a yard wide.

We were prepared for everything.

Except what we found.

THIRTY-TWO

"Twenty seconds."

We were supposed to touch landing skids to the flat crater floor at two hundred miles per hour. Smooth as glass. Then run out four miles while the nose settled.

If the LZ turned out to be hot, we would be taking hostile fire on the way down, and it would intensify after touchdown.

Whump!

It could have been the first landing jolt. It could have been a Slug round gutting us.

Whump-whump-whump. Landing jolts.

Smooth.

The next jolt slammed Munchkin against me so hard I thought she broke my ribs. All around us gear tore free and missiled toward the forward bulkhead.

A loose rifle arrowed at Wire seated across from me, still relaxed and ready for the show to start. It stabbed through his temple like a toothpick through an olive.

His experience hadn't saved him.

The man next to Wire screamed, "Christ. Oh Christ!" He cradled the dead man's head in bloody hands.

We stopped. The lights went out. At first I thought I was unconscious, then somebody swore.

Something dripped in the dark. Somebody puked.

Bam! Bam! Bam!

The explosive bolts along the cabin's top spine fired, the fuselage split like a pea pod and fell away. Ganymede's orange sky surrounded us.

I flipped down my night-vison goggles. We lay right side up, more or less, in gray dust.

"Move it! Out of this coffin, people!"

Even as I looked at the landscape my gloved hands pounded the harness-release plate on my chest. I turned to help Munchkin, but she was already loose and bent forward, unlashing our gun from its floor hooks.

All around us, troops clattered out onto Ganymede's surface.

Clattered. Unlike the moon, the atmosphere here carried sound. Otherwise, it was just as frigid and forbidding.

Munch and I loped in the light gravity, kicking up dust that rose to our ankles. We threw ourselves prone, spaced between riflemen in a defensive perimeter fifty meters out, surrounding our dropship.

Rifles popped as troops cleared weapons. Squad leaders yelled, adjusting positions on the perimeter.

Thunder rumbled behind us and drowned it all out, then Dropship Number Three roared over our heads, its landing skids shaving fifty feet above our helmets.

A football field away it slammed into a mountain and

crushed against itself like a stomped beer can. No flame. Of course not. Only 2 percent oxygen in this air.

Ship Three's wrecked fuselage teetered, then tumbled down the mountain and rolled to within fifty yards of our perimeter.

Mountain?

I levered myself up on my knees and scanned 360 degrees. Instead of the predicted flat plain of the landing zone all around, we lay at the base of the mountain in the crater center, our dropship's nose buried under rubble. Behind us stretched miles of flat crater floor. Half-shadowed Jupiter hung huge and smoky red on the horizon.

We had overshot the LZ by miles and crashed into the only obstacle in an area bigger than Los Angeles. Ship Three did even worse.

And Ship One, with all our vehicles and heavy weapons, was nowhere to be seen.

What the hell had Pooh done?

Pooh!

The dropship cockpit wasn't visible under the jumbled Ganymede rock.

To our left and right, dropships screamed in, skidding and slewing, then crumpling their noses against the shallow cliffs of the mountain that was to have been our sanctuary. Exactly like we had.

Distant pops echoed off the mountain as explosive bolts blew open the surviving transports. Soldiers boiled out like we had, then linked with us into a common perimeter.

I stared across dust and scrambling medics at the split, twisted husk that had been our dropship. Nothing moved.

I fingered the ammo belt in our gun, made sure the

next box was open and ready to load, then said to Munchkin, "I'm going back to the dropship."

"Nobody said you could."

"Pooh's there."

"It's desertion."

"It's fifty yards away!" I scrambled up, shrugging off my pack, and ran hunched against enemy fire. And realized there was none. Ganymede was as still and empty as the big rock in space that it was.

Closer to the mountain, medics already crawled over Ship Three's wreckage. An electric saw whined as they hacked open the cockpit. "Bring that over here!" I screamed, and waved.

The fuselage pinched shut just aft of our dropship's cockpit. No way in, there. "Pooh?"

Nothing.

I scrambled up the rock pile until I stood in rubble just above the cockpit roof. There was an emergency hatch on the fuselage top, somewhere beneath the boulders I balanced on.

It seemed I tore and dug for hours, then I brushed pebbles off the red-stenciled hull plate, OPEN HERE.

Impact had already peeled back the hatch like orange rind. "Pooh?"

Silence. My gut turned to water.

I needed to go into that black pit more than life itself, and I needed to stay away just as badly. I bent, peered in, and saw only darkness.

I tossed my head to drop my night goggles and waited the three beats until they brightened my view.

The hatch opened on the right, above Pooh's copilot. Only floor bolts showed where his seat had attached.

I swiveled my head. He and the seat smeared the windscreen. No need asking if he was okay.

I couldn't look left toward Pooh's seat with my eyes open. I closed them, stopped breathing, turned then looked.

Her seat remained bolted to the floor. She lay in her harness, eyes closed, as though she slept.

"Pooh?"

No movement.

I tugged off my glove, unzipped her flight suit, and pressed my fingers to her throat to find a pulse.

There was no need to search.

The cold flesh I felt held no beating heart.

I had known with absolute certainty that it would be me. It would never be her that was gone. It could not be her.

"Anybody alive in there?"

No. None of the three of us.

Hands from above dragged me away from her. "Give us room to work, man."

Some time later I sat in the dust with my elbows on my knees when they laid her beside me.

Someone spoke. "Neck broke clean. She felt nothing."

Like me. Nothing in all the world.

"What about this one?"

"Dunno. He's just fucked up."

A hand slapped my shoulder. "Yo! Soldier!"

I turned and saw a sergeant from another platoon.

"On your feet!"

"Give him time. They were together." Munchkin's voice.

"We don't *have* time. He'll be together with her again if he doesn't move his ass."

Munchkin tugged me to my feet.

Ari stood next to her. "The sarge's right, Jason."

Around us wounded lay in ragged rows. Medics scrambled from one to the next. Many they just tagged on the forehead "M." Morphine. No other help for those.

Two medics rested a litter beside us. Air splints cased both of the man's legs. His flight suit matched Pooh's, but his sleeve patch read DROPSHIP NUMBER THREE, the one that had overshot us and slammed into the mountain.

He rolled his head and gazed at her through doped eyes. "Dunno how she did it." He held his hands above his chest like airplanes. "Ship One was first on the LZ. Disappeared."

Ari whispered. "Jeeb's overflying the LZ now. The lava plain we were supposed to land on's not lava. It's volcanic dust. Ship One sank like a brick."

"Are they okay?"

"Jeeb's magnetometer says Ship One sank two hundred feet deep."

Ganymede had already buried four hundred GIs alive.

The Ship Three pilot mumbled as he stared at Pooh. "She saw One go under. She overflew and brought Two down against the mountain. She knew the nose would crush on her. But it gave her soldiers a chance."

He shook his head. "Tried to follow. Nobody flies like Pooh."

Flew.

I looked around and counted. Stretched a mile along the escarpment at the mountain's base lay sixteen dropships, each nose crumpled like ours, surrounded by troops digging in and by clustered wounded.

Most of the other pilots, with seconds more to react than Ship Three, had followed Pooh's lead. And died to save the soldiers in their dropships. In a heartbeat she had traded her own life to save thousands.

She had said *I* would do something noble and stupid and die. I stared down at her through tears welling inside my goggles.

Munchkin held my hand and made me look in her eyes. "We should bury her before sunset. It is the Muslim way."

GEF had landed at what passed for dawn in Ganymede's dim rotational period. Hibble's astrometeorologists predicted that the part of Ganymede in "daylight" was calm, then as it rotated into each "night," cooling atmosphere shrank and made wind.

Blown dust shrouded Ari, Munchkin, and me as we laid stones over Pooh Hart. Munchkin said Arabic words and left on Pooh's grave the white rose that Metzger had given her before we entered our dropship. Ari prayed in Hebrew. I wept.

Pooh Hart's was the last funeral I attended on Ganymede.

There was no time for the rest.

THIRTY-THREE

A THOUSAND FEET ABOVE POOH HART'S GRAVE I realized the enormity of GEF's disaster. As part of what was left of HQ Battalion I was among the first to top the escarpment against which GEF had wrecked itself.

I dragged myself over craggy rocks, grabbed a breath, and turned. Even in Ganymede's reduced gravity, and though we sucked manufactured oxygen, we labored. We carried packs as big as clothes dryers and breathed air as thin as at Everest's summit.

Ahead of us, Jeeb flew point, linked to Ari's mind, securing us against lurking dangers. Behind us stretched GEF's remains.

Wrecked dropships and corpses littered the escarpment's foot. From there, the twenty-mile-wide plain we now knew was virtual quicksand stretched to the surrounding crater rim. LZ Alpha lay in Ganymede's rocky quadrant. No ice here. Jupiter's bloodred crescent hung beyond the rim, murky through dust billows raised by ever-swelling wind.

I handed Munchkin up, then General Cobb. Gasping, he turned, too, and followed my gaze. Thousands of black dots spackled the cliff face below as GEF's soldiers swarmed up from the plain.

The general stood still, staring one-eyed into his BAM, then retracted it. Command helmets' HUDs displayed positions of whole units or even individuals. All courtesy of Jeeb, hovering above. The general's earpiece also fed him everything from casualty reports to dinner menus.

He hung his hands on his hips and shook his head as he spoke. "Ship One didn't just cost four hundred good soldiers. We lost our vehicles and heavy weapons. We're gonna complete our mission with what we carry on our backs."

Complete our mission? Impossible.

Already, between the three other dropships sunk in the dust like Ship One and the casualties from the crash landings of the rest, we had lost a quarter of our troops.

I looked over my shoulder. Above the rock shelf where we rested, gray, jagged peaks climbed another two thousand feet. Black smudges among the crags marked cave mouths. Marching GEF up here from the exposed plain was the only logical move. This mountain formed a defensive position as perfect as a medieval castle.

But our mission was offense, not defense. We had journeyed 300 million miles to seek out and destroy the Slugs' capability to strangle humanity. Now we had trapped ourselves on a barren rock isolated from the rest of Ganymede by an uncrossable moat. If the Slugs knew we were here, they could ignore us as if we still sat in the Colorado mountains.

I cleared my throat. "Sir, aren't we screwed?"

General Cobb shrugged. "Battle rarely goes as planned, Jason."

"Yes, sir. We all trust you. You just need to tell us what to do."

He cocked his head. "Me? George Patton said never tell people what to do. Tell them what needs to be accomplished and let them astonish you with their ingenuity."

A wind gust staggered us all. Hibble's astrometeorologists had been right about winds increasing as the eighty-four-hour day ended. Fifty feet away, combat engineers laid fiberglass panels on rock and assembled epoxy sprayers to glue them into shelters. Tents would have been impossible. Already the cold had worsened, even discounting wind-chill. At least the planners had got one thing right.

The next gust knocked the General against me and Munchkin, and the three of us landed in a heap. A wind-borne fiberglass panel skipped across the landscape toward us. I threw myself across General Cobb and Munchkin as it slammed my back like a charging bull.

I peeked at the engineers. Like us, they huddled on the ground. Any fiberglass panels had disappeared. I twisted my head to see the escarpment lip. A trooper fought his way over the top and staggered up. Wind caught his pack, and he toppled backward and disappeared.

The planners had estimated Ganymede's night-storm winds at eighty miles per hour. Hundred-mile-plus gales rocked us already, and it was only dusk.

An engineer crawled to us through the driven dust and screamed in the general's ear. "Sir, it's no good. The shelters wouldn't hold even if we could get 'em stuck together. And we can't."

Howard Hibble and Ari had made the cliff top and

crawled alongside General Cobb. Howard pointed up slope. "These formations are shot through with caves."

Ari shouted, "Jeeb's found some big enough to hold battalions, sir."

The general nodded. "Okay. Pass the word."

An hour later, Ganymede's howling night storm had taken two hundred more troops. The rest of us split up and huddled in a belt line of caves. Hibble's meteorologists measured winds of two hundred miles per hour outside. GEF hunkered down for its first night on another world.

HQ Battalion's cave had a ceiling that arched twenty feet high and twisted back into the mountain fifty yards. I picked out a low-ceilinged side alcove big enough to shelter General Cobb, Munchkin, Howard, Ari, and me, then spread out sleeping bags. No oxygen in the atmosphere meant no campfires, even if Ganymede had wood to burn. But body heat from five of us packed in there might take the edge off the cold.

Hibble and an engineer prowled the cave's main chamber, high-stepping over sprawled GIs who huddled together and wolfed cold rations and sedatives. The army had almost booted me for using Prozac, but it had issued us amphetamines to keep us sharp for the eighty-four-hour days and downers so we could sleep during the long nights. Hibble and the engineer peered up at the ceiling and eyeballed the walls. Cracks spiderwebbed the rock.

They arrived at our alcove, and I listened.

"Igneous. Brecciated. But stable," said the engineer.

I raised my eyebrows at Howard.

He tapped the wall. The cracks spanned two finger widths. "He says the roof won't fall in."

Something bothered me, but my back throbbed where

the fiberglass panel had bruised it, and I was too exhausted to think straight.

Each cave's troops mounted guard at each cave mouth,
though a Slug assault seemed the least of our worries, especially with impassable weather outside.

While the four of us huddled exhausted in our alcove,
General Cobb circulated through our cavern visiting with
individual soldiers, checking equipment, confirming procedures with unit commanders. I was less than half his
age, I'd carried the same load over the same terrain, and
I just sat here an immobile blob of sprains and sores.

Howard, cross-legged beside me, offered chocolate
from his rations while he unwrapped nicotine gum. No
oxygen, no smokes.

"I'm sorry, Jason."

I nodded. Fatigue dulled every emotion, even grief. Or
I was blocking.

"Howard, are the Slugs just going to let us rot here?"

He chewed his gum. "I'd guess not. They like to keep
their enemy 300 million miles away. We threaten them."

"You said they won't be able to fly. They can't get to
us any more than we can get to them."

He shrugged. "We know zip about their capabilities and
tactics. We do know they sacrifice themselves readily."

We had watched whole shiploads of them crash into
Earth as kamikazes for years. "Why do they?"

"Slugs may not be 'they,' but 'it.' A single entity made
up of physically separate organisms. The death of physically separate parts may be as meaningless to the one big
Slug as loss of fingernail clippings is to us." It was
Howard's job to be professorial amid chaos. Serendipi-
tously, it was also his nature.

General Cobb sat down beside us. I swear his joints creaked. "If you're right, Howard, we have to unthink everything. Human armies conserve force. Maybe not to save troops, but at least because resources are finite."

Enemy philosophy suddenly bored me. My eyelids drooped. The last day had wrung me dry. Even Pooh's death left only a dull ache. It had to be the same for all the troops. I pitied those who had pulled guard, condemned to stay close to the outside wind and cold, futilely peering out into impassable darkness.

I zipped into my mummy bag, lay on my back, and counted ceiling cracks until I dozed. I didn't take my downer. Fitful sleep seemed preferable to drugs. Once bitten, twice shy, they say.

Despite all of the day's disasters, the feeling gnawed me that I had missed something, that the worst was yet to come.

I dreamed I was back in the twisting corridors of the Slug Projectile, scrambling for my life, catching toes and fingers in those air vents two finger widths wide. And every corner I turned I found putty-bodied Slugs writhing toward me from out of nowhere.

I half woke in blackness to echoing, muted human snoring.

And something else.

Plop. Plop.

Like big raindrops. I flicked my goggles down and waited until they let me see.

Outside our low-ceilinged alcove, in the main chamber, rain leaked slowly from the ceiling. Well, the astro-geologists said Ganymede had water.

The drops were enormous. They oozed from ceiling

cracks and fell on the upturned faces of sleeping, drugged GIs. But the soldiers lay sleeping, still.

It seemed so odd.

I shrank deeper into my mummy bag. Heated fatigues or no, it had to be ten below in here.

Electricity flashed through me. It didn't rain at ten below.

I came awake as adrenaline surged. I tossed my head to drop my goggles.

Slugs!

Amorphous Slugs by the hundreds oozed from ceiling cracks and wall cracks. Cracks just as wide as the doors in the Projectile walls that I had mistaken for ventilators.

I had seen holos of octopi squeezing through rock cracks an inch wide. It seemed so obvious now.

As obvious as where the stupid humans would land. As obvious as where we would shelter when the night storms came, if any of our ships survived the crater dust. As obvious as the fact that all guards would face out into the night, not inward to sound the alarm.

We had blundered into a massive and perfect ambush.

I turned my head to see a Slug stretch rope-thin from the ceiling to drape itself over Munchkin's face.

"Fuck!" I tore the zipper out of my mummy bag and lunged toward her.

Her arms and legs thrashed as the Slug smothered her, so muffling her screams that Ari slept on, beside her.

I wrestled the blob off her, snatched a rock from the cave floor, and pounded the thing into slime.

Munchkin sat up, gasping and scrubbing her face with her hands.

I grabbed my rifle and began picking off green ceiling

bulges as they appeared. As I fired, I ran among our soldiers, kicking Slugs off them and screaming to wake them.

In moments, constant gunfire echoed. Acrid gun smoke filled and fogged the chamber. Whether the battle raged for minutes or hours I'll never know.

More Slugs dropped and oozed into the cavern than I had bullets.

Few GIs stirred. The Slugs had been at work for hours before I woke.

I backed to our alcove at the side of the main cavern.

The general blazed away with his sidearm, Munchkin, Ari, and Howard with rifles.

The cavern fell silent except for the sobs of too few wounded.

Ari and the others knelt behind the bodies of dead soldiers. He snapped back his smoking rifle's charging handle. "No ammo, Jason."

I looked over my shoulder. A hundred remaining Slugs writhed toward us. We would simply be smothered.

I felt the harness on my chest. Hand grenades. In this closed space, they would be as deadly to friend as enemy. Unless.

My boots straddled a human corpse. I dragged it toward the alcove and piled it on top of the body in front of Ari.

He looked at me. "Wounded are alive out there, Jason."

"They won't be, one way or another."

He nodded, lips tight, then jumped to snatch another dead man. In seconds we had built a flesh wall.

I jumped and rolled across, crouching down alongside the four of them. General Cobb nodded, and we all snatched grenades from our chest harnesses. I froze, staring at mine.

The memory of Walter Lorenzen's dead eyes filled my mind.

"Jason!" Munchkin slapped my cheek, then pulled the pin and threw her first grenade over the barricade formed by our dead.

Thunder reverberated. Shrapnel whizzed like oversized mosquitoes. The five of us hurled grenades into the cavern until we ran out.

Explosive echoes died and left the sound of our gasping and the howl of outside wind.

I pulled myself up and peeked over the now-shredded bodies that had saved our lives. My gloves slid across blood.

Mounded, motionless Slug carcasses lay tattered over hundreds of torn human dead. Nothing moved but pooling blood and Slug slime. Each fluid trickled, then froze in seconds.

The five of us were all that remained of Headquarters Battalion. If the other caves were hit as hard, we could be the five survivors out of ten thousand.

I turned away, slumped, then fell to my knees and threw up my guts.

General Cobb knelt beside me, hand steadying my shoulder.

Drool strings froze as they dripped from my lips, and tears blurred my vision. "I can't do this."

"You just did. I wish I could tell you it gets easier."

It didn't.

THIRTY-FOUR

IN NEXT MORNING'S CALM TWILIGHT, GEF licked its wounds and struggled to survive one more day.

General Cobb knelt in the dust outside the cave that entombed most of HQ Battalion. He rested a hand on a suitcase-size holomap balanced on a flat rock. Previous staff meetings I had guarded took place around a polished synwood conference table with an orderly refilling officers' coffee cups. Actually, this meeting was Munchkin's to cover, but she huddled behind a rock puking.

Today, GEF's staff slouched in a ragged ring around the commanding officer. Most wore new, elevated-rank collar brass. With the nearest promotion board 300 million miles away, GEF had streamlined rules for such things. One staffer was original, a colonel, his hand shrouded in field dressing stiff with frozen blood. He was alive only because he had been checking equipment in a line brigade's cave, instead of with us in HQ Battalion. The staffers he commanded died in our cave. He was alive, but he hung his head like he wished he could join them.

Junior officers promoted from other units stood with helmets askew and uniform jackets untucked. For most, last night had been their first combat. We were beaten, and it showed.

The general looked around. "First thing you do, straighten up your gear."

Vacant eyes stared back at him.

"Now, gentlemen! If we look like whipped dogs, we'll fight like whipped dogs."

New majors and captains snapped to, adjusting uniforms and straightening spines. I buttoned a pocket on my own uniform and tightened a sagging web-gear suspender. Somehow, I felt better. I looked at the others and found light in eyes that had been dull.

General Cobb nodded, then asked an acting colonel, "Casualties?"

He was really a major, new to his job as division Operations officer. He hesitated. "HQ Battalion got hit worst. But some of the other caves were nearly as bad. My battalion—"

"Numbers, Ken."

"We have four thousand available for duty."

Sixty percent casualties after one day! I took a step backward.

For the briefest moment I thought General Cobb's shoulders sagged. Then he pointed to the major. "Reassign troops to restore unit integrity. You'll have to fold some battalions. We'll be spread thin, but that can't be helped. Once we stabilize a defensive position we'll think about offense." The general nodded, then turned to Howard Hibble.

Howard's uniform still looked like the inside of a laundry bag, but that was normal.

"Howard, if the little bastards can't surprise us any more, will they leave us be?"

Howard screwed up his face, then exhaled. "Don't think so. It perceives a threat."

"It?"

"My working hypothesis is these physically separate organisms are a single cognitive entity. Last night bolstered my view. No more individual thought or fear than hair growing."

"So what do I plan for?"

"Frontal assault. Massive and remorseless."

"They may find us tougher in conventional battle. One armed human soldier can take these worms out by the hundreds."

"We've underestimated these worms so far. When Jason fought them in that Projectile, he observed individual weapons and what may have been body armor. Last night it traded weapons and body armor, that wouldn't fit in those cracks, for surprise. Don't expect it to repeat tactics. Expect warriors."

"Still think they can't fly?"

"No evidence of it so far."

General Cobb pointed at the holo and nodded. "Alright. We will prepare to defend against an attack across the plain. We have to assume they can cross the dust. They got into those caves somehow."

Fifty feet away, four engineers tried to epoxy-glue a shelter together. It would blow away like a McSushi wrapper when the twilight gales came.

General Cobb turned to Howard. "Can we be safe in

those caves? Those cracks could still be full of the slimy little bastards."

Bad enough we had no safe place to sleep. Enemy troops could be hiding inside our defensive perimeter.

No Slug could defeat a GI one-on-one. But they didn't need to. We couldn't chance sheltering in the caves, while they could come at us in numbers we couldn't even guess. Exposed out here on the surface, we wouldn't last another night.

General Cobb looked back at the cave that entombed most of Headquarters Battalion and uncountable Slugs, then at Howard. "We *have* to be able to shelter in those caves."

Howard unwrapped a nicotine-gum stick. "It's not as simple as plugging a leaky bucket with chewing gum, Nat."

Futile silence ticked by, broken only by engineer curses as they sprayed epoxy on shelter panels.

I cleared my throat. "Sir? Maybe it is."

General Cobb turned to me. "Jason? You got an idea?"

I held up one of the now-useless sprayers for the epoxy that was to have glued together the panels of our above-ground shelters. The epoxy that we had too much of because some idiot computer clerk sent it instead of fruit. "We've got a thousand palettes of epoxy. It bonds to rock and sets up in sixty seconds stronger than steel. We send an escorted engineer team into enough caves to shelter us for the night and fill all the cracks. Any Slugs still hiding in those walls will stay there."

Burying Slugs alive didn't bother me a bit.

The general turned to Howard. "Will that work?"

Howard shrugged. "I haven't heard a better idea."

The general motioned to a lieutenant who now commanded a platoon-sized battalion, then pointed at the epoxy-spraying engineers. "Do it!" General Cobb pointed at Munchkin and me. "Here's your MG team. I don't need bodyguards."

And I didn't need to go back into a cave full of Slugs. When would I learn to shut up?

An hour later, forty of us lay on our bellies twenty yards outside a cave we had skipped last night. We could, I suppose, have cleaned out the caves where our dead lay. They should have held fewer live Slugs, maybe even none. Instead, a chaplain at each one said a few words, then the engineers sealed them with explosives.

This cave's entrance was a slot as narrow as a double doorway, but, as Jeeb had discovered, it widened inside into a low-roofed cavern that could sleep hundreds.

Beside me Munchkin lay with her cheek against our gunstock, her eyes and mine wide and searching for movement inside the cave mouth. Ari Klein lay alongside us, eyes shut but seeing more than we ever could.

At the cave mouth Jeeb, chameleoned as gray as the stones he scuffled across, disappeared into the dark. Ari's alter ego was literally bulletproof but closed eyes didn't mean that Ari was relaxed. His jaw was tight, fists clenched. Sending Jeeb into a closed space risked Jeeb's "life," and Ari's sanity.

Jeeb was wired with enough ounces of explosives and incendiaries to fry himself to avoid being captured and dismantled. Brain-linked TOTs were new. In their brief history, none had ever been destroyed or had self-destructed. But every time a new model replaced an old TOT, its Wrangler got sedated for a month, just to adjust to the loss. GIs who didn't understand sneered that Wrangler was a cake MOS. I knew better.

I fidgeted and realigned already-aligned ammo belts.

"Klein? What we got in there?" The earpiece voice of the lieutenant commanding this battalion-shrunk-to-platoon cracked with impatience. Combat soldiers may be family, but every family has its jerks.

"So far, we identify a company-sized unit."

We were outnumbered more than three to one. Armies like that ratio reversed when they attack adversaries of equal combat power.

Ari continued, "They're massed behind cover, rocks, and boulders, just beyond the entrance. They're wearing body armor, with just individual weapons. No mines or booby traps we can detect."

Last night, the Slugs had been their own booby traps. This fight would be head to, well, pseudocephalon. They probably intended to give us both barrels at the entrance bottleneck, then fall back.

"Okay. G-men prep in two minutes."

Our lieutenant may have been a jerk, but he was a sound tactician. We couldn't just destroy this cave with artillery, even if we still had artillery, instead of it being buried under two hundred feet of volcanic dust. We just wanted to do a little pest control in our new sleeping quarters. Flamethrowers excel at cleansing enemy holes, but nothing burns on Ganymede.

That left us to apply Infantry's unique, dirty genius: controlled, selective violence.

Each squad had two grenadiers armed with repeating grenade launchers. With round magazines, the launchers looked like the early-1900s tommy guns the old federal police "G-men" carried.

Seconds ticked away.

Thok.

Even cartridged for Earth gravity, much less the reduced Ganymede load, grenade launchers whispered and the round crawled so slow you could see it. A single grenade looped into the cave mouth. A grenade launcher is an indirect-fire weapon. The round arcs above the line of sight between the weapon and the target, the difference between a fly ball and a line drive. No explosion. It must have been a dummy ranging round, lobbed in by our most accurate grenadier.

More seconds ticked.

"Fire for effect!"

Thok. Thok. Thok.

From up and down our line, fist-size antipersonnel grenades arced like Texas League singles at a combined eight hundred rounds per minute.

Nothing. Could the Slugs keep our conventional explosives from detonating, too?

Before my heart beat again, flashes flickered in the cave's darkness, and detonation bangs merged into a constant rumble. As small as each individual grenade may have been, the ground shook beneath my belly.

Munchkin whispered, "Wow!"

"Cease fire!"

I looked over at Ari. He nodded, eyes still closed as he spoke to the lieutenant. "There are probably forty of them still moving."

Forty on forty was more like it. Now we had to do what Infantry had done since before Thermopylae. Dig the enemy out of his hole and bleed doing it.

"Even squads advance."

My heart skipped.

Our gun was attached to First Squad, so Munchkin joined the rest of our squad and rattled rounds into the cave while Second and Fourth Squads ran forward, on-line, and crouched. I had red tracer loaded every third round and watched Munchkin stitch every shot straight into the cave. The others deluged the cave rim and exploded rock chips in a shrapnel storm so violent that Squads Two and Four dropped and covered.

"Cease fire! Odd squads advance!"

I had already loaded a fresh ammo belt. We stood, along with First Squad. Ari stayed behind, too valuable to risk in a firefight. His jaw hung slack. The grenades hadn't trapped Jeeb inside and bullets and shrapnel would barely scratch a TOT's paint. Ari's Moment of Truth had passed. Ours lay ahead.

Munchkin folded our gun's bipod legs back along the barrel, then raised it to her shoulder. We shuffled forward, on-line with our squad mates, our gun as long as she was tall. But I wouldn't want to be a Slug in front of that muzzle.

After another leapfrog round and a half, our squad was first into the cave. We paused in the cave mouth for our night-vision goggles to adjust. Just long enough to be silhouetted as targets.

On my right, a Slug round struck a rifleman's forehead. Our helmets will deflect a grazing round, maybe even a small-caliber bullet direct, but Slug rounds come big and fast. His head tore off.

I shoved Munchkin down as I dropped, and we both hit the cave floor before the headless rifleman's body fell across us. There was no time to think about who he had been or where he was going, just to shove him aside as his arterial blood pulsed onto our gun's barrel and sizzled.

Munchkin returned fire as the Slug who shot him slunk behind a rock. If we hadn't been green and exhausted, we would have crawled in the cave entrance instead of making silhouette targets of ourselves. Careless soldiers are dead soldiers.

The little bastard was pinned down, but there was no rushing him in force. His position commanded our axis of advance, which had to be single file between rock walls. He could stay behind his boulder all day and pick off any single soldier who tried to get through. He was too far away to throw a grenade at him, the roof too low for a G-man to lob one in. The Slug just had to keep us outside for a few hours, until the nightstorm could kill us.

"Now what?" I muttered.

Munchkin shifted her aiming point to the rock wall six feet behind the boulder, thumbed her selector switch to FULL AUTO and cut loose twenty rounds.

"What—"

Her burst thundered against the wall and a hail of ricochets peppered the cavern. Half of them deflected behind the boulder.

Our gun's echoes died.

The Slug flopped out from behind the rock, his armor shredded. Ricocheted M-20 rounds were too small and slow to penetrate Slug armor, but when an M-60 talks, everybody listens.

Before any of the dead Slug's buddies could take over his little sniper's nest, we were through the gap.

"That was amazing!" I told Munchkin.

"That was bumper pool." She shrugged.

Once we got a couple squads into the main cave, it was a mop-up. We took no prisoners, not from rage but because the Slugs fought until they died. We lost two KIA. Slug firefights, we were learning, left few wounded. Their rounds tore GIs to pieces.

We secured that cave and a couple of others and copped a night's rest while the nightstorm howled.

The next morning, Munchkin and I were back on PSD with General Cobb. He huddled up for a staff meeting with his back to a rock wall.

He looked up at the commander of the surviving combat engineers. A skinny lieutenant where there had been a colonel.

The general's finger inscribed a circle along the holo-model escarpment, making a ring all the way around the mountain, a thousand feet above the plain. "Son, can you blast a trench ring along the military crest?"

"One thing we got's explosives, sir."

"Off you go."

The lieutenant saluted and double-timed away.

An hour later we heard the first boom as the engineers began blasting our trench system.

An hour after that Munchkin and I were breaking our backs digging trenches to shelter headquarters when messages beeped up on my Chipboard and Munchkin's simultaneously.

We both read halfway through the orders, then she turned to me, eyes wide. "We're reassigned to a line unit, again."

"You know the casualty numbers. General Cobb figures he can take care of himself. They need our gun on the perimeter."

We gathered gear and trudged around the mountain toward our new outfit, bent under our gun and ten thousand rounds. As we moved, all along our perimeter, soldiers dug blasted rock from the trenches like their lives depended on it. They did.

We found the line segment held by the platoon to which we were loaned.

Their platoon sergeant had never made it out of their dropship. Their platoon leader bought the farm in a cave the first night. They had shrunk below half strength, otherwise.

Therefore, the platoon's current stud duck was a corporal from Chicago. We found him squatting beside a boulder, drinking coffee from a therm cup that likely warmed it just enough to unfreeze it. He looked up, and coffee slopped onto his field-jacket front. He didn't clean it off.

"Just you two? That's all they sent?" He eyed our gun. "We can use the weapon." He pointed us at a rock pile a hundred yards along his platoon's sector of the perimeter. "Set up there."

I looked around. "You mind a suggestion?"

He tugged down his face mask and scratched an unshaven jaw. "Free country."

The platoon's sector included a ridge that stuck out from the mountain like Florida stuck out from the United States. "You got a salient here to cover."

"No shit." He grimaced. A salient is a bulge in an army's line. The trouble with bulges is bad guys can attack you from the sides as well as the front. If they succeed when they attack your flanks, they pinch off your salient and encircle the troops left inside. The German

General Staff in World War II assaulted the poor bastards pocketed in a salient at Bastogne. The Battle of the Bulge nearly turned the war for Germany. Salients attracted enemy attention.

Salient or not, there was a right way to defend it. "Your—our—sector's mostly unscalable cliffs. Except for that ravine, there." I pointed. "It's the most likely avenue of approach. Lay our gun to cover it."

He shrugged, weary. "Suit yourselves. I'm just a grunt. They were supposed to send us a new platoon leader. No loss. He was just some enlisted weenie detached from HQ Battalion."

Under my fatigues goose flesh rippled my forearms. Besides Munchkin and me, all that remained of HQ Battalion was Howard, Ari, and General Cobb.

I pulled out my Chipboard and read the part of my orders I'd skipped. I swear my pack gained a hundred pounds. "Acting second lieutenant . . . assume command effective immediately."

I pulled Munchkin aside and held my Chipboard so she could read my orders. I whispered, "This is a typo. They don't jump specialist fours to platoon leader. I'm a twenty-one-year-old grunt."

"Who General Cobb probably recommended for the job personally, because he knew you could do it."

"Why not you? I'm not even the boss of this gun, you are."

"I wasn't born to this. Judge March saw it in you, Jason. So did Sergeant Ord. I believe this is your destiny."

My head spun. Destiny, shmestiny. I'd think about that tomorrow. "What do I do?"

"Your job."

I took a breath and turned back to the corporal. "I'm Wander. The weenie from HQ."

I expected him to roll his eyes, and say, "Oh, sure." Instead he stood up straight and saluted. GEF was on the ropes, but we were soldiers, after all.

"Yes, sir. I didn't know, sir." He stared at me waiting for orders. I prayed to God for a clue. God, as usual, ignored me.

I tugged the corporal's unfastened equipment harness. "First thing you do, straighten up your gear. If we look like whipped dogs, we'll fight like whipped dogs."

"Yes, sir."

An hour later, I'd walked our sector with him, met my soldiers, repositioned a few, and contacted the platoon leaders to our left and right. Our coverage wasn't just thin, it was onionskin.

I headed back to the center of our sector, where I'd left Munchkin and found her position.

She had dug in on the escarpment at the military crest, the line below the high point where a soldier could see her field of fire but wasn't silhouetted against the sky. I crab-walked sideways down loose scree, and she turned at the sound of cascading pebbles.

"Hey."

"Hey." She eyed the bar on my collar, which the corporal had recovered from his platoon leader's body.

"I mean, 'Hey, sir.' "

I smiled. "You ready?"

She pointed over her gunsights at her ravine. "Ravine" was descriptive but a misnomer. No water had flowed on Ganymede to sculpt it. However it got there, the feature was a rock-strewn funnel that narrowed toward Munchkin as it rose from the plain a thousand feet below us.

She pointed downslope, where her new loader threw together rock cairns that would serve to mark range to target. I picked out other cairns that defined where her sector of fire ended and those of the riflemen on her flanks began. Her loader turned and circled his gloved thumb and forefinger. She waved in acknowledgment, and he began the climb back to her position.

"Ready," she said.

My earpiece chirped. The corporal had also recovered the platoon leader's radio for me. The microphone smelled of my predecessor's blood.

"Jason? This is General Cobb."

So much for proper radio-telephone procedures and chain of command.

"Yes, sir."

"Your troop dispositions look fine." I hadn't mastered my platoon leader's HUD enough to eyeball them myself, so I'd take the general's word for it. But the division commander was monitoring where I dug in twenty-five riflemen? My heart rate rose.

"How's morale there?" Static crackled the general's voice.

"They took it on the chin last night. Better now."

"I hope you're right, 'cause they're gonna take it again."

"Sir?"

A barely visible shape flitted against the sky at the edge of my vision. Jeeb.

Hair stood on my neck.

GEF's one-and-only TOT sat tight above our position. The commanding general had placed a handpicked sol-dier, whose judgment and communication skills he knew personally, in charge of this unit. Said handpicked soldier was at this moment patched through direct to said commanding general, leapfrogging the intervening company, battalion and brigade commanders.

"Sir, are we in for trouble?"

"Look to your front."

THIRTY-FIVE

I SNAPPED MY HEAD UP. The only thing moving in Munchkin's ravine was her loader, now twenty yards from us and puffing audibly as he climbed. I raised my gaze to the wide, distant end of the funnel, then to the gray, volcanic-dust plain beyond. Nothing.

Except a thin shadow on the dust, miles away.

General Cobb's voice buzzed in my earpiece. "See 'em?"

I popped the BAM over my right eye and chinned the laser-designator function. It fired a beam that painted targets so smart bombs could see them, but it also made good binoculars.

I found the smudge of the shadow, then blinked for focus.

At first, it looked like a million snaking poppy seeds, shiny, black, and rounded.

I blinked up the magnification. Even though I expected it, my heart skipped.

Slugs.

Slugs gliding over the dust like the footless snails they were. Slugs encased in shiny, black armor like the hollow cornhusk I had tripped over when I invaded their projectile. The armor curved around each Slug's body like a scimitar, exposing flesh in two places. Where a face should be, a green oval showed. Above it hooked a helmetlike visor. From the left side of the body, halfway down, protruded a tentacle, what Hibble's freaks called a pseudopod. Each warrior's tentacle wrapped around a twin to that curved, sword-edged individual weapon I had fired once. Replicants of the soldiers we had battled in the caves, but these stretched across the horizon.

I glanced at Munchkin. She had followed my lead and peered through her LD, too. She muttered in Arabic.

My earpiece buzzed. "Jason?"

"I see them, sir." The line moved toward us fast enough that dust kicked up behind it. From my vantage point, I could only tell that they were moving closer to our mountain. "Have you defined an axis of attack, sir?"

"Your salient is it, son. The TOT above you has counted fifty thousand of them."

Fifty thousand against twenty-five. Not twenty-five thousand. Twenty-five. If every round we fired killed a Slug, thousands would remain to overrun us when we ran out of ammo.

The fact that I wasn't surprised didn't keep my stomach from knotting. I shivered, blurring the image of charging Slugs in the LD.

"What's left will reach small-arms range in twenty minutes, Jason."

"Left?"

"*Hope*'s orbit brings her into firing position in fifteen minutes."

I stared through the LD while my jaw dropped. Of course. Fire support.

Even though *Hope* still sped above us miles beyond the horizon, I stared at the sky. As usual, Metzger was above the battle, literally, and poised to make things better by a button push.

"Jason, I'm switching your audio feed direct to fire control. Give 'em hell, son."

My earpiece went dead while I watched the Slugs advance. I switched my radio to my platoon net to give my people a heads-up.

"—must be a million of them."

"Anybody got extra rounds?"

Both voices quavered, but they were firm.

I switched my radio back to fire control net and prayed I remembered procedure.

"This is fire control, over."

"Fire mission, over."

"Fire mission, aye."

"Target, troops in the open. Coordinates . . ." I looked into the LD at red numbers that shifted constantly as I shifted the LD over the miles of onrushing Slugs. "Fuck! Just wax the whole place!" I paused. "Over."

"Just play your designator up and down the line. We'll bring the goods." Field artillery rarely sees the enemy, but they're a combat arm like us and proud of it.

The Slugs were close enough now to make out individuals without magnification.

Thunder rumbled somewhere.

I looked again through the LD. No, not thunder. As they came, the Slugs pounded their weapons against their armor, in unison, *boom-boom-boom.*

They might be doing it to keep cadence. They might be doing it to scare the crap out of their enemy.

The last part was working.

A few of them fired their weapons. Howard's people had examined the ones we captured in the cave. They decided the weapons were magnetic sling guns. Whatever.

Their rounds fell way short and kicked up dust fountains on the plain.

I craned my neck and wondered where the hell *Hope* was.

Pop—pop—pop.

I jumped. Alongside me, Munchkin lay with her cheek along the gunstock. Smoke curled from the barrel. Just a three-round clearing burst.

Below us, dust fountains from the exploratory Slug firing kicked up at the funnel's base, walking closer to us by the moment.

I looked to the sky again. The silver dot that was *Hope* came into view, crawling across the sky, and silhouetted against Jupiter's striped bulk.

Below, Slug rounds now impacted a hundred yards from us.

I flicked on my laser designator and a thread-thin red beam painted the charging Slug battle line. I ran it back and forth while I peeked up with my uncovered eye.

Sparks detached themselves from *Hope*'s dot and drifted toward us.

My heart pounded.

Crack.

A Slug round shattered rock ten yards to our right.

Thump.

Out on the plain, a yellow flash flicked in the Slug line's center. Then another.

Those little thumps were two-thousand-pound bombs. We were probably a mile from the impacts, but the mountain shook under my boots. A dozen dead Slugs littered each impact point. Great. But at that rate, forty-eight thousand of them would overrun us instead of fifty thousand. I stared through my LD as the Slug wave rolled toward us.

"Adjust fire? Over." The voice in my earpiece made me blink. These first bombs were ranging rounds. I was supposed to be telling them whether to adjust aim long, short, left, or right.

"Uh. No. You're on target."

A bomb flicked through my field of vision as it burrowed into the dust amid charging Slugs. Dust erupted, the ground thumped and a handful of Slugs bought the farm.

"But you're not killing dick. The dust swallows the bombs."

Silence.

"Fuck!"

At least I knew I was talking to a GI.

The voice continued, "We racked thuds fused for ground bursts." Assuming our LZ was rocky, our artillerymen had set fuses so the bombs would explode just after their noses touched the surface. That way the bombs would shatter rock into deadly, secondary splinters. Instead, our bombs were plunging into the plain before exploding, so the dust muffled their effect. The bombs should have been fused to burst in air fifty feet above the Slugs.

The artilleryman's voice sagged. Artillery's creed was "On target, on time, every time." On the most important fire mission in history, it wasn't.

"How long to reset fuses, fire control? Over."

"Too long. We got airburst racks coming from the magazine."

In my mind I saw *Hope*'s space squids racing racks of properly fused bombs to elevators for the trip from the ship's core to the weapons bays. If *Hope*'s computer net picked this moment for one of its too-frequent blackouts, the elevators would freeze, and we would be toast.

In front of me, fifty thousand Slugs closed to where I could pick out individuals with my naked eyes.

One of my guys cut in, on platoon net. "Lieutenant? Where's our fire support? There's a million Slugs to our front."

"Hang on. Aimed shots when they come in range. Out."

Minutes crawled. Aimed shots would be worthless if the sky didn't rain bombs, pronto.

Munchkin turned her eyes to the sky, and her lips moved. She always prayed for serenity.

I followed her gaze and prayed for shrapnel.

The Slugs had closed to where their ranging rounds struck around us every few seconds.

Fire control said, "On the way."

God bless squids. God bless *Hope*'s computers.

Our incoming painted heaven, now. The bombs' heat shields burned away as they dropped through the atmosphere. They left fire trails like shooting stars crossing Ganymede's dark sky.

Bombs began exploding in an accelerating crescendo, like popcorn in a microwave. Each detonation took out Slugs by the hundreds.

I switched my radio to platoon net. My guys whooped with each explosion.

I held the LD on the Slugs, even though smoke—no, not smoke, nothing burned, here, dust—obscured them.

When the dust broke, I saw, at each explosion's epicenter, Slugs vanish. Just body fragments littered the next ring out from the bull's-eye, then still, whole carcasses beyond that.

Slugs were inhuman. They had murdered my mother and were out to kill me. Yet for a moment, as high explosives flung them like sacks, a pang touched me for living things now dead.

The dead Slugs' comrades in arms shared no such grief. The rear ranks skimmed over the fallen without pause.

It seemed our ordnance pounded them for hours, but *Hope* was only in firing position for minutes each orbit. Nothing but dust showed in my LD's eyepieces.

Echoes of our last bombs died, and I squinted at the dust cloud below.

Boom. Boom. Boom.

At the base of the funnel, Slugs emerged from the dust, climbing toward us and pounding their armor.

"Shit!"

Their front line came even with the most-distant of Munchkin's range markers, and she squeezed off a three-round burst. Three Slugs dropped. So their armor wasn't bulletproof.

It didn't need to be.

They advanced on-line, as fast as a sprinting man. Odd numbers leapfrogged ahead while even numbers fired, then advanced. I sighted on one who would soon stop advancing and present me with a still target.

Just as their pattern emerged, they switched. Random groups advanced, and others covered. I swore and swung my sights.

No Slug slowed. No Slug hesitated beside a fallen comrade. No Slug broke ranks. Perfect Infantry.

If our bombs had slaughtered tens of thousands, they also missed thousands. Too many. Too close. I dialed up platoon net. "Fix bayonets."

I reached to my belt, slid my stubby bayonet from its scabbard, and clicked it below my rifle muzzle.

Munchkin kept firing. Slugs kept dropping.

More kept coming.

I squeezed off aimed shots while her loader changed barrels. M-60 barrels overheat. The loader uses an insulated glove like an oven mitt to unscrew the barrel and replace it.

While she waited she looked at me. "Jason, I need to tell you—"

Her loader finished and tapped her helmet. She turned her head back and resumed firing.

Ricocheting Slug rounds cracked all around us, now, but it seemed Slugs were crappy shots. Maybe they really couldn't see us in our red armor.

But we saw them from fifty yards, which is how close their lead soldiers were.

"Switch to full auto." At this range, aimed shots wouldn't save us.

My words were intended for Munchkin, but I saw her

thumb the selector switch on our gun even as the words left my lips. I switched my rifle to full auto and blazed away.

I don't know how many magazines I changed until I reached to the ammo pouch at my waist and felt nothing but empty fabric.

A Slug warrior lunged at me with his weapon's edge. I parried, then stabbed my bayonet into the green place where his face should be. His insides sprayed my sleeve as he fell, twitching. I braced for the next ones and prepared to die.

I stood my ground, arms shaking, for minutes before I realized there were no next ones.

The first breeze of Ganymede's coming night blew dust away. Black Slug corpses carpeted the ravine floor in front of me, stacked one on another in places. The one I had bested in hand-to-pseudopod combat was their high-water mark. Two armies had journeyed light-years to fight a battle decided by knives stabbing flesh.

I looked around and saw Munchkin's loader sprawled alongside the gun, a neat hole in his forehead.

She lay still, facedown alongside him. My blood froze.

"No! No, no, no!" I knelt beside her, and her fingers twitched. Thank God!

Then I saw the stiff, red stain on her jacket shoulder.

I turned her on her back, slow and careful, then cut away her clothing. The wound was eggcup deep and showed shattered bone. Coagulant powder would stop her bleeding, but she must have lost a quart already. I bit my tongue as I sprinkled antiseptic/coag powder, then packed the hole with a field dressing.

"Jason?"

"You're fine, Munchkin."

"I'm cold."

Shock. Blood loss. I propped her feet higher than her head with a rock. One thing Ganymede had was rocks.

Her loader lay dead, in battery-heated clothing he no longer needed.

It took minutes to strip his stiff corpse and wrap Munchkin in his clothing. I overrode his thermostat so his batteries warmed her and started an IV with plasma from my backpack.

She needed more.

I fired up my radio.

"Jason? What the hell happened?"

General Cobb's voice snapped me back to my job. "We stopped them, sir."

"The TOT shows me that. Why didn't you report?"

Because I thought Munchkin was dead. "Tending wounded, sir. We need medics here. Bad."

"Everyone does. We'll send what we can. Jason? Howard thinks they'll come again. You need to regroup."

"They can't come again. They didn't retreat to regroup. We killed them all."

"He thinks they've got a hatchery someplace. They'll keep making more until we run out of troops and ammunition."

Cheery news.

Munchkin sobbed.

"Sir—"

"I know. See to your troops. Out."

I switched the BAM to display the vitals of my platoon before my eye. Sixteen solid, green bars showed survivors. Munchkin's bar was green, but blinking for wounded. There were nine blinking red crosses. The corporal from Chicago was a red blinker.

As the night wind kicked up, we withdrew to a Hibble-sanitized cave behind our sector. Moving Munchkin made no sense, but she couldn't stay outside. I shot her up with morphine and carried her fireman-style across my shoulder. She never let out a peep until she lost consciousness. Then she screamed with every step I took.

I may have slept that night, huddled against Munchkin in frigid blackness while unbreathable wind howled. But mostly I half dreamed of dead people. Mom. Walter Lorenzen, who gave his life for me but never won a medal for his mother. Wire, the sergeant major. Pooh. The loader with the hole in his head, whose name I didn't even know. Eight other GIs I only knew as blinking red crosses who had just died because I hadn't known how to save them.

At first light, such as it was on Ganymede, the gale abated and the Slugs came again. This time artillery cracked them hard, miles out on the dust plain.

I pulled triple duty, commanding, firing our machine gun, and loading it myself. The closest remaining Slug took a fatal round a hundred yards downrange from me.

But we still lost three more men. Little by little the Slugs would wear us down. I ached from toenails to scalp follicles. I radioed my report to HQ, then cleaned the gun. I could strip it in seconds, normally, but it took me three minutes.

What was the point of continuing? Eventually, the Slugs would overrun us. Home was a pinprick in the sky. The woman I had hoped to spend my life with was gone. The woman who had become my sister lay dying. I was cold and hungry and alone. Next assault, I would fire up all my ammunition but, when the Slugs overran us, as they eventually would, I would just relax and let it happen. I was just too tired to fight anymore.

Captain Jacowicz had said something to me a million years ago. That commanders measured their failures in the letters they wrote about soldiers killed under their command.

At Gettysburg, the Confederate General George Pickett hurled his division against a Union strong point. Pickett's Charge became synonymous with futile slaughter. Pickett returned to Confederate lines, dazed. His commander, Lee, told him, "General, see to your division!" Pickett responded, "General, I have no division."

Now I understood Pickett and Jacowicz, perfectly.

After I walked our line and made sure my guys were fed, I dragged back to the cave and sat cross-legged next to Munchkin. I spooned lukewarm broth into her, while my remaining troops cleaned weapons in their trench-line positions. The morphine eased her pain but she had sunk overnight. Without more help than I could give, she had hours. She drifted back to unconsciousness.

"Major Wander?"

I looked up to see a medic, out of breath, his rifle slung. He saluted, and I returned it. That still seemed unnatural.

"Finally. She needs help. And I'm just an acting lieutenant, not a major."

Confusion flashed across his face. "Not anymore, sir. You have Third Battalion of the Second, now, Major."

"What?"

"Yesterday was bad, sir. Lots of field promotions."

I knelt beside her and peeled back her jacket, exposing

the monitor leads for the medic to plug in his field-analysis reader. "Look. Thanks for the news. You're a medic. She needs a medic. Go to work."

"You don't understand, sir. I'm a medic, but I'm here as a runner. Radios went out after you reported this morning. My orders are to escort you back to HQ. Without delay."

My head spun. Insanity spread each moment.

"Sure. We'll take her along."

He looked down at her. "Moving her will kill her."

I had lost twelve soldiers. I wouldn't lose Munchkin. "Then I'm staying with her."

He fingered his slung rifle. "General Cobb issued my orders, himself. If I have to take you back at gunpoint—"

Purple images of Mom and Walter Lorenzen and Pooh Hart and dead soldiers I never even knew ached in my head like tumors.

I snatched up my rifle and thrust the muzzle against his forehead. "Gunpoint? How's this for gunpoint?" I pointed my trembling free hand at Munchkin. "You save her life, or I blow your brains out."

The medic's breath caught in his throat.

I thumbed off the safety. "She's my family. Her husband is my best friend. He's up in orbit, now, expecting me to keep her safe. You understand that? I won't let my family die. Third Battalion of the Second can go to hell."

He stood as still as marble, except for his hands, which uncoiled the lead wires from his field-analysis reader while his eyes focused on the gun muzzle pressed in his flesh. "Sure, sir. Let's get a read on her."

I pulled the muzzle back as he knelt and fastened the lead wires to her with shaking fingers.

We waited until the reader beeped and he tilted its screen toward his eyes. "Blood loss. Mild infection. The round shattered her clavicle. But that won't kill her. Overall, critical but stable. Somebody took good care of her. Baby's fine, too."

"Baby?"

Munchkin turned her face away, and I knew it was true. It was so incomprehensible I wasn't even sure whether it violated regulations.

"Munchkin, what about after-pills?" Unwanted pregnancy disappeared courtesy of Squibb twenty years ago.

"I've got two more months for that. I'm mission-capable."

"You've been puking every morning."

"So have a lot of men." She was right. The army tolerated tobacco smokers' morning hacking. She could do her job, now. In a month, if need be, a pill could make her body resorb the fetus.

"But why?"

"If I lose Metzger . . ."

If I could make some part of Pooh or of Walter, of my family, survive, would I break a regulation? Of course. I had just nearly killed a medic to save Munchkin.

"Metzger'll be fine." I wasn't shining her on. The Slugs had no antiaircraft. The Numbers were right. Metzger was safe. But The Numbers said Pooh should be alive, too.

"Jason?" Munchkin's hand gripped my sleeve. "You need to go. It's what you signed up for. I'll be fine. And if I'm not, it's what I signed up for."

Neither of us blinked. It was also what Walter Lorenzen and Pooh and twelve dead soldiers who had died under my command had signed up for. They all died trying. I could do no less. I wouldn't leave Munchkin for the flag or the UN or to kill Slugs. I would leave for Walter and for Pooh and, in the end, for Munchkin herself, even with child.

"Does Metzger know?"

She shook her head.

I shouldered my pack, then said to the medic, "I'm ready. And you can write me up when we get back to HQ."

He shrugged. "Long as you're going, I don't need to leave. Plenty of work here besides her. She's not out of the woods, but I've got tricks in my bag. No soldier writes up another soldier. We're *all* family."

I bent and kissed Munchkin's forehead. "Thank you."

I turned and loped back toward HQ. As I ran, I peered out across the plain. A black shadow line bigger than yesterday's formed on the horizon.

THIRTY-SIX

I RAN THROUGH OUR MOSTLY EMPTY TRENCHES toward HQ, listening as *Hope*'s bombs began pattering like raindrops out on the plain. Then they stopped.

I looked up, steadying my helmet with one hand. *Hope*'s silver dot floated overhead, clearly still in firing position. Odd.

Minutes later, the Slug *boom-boom-boom* echoed off the crags. The Slugs had advanced within small-arms range but *Hope* had barely fired a shot.

As I ran, I wondered whether I would really have shot the medic. I wondered whether I should tell Metzger that Munchkin carried their child. I wondered how badly we were hurt that a specialist fourth class commanded a battalion after two days' battle. Three leg-infantry companies and a weapons company made a battalion. If the battalion was at full strength, which, of course, it wasn't, eight hundred soldiers would live and die on my orders.

By the time I rounded a bend, and HQ came in sight, battle sounds had died. We had beaten back the Slugs again. Since I'd left, the engineers had rigged a roof, of sorts, over HQ and topped it with loose rock. Antennae sprouted from it, and below I saw soldiers move.

I got closer and realized that the movement was the hauling of wounded. Slug carcasses draped HQ's parapet by the hundreds. If the Slugs had got this close to our HQ, the next assault would be the last.

I ducked under HQ's low ceiling and waited for my goggles to adjust. The first person I recognized was Howard Hibble. He sat with his back against the trench wall, a rifle across his bony knees. Its stock had shattered. Howard never touched rifles if he could help it.

A medic knelt beside him, dressing Howard's bloody forearm.

"What happened?" I asked.

The medic tied the dressing. "Slugs breached HQ. Major here mowed down fifty. Clubbed the last two with his rifle butt."

I almost smiled. "Holy Moly, Howard!"

He rolled his head back against the rock. "I'd kill for a cigarette."

"You still think they're a hive entity?"

He nodded, slowly.

An orderly entered the room, saw me, and snapped to attention, head cocked below the ceiling. "Sir!"

"I'm Wander."

"General Cobb said to bring you to him as soon as you arrived."

The orderly led me deeper into the warren of roofed trenches that had become HQ since I'd left. Unit radios squawked. Litters of wounded were ranked along trench walls. Too many were no longer wounded.

He handed me off to another orderly, who led me to the wide trench that formed GEF's nerve center. The roof had been breached. Dead Slug warriors slumped in the opening. Don't mess with Howard Hibble.

"I'm Wander. New CO of the Third of the Second."

"No, sir. You're not."

"What?" Rage surged in me. I'd abandoned Munchkin for nothing?

"Jason!"

I turned. General Cobb lay on a litter, a pressure dressing banded across his eyes with blood-soaked gauze strips. I knelt beside him. He groped for my arm, frowned as his fingers slipped in blood. "You hit bad, son?"

I looked down. A metal splinter jutted from my bicep. I hadn't even noticed. "No, sir. You—"

He shook his head. "I can't command what I can't see."

Somebody cried for her mother. I looked around, then back.

"You've done okay with your platoon. You'll do okay with the division."

My ears rang. Not just from the cacophony around us. I was supposed to play one poker hand for the future of the human race? I didn't even know the rules. And I had no cards. "Division, sir? I never. I can't."

"You will. Hell, it's not much more than a battalion left, now." He reached to his collar, fumbled with his stars, then pressed them into my palm.

"Coffee, General?" A private held out a canteen cup in a shaking hand. To me.

I shook my head, pointed to General Cobb. The kid

took his hand, pressed the cup into it. Then the private asked me, "What do you need, sir?"

A fucking clue, for starters. I sat still and breathed.

General Cobb reached up, groped for the back of my head. He tugged my ear down to his lips and whispered. "Jason, you're in command! The one thing you can't do is nothing. Do *something,* even if it's wrong!"

I turned to the private as I pinned the stars to my collar. "Get me staff. Now." I needed information.

"Sir, there hasn't been a live staff officer for twelve hours."

Somewhere a wounded man screamed.

Of course there was no staff. Why did I think an acting lieutenant had been jumped over colonels, majors, and captains? They were dead.

"You have any idea what our strength is?"

"Eight hundred available for duty, sir."

"What about the other brigades?"

"All brigades. Eight hundred left in the whole GEF, sir."

"It can't be."

"It is."

We needed fire support more than ever.

"How do I talk to *Hope*?"

He pointed across the room, at a radio console on a folding table.

"Why isn't somebody manning that?" I asked.

He stepped to it and turned it, displaying a line of holes across the back. "It got shot up today."

No wonder we'd lost fire support. I would have blamed the ship's computers.

"Nobody's talked to *Hope* in hours. Except the cooks, of course."

"What?"

He pointed across the room. A corporal wearing mess fatigues sat at a radio, talking.

"They been sending up menu orders, just in case *Hope* can get some hots down to us. You know how General Cobb feels about feeding the troops."

The firepower to destroy a planet hung in orbit above us, and the only working uplink was being used to order stew.

I jumped up, snatched the corporal's mike, and spoke. "Who is this?"

"Who is *this*? 'Cause this is *Senior* Mess Steward Anthony Garcia and I got work to do! So get off my net, dick brain."

"This is Division Commander Wander, Garcia. It's my net. If you want to stay senior anything, you patch me through to Commodore Metzger on the bridge. Now."

Silence. While I waited for the patch, Howard Hibble and Ari came in, along with a handful of surviving junior officers. Except for Howard, their combined age matched a Scout troop.

Ari said, "Heard you got a small promotion. Sir."

I nodded, then held up a finger as Metzger's voice came through. "Jason? You're commanding?" He didn't have to say what he meant. If I was in charge, things had gone to unimaginable shit down here.

"I'm commanding. How's fire support? 'Cause we're hurting down here."

Static roared. The mess uplink had been the general's indulgence. It was an obsolete radio with a line-of-sight antenna. We'd have to wait for *Hope*'s next orbit to talk again.

I turned to Howard. "How do we stop them, Howard? Because even if *Hope* can bomb the Slugs back for another attack, eventually she runs out of bombs."

Howard sucked his teeth. "It. Stop it. There's probably a single central point, a brain if you will. It breeds troops there, thinks there, fabricates Projectiles there."

"You *know* this?"

"Wild-ass educated guess."

A lieutenant, real, not day-old like I had been, seesawed his hand. The jerk who had been impatient with Ari when we assaulted that cave. "More likely they decentralized their command and control structure. They're not dumb."

Howard shrugged. "Never said it was dumb. Just different."

I looked around at all of them as we hunched under the low ceiling. "Howard guessed right about the frontal assault. Anybody got a better guess?"

Feet shifted, but no one spoke.

I slapped my palms on my thighs. "Okay. We need to find this brain. Fast."

The lieutenant spoke again. "If we had choppers . . . or if we had time to get patrols out across the dust bowl . . ."

I looked at Ari. "Jeeb."

Ari nodded.

The lieutenant shook his head. "Sir, doctrine is we keep the TOT tight to the division. It's too valuable for patrolling."

Adrenaline surged in me. This lieutenant was probably incredulous that I got jumped over him. My spec-four patch remained sewn on my sleeve, even if my collar brass said different. The last thing I needed now was attitude from somebody who was supposed to be working for me. And I was the by-God division commander! "Lieutenant—!"

He winced.

I bit my tongue. The medic I had nearly killed an hour ago had said it. Ord had tried to teach me an eternity ago. This lieutenant had been through hell. We all had. Together. We were family.

Ari nodded, again. "He's right, Jason. About doctrine."

Why conserve Jeeb? So he would be here to see the last of us die on this rock? "Thanks for the perspective, Lieutenant. But doctrine got us in this mess. Ari, what can Jeeb look for?"

Ari walked us over to the suitcase-size holotank that showed us what he saw through Jeeb's eyes.

He pointed. "These depressions at the crater rim are the staging area where the Slugs formed up. This"—Ari drew his finger along parallel lines in the dust—"is a trail back to somewhere."

We watched the view change as Jeeb zoomed down and shot along scant feet above Ganymede's surface. Miles flew by, then the dust trails disappeared. Jeeb stopped and hairpin-turned, then the view was right at ground level. I imagined Jeeb picking his way across Ganymede on six legs.

"They crossed solid rock, here, no tracks."

"So?"

Ari closed his eyes and made a scooping motion with one hand. "Sampling. Jeeb's taking the rock's temperature." Ari opened his eyes. "Okay. We switched to passive infrared. The Slugs left a trail a quarter degree warmer when they crossed this rock pile."

The infrared holo shimmered, not like the visual-spectrum image. But the Slug trails crossed the rock, as obvious as pale smoke. Jeeb crawled slowly as he followed them.

"Sir?" Lieutenant Negative broke in.

I nodded and he continued. "If the TOT doesn't find something before nightfall, the storm and the temperature drop will wipe out any traces. We'll be nowhere."

I shot Ari a glance.

He said, "Lieutenant's right, Ja—sir."

If I'd bitten Lieutenant Negative's head off the minute before, he would never have offered the second bit of advice. The remaining eight hundred of us wouldn't last to try again after the following day's attack. It was now or never.

"So, what do we do, Ari?"

"If Jeeb switches from passive infrared to active, he can track while he's flying." Ari's face darkened. "But it's like shining a searchlight. He gives himself away to any observer who sees in the infrared spectrum."

I shot Howard a glance. Sluggo's autopsy and two nights on Ganymede had taught us that Slugs saw in the infrared spectrum. Ari would be risking not just a metal robot, but the flesh of his flesh, the blood of his blood. As I had risked Munchkin.

I turned back to Ari. "Do it."

He hesitated one heartbeat, then closed his eyes. "Yes, sir." The image rolled across the holo faster.

An hour later, the trails disappeared again, against a cliff.

Ari said, "I don't see anything. If there was a door, you'd expect straight lines. The rarest thing in nature."

"No. Slug doors are circular, with curved panels. Like a camera's iris."

Ari moved his hands and the holo image got herky-jerky again, as Jeeb climbed the vertical cliff. Ari made his hands flat and stabbed the air. In the holotank, I could see from Jeeb's viewpoint. He hung fifty feet above the ground, his forelimbs probing for joints in the rock.

Above our heads, pebbles rattled across the roof as afternoon wind heralded the nightstorm that would end Jeeb's search, and all our lives.

Ari opened his eyes and exhaled explosively. "Nothing. I'm not saying nothing's there. We just can't find it."

Before Jeeb moved again, the horizon in the holo rotated.

I stabbed my finger. "There! It's there!" A hole grew as the door-panel petals expanded. Jeeb was hanging from a moving door panel as it rotated open. It looked ten feet thick.

The holo went black. I shot Ari a glance.

"Jeeb only cuts contact when he thinks he's detected. They picked up his infrared."

"He knocked on their door?"

"Now he'll switch to passive sensing and try to sneak in that door."

Ari's face was chalk and I knew why. Jeeb was nearly indestructible. But he couldn't drill through a ten-foot-thick blast door or tunnel out from under thousands of feet of solid rock. The Slugs wouldn't open that door again. If Jeeb got inside, half of Ari was imprisoned for life. And if the Slugs caught Jeeb and dismantled him, Ari would feel it like he was being broken on the wheel. No. Jeeb would blow himself into rutabagas if they tried that and take a bunch of Slugs with him. For Ari, it would be like spectating at his own suicide.

Lieutenant Negative pulled up his jacket sleeve to read his wrist 'puter. Seconds trickled away.

Suddenly it hit me. I whispered to Ari, stupid since the Slugs couldn't hear me, "Jeeb can't transmit from under a mountain!"

Ari closed his eyes and held up his palm at me.

The holo flickered, then fired up.

Ari whispered, too. "He's okay. He's transmitting ultralow frequency, now. ULF just means he has to be in contact with the rock to send signals through it. His passive night vision's working. They may suspect he's in there with them, but they'll never find him."

The cave corkscrewed like the passage I had navigated in the Slug Projectile, but bigger. Then it swelled into a cavern big enough to swallow Lake Erie.

Ari lifted his arms and Jeeb drifted along the curved ceiling. Below, around the chamber's walls, bulging, churning organic machines spurted out Slugs like green bread loaves. Near the chamber's center, finished products in their body armor circled a spherical sack a hundred feet tall, like Muslim pilgrims around the K'aaba stone.

Howard Hibble whispered, "Jackpot."

I looked at my wrist 'puter. *Hope* should be in range, now. A corporal stuck his head in the room. "Sir, we got Slugs outside! Must've missed some cave cracks. They pulled down the uplink antenna to *Hope*."

Whatever else the Slug common intelligence was, a

slow learner it wasn't. It realized what we were up to. It realized Jeeb had blown its cover, even if it couldn't catch him. It had communicated to the Slugs inside our perimeter, and they attacked the one thing that we couldn't live without, that uplink antenna. If we didn't contact *Hope* on this pass, night would fall, and the game was over.

Ari stared at me. Jeeb's only way out was if *Hope*'s ordnance cracked open Slugtown and busted him loose. Jeeb could survive anything short of a nuke, but he couldn't dig for crap.

Before I could speak, Ari picked up a rifle and tore for the trench exit.

I ran after him.

Outside, Ari had already dropped three Slugs. Two more hunkered in rocks; the drooping antenna mast laid down behind them. There was no question we would get the bastards. But late was never, and Ari knew it. He charged out firing and made it all the way to them before the last surviving Slug sent a round point-blank into Ari's chest. I ran up and shot the twitching Slug. In fact, I emptied my magazine into it. But it was over.

I stood panting.

"Sir?" A soldier who had followed me touched my elbow. I turned, and he nodded toward Ari. A medic knelt alongside him, attaching monitor leads.

"Jason?"

I knelt there, too, and drew back Ari's blood-sodden field jacket with two fingers. The Slug round had penetrated a seam between plates of Ari's body armor, then it had twisted through him like a ferret.

Munchkin's wound, horrible as it was, had been a

lucky nick. Inside Ari's jacket, lungs, liver, arteries, all those miraculous human complexities, pulsed like lacerated table scraps. I gulped a breath and bit back nausea.

His breath sighed between his lips in pink froth. "Would you—?"

"Relax." I laid my palm on his brow.

He shook his head. "No time."

I looked at the medic. He gave me a one-inch headshake as he unwrapped a morphine syrette.

Ari pushed it away. The effort of moving his hand made his eyes tear. Or maybe it was something else. "I need to go fast. Jeeb feels what I feel." Ari gathered himself to speak again. "Jason, he's alone now. He doesn't understand. He's an orphan, like you."

The medic looked blank, presuming Ari's delirium.

"Take care of him?" Ari asked me.

"Sure. Always." With those words I adopted a steel-and-plastic orphan.

Ari relaxed and lay back against hard stone. I saw his eyes close through my own tears.

Behind me, troops raised the mast.

By the time I got back to the radio, Metzger's voice crackled. "Jason?"

"Wander here. Over."

"What's happening down there?"

"Too much. We need everything you've got. I mean everything, delivered on the coordinates the TOT's transmitting to you now."

"Jason—"

Even radioed from orbit I could hear it in Metzger's voice. "What?"

"We got nothing. Computers are down."

"Fix 'em."

"We're trying! By next orbit—"

"There is no next orbit!" I told him what was going on.

"Those coordinates are halfway around Ganymede," he said.

Silence.

"Jason? How is she?"

"Alive. Hurt, but alive."

"You believe this Slugtown is the real deal?"

"Ari believed it enough to die for it." There was no time for tact. "Munchkin's pregnant."

More silence.

"Okay. I'll take care of everything. Good-bye, Jason."

In that moment, after a lifetime together, I knew exactly what he meant.

I dropped the mike, walked out into Ganymede's twilight, and looked to the sky. *Hope* drifted into view over the horizon, one hundred miles high, silver against Jupiter's red disk. Sparks flickered from her and drifted down toward us. Escape pods. *Hope*'s crew was abandoning her, on Metzger's orders.

One pilot in the world could fly *Hope* alone, without computers, lying on his belly in the Navigation Blister while Ganymede's horizon stretched before him. One pilot in the world could calculate and execute course corrections to bring her mile-long bulk screaming down on Slugtown in half of an orbit.

Metzger chose to end his marriage where it began, in that star-spangled crystal dome.

Hope streaked flame red across the sky, now, as she dropped into the atmosphere. By the time she reached

Slugtown in Ganymede's opposite hemisphere she would be a molten mass, trailing fire miles wide.

She disappeared over the horizon. I held my breath.

The flash came first, blinding even half a world away. I threw myself on the ground as the blast wave and then seismic quakes rocked Ganymede.

History would say that Metzger died to save the human race. History would lie. Metzger sacrificed himself to give his wife and unborn child and the rest of us on this rock a chance at life.

The next morning, Jeeb sent images back to the holotank as he flew home, his course erratic. The electronics people said the explosion had freed him from the Slugtown cave, but scrambled his circuits. I believed it was grief.

Hope's impact had rent the very fabric of Ganymede. Lava and liquid water flowed in a flaming, steaming, unending mass across the other side of this world. This world that the Slugs no longer held. The volcanism lit the sky dull red as the seven hundred of us who had survived settled in for a long, cold occupation.

We reestablished radio contact with Earth and got thanked. Politicians radioed that a grateful world had awarded me the Medal of Honor. I had it presented to Walter Lorenzen's mother.

That afternoon, before the nightstorm came, Howard Hibble and I scaled the crag above HQ and looked out across the battlefield.

Howard tucked his bandaged arm against his side. "In the end, gadgets didn't matter. Soldiers who could choose to live or to die for one another fought perfect soldiers that died without thinking. We should have lost. But we won."

Below us, dead Slugs blackened the plain and the mountain.

There, too, lay nine thousand children who traveled 300 million miles and made Ganymede their orphanage forever. The dropships Pooh Hart had led littered the foot of the escarpment, and I imagined I could see her grave from here.

"Won?" I shook my head. "Wellington defeated Napoleon at Waterloo. He said there is nothing so melancholy as a battle lost, except a battle won."

I sat on the cold stone of Ganymede, laid my elbows on my knees, and cried.

THIRTY-SEVEN

I RUN MY HANDS ALONG the vibrating viewport frame as the new ship hangs in parking orbit above United Nations Base Ganymede. So much a part of me is the ship's vibration that I notice it only when I have time to think, like now.

The *Metzger* class is so much *Hope* never was. Beyond the viewport at ten-mile intervals orbit the other four cruisers of the *Metzger* class. Synchronous with us, they glisten silver against space's black velvet. Utility barges one hundred feet long scurry around the cruisers like ants around logs. The new ships' antimatter bottles alone are as large as *Hope*'s entire payload section was.

The new cruisers have better gravity. That means real showers instead of years of sponge baths. Their agriculture labs grow hydroponic fruits and vegetables for us grunts, not just bootleg vodka. Maybe best of all, the *Metz*'s antimatter interplanetary drive gets here from Earth in half the time. After decades of drift, war made us leapfrog direct from chemical propulsion past fission, fusion and plasma to AMat. Metzger would be proud of the class of ships they named for him.

Below the viewport green streaks are visible on Ganymede, even from here in orbit. The lava flows and liquid-water floods touched off by *Hope*'s impact continue even now. Eons ago, meteors did the same thing to Ganymede's sister satellite, Callisto. But with these flows heat was released from Ganymede's depths. Evaporation released oxygen into the atmosphere. Oxygen content reached half-Earth-normal last year and climbs annually. And the heat has increased the surface temperature so high that the ag-lab wizards are growing things down there. Just primitive lichen, so far.

Nonetheless, along with death and destruction, war brought life to Ganymede. War forced men beyond the moon, and now to the stars, where we might not have ventured for centuries. Horrible trades that those were, they are no less fact.

I step away and turn back into my stateroom. Rank hath its privileges. As embarked-division commanding general, I have a tree. Just a foot-tall bonsai juniper, but green, alive, and all mine.

A six-legged football preens beside my juniper. The stateroom's not all mine. I share with Jeeb. His combat circuits fried when he escaped Slugtown. As an obsolete J-series, they decommissioned him, extracted his self-destruct explosives, and let me buy him for scrap. Machines have no personality, of course. But I see Ari in him every day.

I sit at my desk and read the screen. I read a lot during the years it took for relief to reach Ganymede. Enough to earn my master's in military science and validate my field promotion. The longest-distance correspondence course in human history, completed while on the most boring diet. Rations for a force of ten thousand fed us seven hundred survivors, but we were glad to see peaches when relief arrived.

They busted me back from division commander to second lieutenant, correspondence degree or not. Why and what happened then are stories for another time.

The Battle of Ganymede was a miraculous victory. It will never be miraculous to us who left brothers and sisters beneath Ganymede's cold stones, but it was miraculous, nonetheless.

Pooh Hart sleeps beneath those stones. I always visit on her birthday. I always leave white roses. I always cry.

Pooh won the Medal of Honor and the Distinguished Flying Cross, posthumously. In all, 307 soldiers there won their nations' highest awards for valor, including Ari Klein and Nathan Cobb. I told Walter Lorenzen once that medals recognized an army's mistakes. That may be, but it doesn't diminish the courage and sacrifice of those who win them.

The First Battle of Ganymede didn't make the killing stop. It wasn't the end of the Slug War. It wasn't even the beginning of the end. But, as the British Prime Minister, Churchill, put it a century ago, it was the end of the beginning.

Even AMat would take centuries to get us just to the Slug Outpost Worlds. So, how we stole Temporal-Fabric Insertion Technology from the Slugs is another story. So is our use of T-FIT to find the Slugs' homeworld and to equip the Metzger Class with T-FIT so we can pay them a visit.

The after-action analysts eventually found out that Slugs hibernate. A few Slugs we had epoxied into their cave cracks got dug out alive.

The cryptozoologists and psyops spooks had little luck interrogating their first prisoners of war, even with Howard Hibble asking the questions. We've been working for years to figure out what makes the Slugs tick, so we can make peace, make it stop. Peace is what every man and woman in this army wants.

If the Slugs won't make peace, well, payback's a bitch.

My command sergeant major raps on the hatch frame, then sticks his head in. "Sir, the spec four you wanted to see is out here."

Another of rank's privileges is you can cherry-pick your cadre. I pulled strings and got my division sergeant major shipped up from Earth aboard the *Metz*. He is the finest NCO in the armed services, bar none. Without him this division wouldn't be worth a rat fart. "I'm ready, Sergeant Major Ord."

"Sir, Specialist Trent reports." She snaps off a salute so crisp her fingers quiver. I could cut my fingers on her fatigue creases.

I smile. We are the finest unit in military history. I'm just being objective, even if it's my own division. "Take a seat, Specialist."

She sits. The prettiest M-60 loader I ever saw.

"The general sent for me?"

But not the shyest.

"Your platoon sergeant tells me you are the biggest troublemaker in your company. You beat the snot out of a squad mate."

"A guy, sir." She looks smug.

"Another soldier!"

Her shoulders sag. "Is the general advising me that Articles have been drawn? Because I want to stay in sir. I need to. I lost my family—"

"I've read your file. Your platoon sergeant also tells me you are potentially the finest soldier he has ever trained. You finished college. You enjoy being a loader?"

She squeezes her lips together, opens her mouth, closes it, then speaks. "Rather be a gunner. They say I'm too small to handle the gun. But they're fine with me humping the ammo, sir."

I smile. "My gunner was smaller than you are, but I never saw the gun handled better."

Her eyes get big. "I knew the general received battlefield promotions. But from spec four to general?"

I nod. "However, I don't recommend the career plan. Would the specialist care to make a deal?"

"Sir?"

"No Articles will be filed."

She straightens but her eyes narrow. "What do I have to do, sir?"

"You return to Earth tomorrow on the *Powell* and attend OCS on my personal recommendation."

"Officer Candidate School?" Her jaw drops, and she forgets to say "sir."

"And"—I lift two boxes from my desk drawer—"you will personally deliver these to the addresses noted, with my regards."

"Sir? I should know what they are."

"With a general's return address on them, the MPs won't give you trouble. But they're not secrets. They're gifts. Ganymede rock made into paperweights. You'll deliver one to the senior juvenile judge in Denver. Plan to spend an hour visiting him. He's Infantry, too."

She nods and places the first box in her lap. "The other?"

"To my godson. His mother was my gunner." Munchkin lives in the Rockies foothills, now, not so far from Camp Hale. She prefers cold to Egyptian heat, after Ganymede. On her pension and Metzger's, she raises Jason Udey Metzger, the first extraterrestrial-conceived and -born human. They say Jude is . . . different.

My visitor's eyes glisten as she gathers up the second box.

"Godspeed, Specialist."

She stands, and I return her salute.

"Sir!" Her about-face is crisper than hydroponic-grown lettuce. Before she reaches the hatch, she whispers, "Thank you, General."

She's out the hatch without hearing me whisper, "No, thank you."

I don't tell her that if things really work out the way I hope, she'll never come back here. At least not as a combat Infantryman. With luck we'll end this war before she or any other kid has to fight another lick.

Ord slips in the hatch before it closes behind her, a holobox in his hand. "Thought you might like to see this, sir."

It is a picture of the old company street at Indiantown Gap. Alongside the mess hall a solitary tree stands, covered in green leaves. The sky behind glows faint blue, like before the war.

"Trees are leafing out all over Earth this spring, General. First time since the war started."

I step to the viewport and look out into space. I stand silent with my feet spread shoulder width apart, hands clasped behind me at the small of my back. In Drill and Ceremony, the position is called "At Ease." For the first time in years, it is also how I feel.

Someday maybe I'll see trees again. For now it is enough to know they are there.

About the Author

Robert Buettner is a former Military Intelligence Officer, National Science Foundation Fellow in Paleontology and has published in the field of Natural Resources Law. He lives in the Colorado Rockies, creating the sequel to *Orphanage* and snowboarding passably. Visit his Website, www.RobertBuettner.com.